AF445635

ROBERT S. CAMPBELL'S

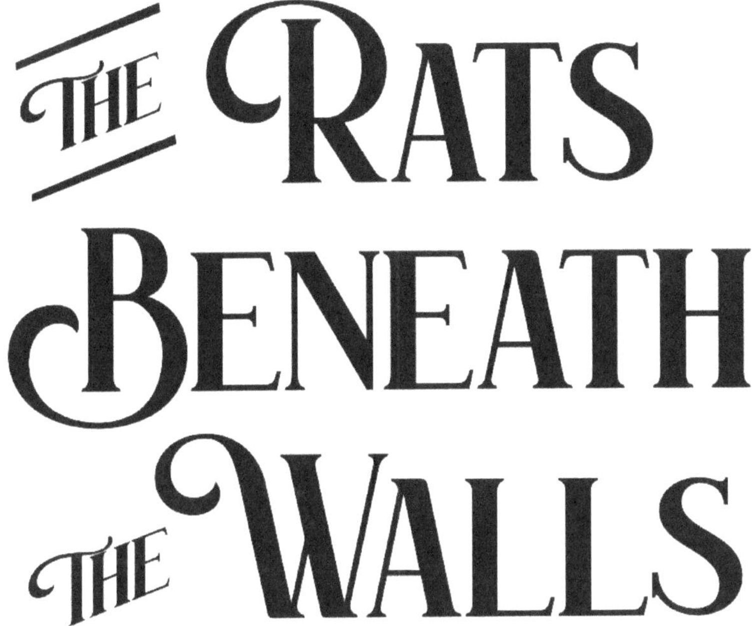

THE RATS BENEATH THE WALLS

Squeezed Lemons Publishing

www.squeezedlemonspublishing.com

For Andrea

I thought my story was over,

but she showed me, like all good books,

there is a second chapter.

℘ROLOGUE

"Where are you, my love?"

A pallid moon shone through the narrow window, casting its sickly glow upon Walter as he awoke with a start, his sleeping-gown drenched in icy perspiration. Still lost in the throes of the nightmare's grip, his wide eyes darted frantically about the shadow-shrouded bedchamber, straining to pierce the gloaming darkness.

The far off cheers from raised goblets echoed through the stairway beyond his door. The lustful merriment was undoubtedly the source of his fitful slumber.

The feast was underway. This was the appointed hour.

Dread clutched his heart like an icy hand and twisted his insides most horribly. He cringed back into his dampened sheets, beseeching the Almighty to spare him from what must be done. To stay him from the dire deeds to come.

Then, from somewhere deep within the ancient walls, came a faint, hellish scratching. Subtle at first, but growing ever louder, ever more maddening. Clapping his hands over his ears in a futile attempt to dampen the nerve-rending noise, Walter leapt from his bed and hastily drew on his robes.

Snatching up a candlestick, he stole from his chamber and down the worn stone steps, through halls and galleries lit by candle and moonlight. The scratching faded, replaced by the distant clink of cutlery on platters and the boisterous cries of revelry.

Turning the final corner to the Banquet Hall, the ruddy glow of flicking candlelight revealed the long feast table surrounded by gluttonous revelers, consumed with their midnight feast and debauchery. The sight filled him with horror and revulsion. Upon seeing him, his portly cousin stood and beckoned him with grease smeared fingers. Over the pounding rush of blood in his ears he heard his name cried out in amusement by the merrymakers. "Walter!"

When next his mind was able to comprehend his surroundings, he stared in numbed incomprehension at the blood dripping from the carving knife clutched in his shaking hand.

From around the banquet table came wet gurgling gasps and fitful thrashing, then silence. Slumped across the table lay the bloodied corpses of the feasters, their lifeblood still dripping and pooling on the stone floor. Surrounding Walter stood four wide-eyed servants, bloody knives clutched in their own hands. Meeting Walter's terrified gaze, they slipped from their stunned silence, solemnly acknowledging their deeds.

Steeling himself, Walter wiped his bloody hands on the tablecloth. Dropping his knife, he instead reached out to grip a ceremonial cutlass from its wall mountings. He clenched the blade in his clammy hand, testing its weight. Finally finding his voice, he rasped "It is time."

"Aye, m'lord," the servants intoned as one, nodding, clutching their knives as if they were holy crosses.

Ascending the spiral stone stair to the topmost level of the priory, Walter came to a carpeted hall lined with portraits and doors. A robed guard stood quickly from his chair when he spied Walter. "M'lord, 'tis late for thee to..." The guard faltered as he saw the other menials behind Walter. Just as the guard began to shout, Walter lunged forward, clamping a hand o'er his mouth and plunging the cutlass deep into his vitals. The gurgling guard kicked against the unyielding stones, toppling his chair, but soon grew still. The servants regarded the scene with mounting horror.

A heavy oaken door suddenly creaked open. "What is this..." A comely young woman in her sleeping-gown rubbed the last vestiges of slumber from her eyes, then stared in disbelief at the bloody tableau. "Walter...?"

With a quick jerk of his head, Walter directed his men, who rushed the maid with daggers bared. She screamed as they forced her back into her chamber.

Walter wrenched his blade from the impaled guard and strode swiftly down the hallway. His servants kicked open doors in his wake, cries of alarm and shrieks of violence erupting behind him.

"What are you doing, my Love?"

Breathing heavily, Walter moved with grim purpose toward the door at the corridor's end. With a resounding kick, the portal flew open, revealing the master bedchamber beyond.

Upon the bed, clad in her night-robes, was an attractive woman, seemingly in her early thirties. Lady Adelaide drew the sheets higher, startled. "Walter...?"

Walter stood framed in the doorway, blood dripping from his saber. "Mother...", fear and shame overwhelming him. "I cannot do as thou biddest. I mustn't!"

Lady Adelaide slid gracefully from the bed, maternal concern writ upon her features. "Oh, my dearest." She tenderly clutched his face in her hands. "Can you not see? Their lives are meaningless. I care only for you."

The other menials appeared, their robes stained with splattered crimson. Walter regarded his mother silently before pushing her hands away. "Restrain her."

The servants rushed to grab the lady, dragging her forcibly to her knees. "Walter! I beseech thee, do not do this!"

Walter raised his blade on high. "Mother! Thou art an abomination in the eyes of God!"

Lady Adelaide's visage twisted in sudden fury at the word. "God!?", she spitted like a curse. Walter's strike was halted by the sheer force and volume of the cry.

With little effort she crushed the wrists of the men holding her fast. They shrieked out of disbelief and agony.

"Allow me to demonstrate the power of a god!" Slowly she rose, releasing the servants' mangled appendages. The one still clinging to her from behind was lifted clear off the floor by her preternatural strength. Walter recoiled in horror as she reached behind, plucking the man off her back and dashing his skull upon the unforgiving stones. The fourth servant lunged, dagger glinting in the firelight. She slapped the blade aside and closed her fingers around his throat, hurling him across the room as if he were a discarded garment. The lady turned her baleful gaze upon her son.

"You dare strike against me!? You ungrateful..."

Walter's lunge sank the cutlass tip deep into her breast, cutting short her vitriol. She gazed at him with unbridled wrath. A blood-curdling scream burst from her lips as she hurtled toward Walter, knocking him to the floor and dashing the sword from his grasp. She loomed above him, face contorted in unholy rage.

Spying himself before the hearth, Walter reached into the flames and snatched up a burning length of wood. He struck at the lady's raiment, swiftly igniting the fabric.

Again she shrieked, seizing Walter and slamming him against the unyielding stone wall. She cursed him in a strange tongue as the flames engulfed her, scorching the pinned Walter.

Suddenly, a blade tip pierced her breast from behind. She glanced down in disbelief before wheeling around to behold the cowering menial who had run her through with the discarded cutlass. Still clutching the flaming brand, Walter swung with all his might, striking his mother squarely on the back of the head and felling her to the floor.

As the burning body twitched and jerked, Walter continued to hammer blows upon his mother's form until she moved no more.

The four servants, unbelievably still drawing breath, huddled around Walter, clutching their wounds. One grasped at Walter's smoldering coat. "My lord!" Together they stripped off the smoking garment.

A low rumbling could be heard, like the swelling of some eldritch storm. The portraits and furnishings began to shake, vibrating against the walls.

Walter's eyes brimmed with primal terror. "We must flee!"

He flung the flaming brand onto the bed as they retreated from the chamber, a baleful orange glow kindling behind them.

As they raced madly through the maze of corridors, the deafening rumble was joined by a new sound - a million skittering claws and mewling shrieks echoing up from the bowels of the earth.

Things began to fall from the walls. Tapestries swayed and undulated as if concealing squirming entities. The menials scrambled in mounting panic as they ran. The rearmost follower glanced back and was overcome with the horror he witnessed surging behind them. In their panic, he stumbled to the flagstones. His scream was silenced instantly by the pursuing darkness.

Walter and the three survivors burst through the doors into the courtyard, fleeing mindlessly through the open gates of the priory as flame and damnation exploded behind them.

From a vantage on a nearby hillock, Walter silently observed as the roaring flames consumed the priory's highest reaches. The priory's timeless stone structure stood unbreaking, but orange flames burst through the windows and flicked across the roof. The swirling smoke glowed lurid in the heavy night, pierced by shrieking wails from far below.

"What hast thou wrought, my love?"

"By God's grace, I did what was necessary," Walter whispered, his body shaking in the cold midnight air.

A servant approached the stoic Walter, trembling. "M'lord, the priory is no more. Your family is gone. Whither shall you go now?"

The barque slipped through the waves, its newly milled oaken hull creaking beneath its vast squared sails. Looking across the mist-shrouded harbor, Walter De La Poer stood at the rail, gazing back at the grey, overcast banks of his homeland. Baron no more, he felt the clean breath of freedom for the first time.

Above the din of labor, a sailor cried out to his mates, "Catch the wind, lads! We sail on till we make Virginia territory!"

CHAPTER

1

$\mathcal{A}$ rainy day in Pittsburgh. A young 26-year old sits alone in the outdoor patio of a coffee shop, rain thumping on the umbrella of his table. He is reclining in the metal chair, wearing sunglasses and napping - one hand still protecting his 10-speed leaning against the table. He is alone in the patio - other customers huddle in the coffee shop from the downpour - some eyeing him through the windows with bemused curiosity.

Markus is startled awake by his jarring cell-phone alert. It strobes the screen with the sounds of klaxons. Tilting down his glasses, he fishes out his phone from his jacket and swipes on the screen. A new delivery. He's got work. He takes a sip of his coffee - grimaces at its lukewarm temperature - and tosses it into a recycle bin. Rising, he sweeps up his bike by the handlebars as he hurriedly guides it past chairs and tables to the gated patio exit. In one swift move, he straps the bike helmet to his chin as he kicks his leg over the seat and begins riding across the rain-slick downtown sidewalk.

Markus cuts through the headlight-illuminated mists of the streets, weaving deftly through traffic and the occasional pedestrian. The glass buildings of downtown Pittsburgh reflect the gray and dismal sky.

Markus hops off his bike and carries it up the steps to the building entrance. Unstrapping his helmet and walking his bike across the open lobby, he heads to the familiar reception desk. Connie is working today.

A young woman in a business-casual dress looks up as he approaches. She smiles genuinely, "You again?" Markus smiles back shyly. She leans towards him, "Are you the only person working at that delivery service? I swear this is the fourth time this week you've been here."

"Yeah...", Markus grinned awkwardly. It was actually the fifth time, but he wasn't going to correct her.

She slides a large package across her desk before him. "Do you ever get any time off?" She looked up at him with flirtatious eyes. Markus wanted to be smooth and suave, but instead he stammered, "Uh... not often." He grinned at her. Her look became confused. Markus awkwardly reached for the package and hurriedly put it into his saddlebag. Nerves and self-loathing prevented him from looking back at her as he quickly walked away.

As Markus glided through the wet city streets, he berated himself. Connie was nice, and available, but whenever he met a girl, he was overcome by crippling self-doubt. In all of his 26 years he never had a real girlfriend. He'd never had any real relationships - friends or family. Spending your whole life in an orphanage makes it difficult to connect with people, he was once told. But why did it always feel like it was his personality and failings that drove people away?

Lost in his thoughts, he passed a parking lot, when a scene caught his eye. A family with two young children were getting into their car.

The mother buckled a cooing and grinning baby into a child seat. The father, shaking an umbrella, watched as his other daughter splashed carelessly in the rain puddles. Feelings of warmth and longing welled up in Markus. Here was something he had spent his whole life yearning for - the comfort of family. Of belonging.

A car horn brought Markus back to reality. The spell of yearning broken, he pedaled hard as the rain began again.

Spending the rest of the day searching his phone for work, no worthwhile gigs came up. As night descended on the downtown buildings, Markus began the long ride to his apartment.

His apartment building was not in a good part of town. The neon signs for massages and liquor reflected in the greasy-wet streets as figures huddled beneath eaves to keep dry. Guiding his bike into the entrance, he checked his graffitied mailbox for bills. Hefting his bike over his shoulder, he climbed the two flights to his studio apartment. Unlocking the various dead-bolts, he was greeted by a tiny, spartan room. A couch, which doubled as his bed, a small TV, and a short table that still held last night's take out.

Leaning his bike against a wall, he dropped heavily on his couch. The rain beat heavily on his window, as he clicked on the TV and picked through leftovers. He was tired from his long day, and hungry, but the rent was due in a few days, and he had to keep things tight. He flipped through channels, settling on a black-and-white detective movie. It wasn't long before he was asleep.

Markus had always been an "active" dreamer, having vivid dreams almost every night. It made for some entertaining lucid dreaming -

but also for some dark nightmares. This night was no exception. Markus dreamed of that family he saw getting into their car, only he was the father. The little girl in her rain coat splashed through the puddles and looked up at him smiling. She raced into his arms and he held her tightly, feeling her warmth and hearing her giggling voice. Slowly, she dissolved in his grip. When he looked for her he found himself at his orphanage. He was in the play yard. He was 8. Surrounded by other boys and girls. They pointed at him and leered. "Your parents are dead!" one shouted gleefully. "Nobody knows who you are! Nobody even knows your name!" a chorus of children teased. The large bully standing in front of him pushed him hard, "Nobody wants you!". He fell back. Back into darkness.

Snapping awake, Markus sat upright on his couch. God, he hated that nightmare. The day he aged-out of that orphanage was one of the best in his life. He punched at his sagging pillow, determined to get a few hours of sleep.

Laying back, he stared into the glow of the TV's late night infomercial.

"Have you ever wondered who your great-great-grandmother was?", the narrator's voice began. "Have you ever wanted to know where your family tree grew? Where you came from?"

Markus blinked his eyes and began to pay attention.

"We have traced the genetic lineage of tens of millions of people as far back as the Roman Empire. We have helped thousands of people find long-lost family members - and even whole family trees they didn't know they had."

Markus sat up, paying full attention.

"Every membership to GeneticHeritage gives you access to our world-wide tree of ancestry. One simple DNA swab will open connections to the family and ancestors that make you - you."

A logo flies onto the screen. "GeneticHeritage.com - Find out where you belong."

CHAPTER
2

The next morning, Markus awakes with a mission. A quick

shower, change of clothes, a bite of a stale bagel, and he was out the door. Making his way into the downtown area, he headed straight for Independence Library. Locking his bike, he strode into the musty library, forgoing the shelves of books and heading to the public computer area. Finding an open machine, he sat and clicked on the internet icon and typed in "GeneticHeritage.com". The website resembled the infomercial, spinning the same facts and dreams for anyone curious about their lineage.

Markus had never known his parents. On a cold morning in December of 1998, an officer Smith happened to hear crying over the biting wind. Following the sound into an old cemetery, he found a baby swaddled in blankets in the snow at the base of a grave. The officer took him to Family Services and eventually into the foster care system. Markus was told that Officer Smith had given him the name "Markus" from the grave he was found on.

Markus barely remembered Officer Smith, but knew that he would visit him on his birthday - as no one knew his actual birthday, it became December 5th, the day he was found. When he was seven years old, he was told that Officer Smith was shot in the line of duty. This became the start of his misery.

Young Markus only wanted a place to call home and a family to love him. But each new family would last a short while before he was put back in the system.

When he became a teenager, he was a typical depressed and angst-ridden youth who would self-sabotage any potential family, before they could return him themselves. When he aged-out from the system, he was given his whole file - a meager police report and "Inconclusive Parental DNA" results.

Lost in his thoughts, his cursor hovered over the "Sign Up" button of the webpage. He held his breath and clicked.

Entering his address, a DNA collection kit would be sent to him. He tried to temper his excitement with reluctance. Most likely nothing would come of this.

A payment screen appeared, prompting for a credit card number. Reaching for his wallet, Markus fished out his one and only credit card. The ancient plastic card was presented to him on his sixteenth birthday when the orphanage established a banking account for him. It was his first taste of freedom. But now the old card was showing its wear, as he tried to decipher a few of the scraped bare numbers.

His information was accepted. He sighed in anticipation. All that was left was to wait.

His days continued like they always did. Wake up, chase any gigs that pop up, eat when the time permits, check the mail, crash on the sofa, sleep.

After a week of waiting, a tiny package was waiting in Markus'
mailbox. He snatched it excitedly, holding it in his mouth as he
hauled his bike up the stairs to his apartment. Ripping open the
box, he found inside a plastic vial, a swab, a colorful instruction
pamphlet, and a return envelope.

Following the instructions, Markus scraped at his cheeks and
sealed the swab in the vial. Sealing the vial in the return envelope,
he raced downstairs and dropped it into the outgoing mail. He
could hardly sleep that night, daring to hope for a result that would
change his life.

Markus awoke to the flashing klaxons of his phone. There was work
to do. Life goes on.

More passing days. Having something to look forward to made the
monotony of the daily grind seemed less oppressive. Each day he
would return to the public library and log into his GeneticHeritage
account - but each time it was the same - "No Results Yet".

A week went by. Still no results. He was beginning to doubt he
would ever get the results he hoped for. He rationalized that the
test might be inconclusive, or simply not provide any answers. He
should prepare himself for disappointment.

Another week passed. His anxiety manifested as nightmares filled
with taunting children. "You are nobody. You'll always be nobody."

The day was rainy. Markus made his way to the library, shaking the rain from his jacket as he entered. Back to the same terminal. Punching in the same URL. Waiting for the slow internet to eventually load. Preparing for disappointment.

"You have a new message!"

Markus blinked in disbelief. Overcome with excitement, he furiously clicked on the messages tab.

"We have matched your DNA profile! Click here for results." Markus clicked and began scrolling down pages of information: his genetic makeup, disposition for genetic diseases, and other stuff he didn't care about. Finally he arrived at the section named "Family Tree". Holding his breath, he clicked on the link.

His name appeared - along with two connections. Both connections had a name and a picture. "Theodore Delapore" and "Margaret Delapore". For the first time in his life, he was looking at his parents. Tears welled up in his eyes.

Quickly looking through the available information, Theodore and Margaret were US citizens living in Amsterdam. Apparently littlewais known about them. One was an engineer, the other a school teacher. They left Europe and returned to the US with their newly born son, Jason.

Markus covered his mouth to stop a gasp. His name was Jason. Jason Delapore.

He quickly pieced together why his orphanage hadn't been able to find any birth certificate - they were only looking in the US. Still, why has his parents abandoned him? He read on.

Theodore and Margaret had both died tragically in an apartment fire only days after returning to the US. Apparently there were suspicious circumstances, but no suspects were charged. Weird.

His mind churned with possibilities. Could they have been murdered? Maybe they knew they were in danger. Maybe that was why they had abandoned him to that cemetery so long ago. Perhaps that's why they left Europe all of a sudden...

Scrolling around the page, he saw that his parent's had connections to other family, and still others. Scrolling down, the list of family connections went on and on and on. He had family - uncles, aunts, dozens of cousins - an enormous family.

Overwhelmed with a feeling of connection he had never experienced, he clicked into his user profile and changed his account name. Gone was Markus Smith.

He was Jason Delapore.

CHAPTER

3

$\mathcal{H}$e awoke the next morning well-rested and surprisingly happy.

For the first time in a long while, he had no dreams, only a deep feeling of contentment - of belonging.

On the job, the day was bright and crisp, the traffic light. As he crossed the lobby to Connie's desk, she looked at him surprised. "Did you change something?", she moved her hand indicating her head and hair.

Jason, grinned. "Just my name."

Connie smirked, handing him a package, "well it looks good on you."

Back at the library, he made a nest of jacket, bike, and coffee around the computer system. The more he researched his family, the more he was fascinated.

Scrolling around the current year, he had noticed a number of relatives - but all deceased. One by one he pulled up their information. One had died in a ship fire. Another had died from a dog attack. Another was asphyxiated in their home by carbon-dioxide. Anther was struck by lightning. Each death was abnormal, to say the least.

"Goddamn", Jason muttered, "My family is cursed."

Following the links on his father's side of the family, he scrolled through names. Theodore, born in 1971 was the only son of Thomas and Harriet Delapore. They died in a freak mid-west tornado storm in '85. Thomas, born in 1949, was raised by his grandfather Samuel Delapore in Kentucky. Samuel, born in 1902, was a renowned outdoorsman and tracker, traits he inherited through his grandfather Nathaniel Delapore who was somewhat of a legend in the expansion of the West. His death while fighting a rabid grizzly was made famous in a certain dime-store novel.

Jason couldn't help but laugh out loud. "My great-great-grandfather wrestled grizzlies."

His narrow line of genealogy could be traced back to one interesting, yet strange person.

Randolph Delapore was born in 1828 in the Carfax estate in Antebellum Virginia. Only a teen-ager, he fought in the Mexican-American war in 1846, returning home in 1848 to some acclaim. In 1857, the Dred Scott case had set off a fuse in the slave-owning south. Randolph, much to the dismay of his family, spoke out against his family's ownership of slaves, calling himself an Abolitionist. Only a year later, he married a "Black Woman", which caused his family to shun him and expel him from his ancestral home of Carfax.

"Good for you Randolph", Jason grinned. "Screw those guys."

His wife was well-known as a daughter of a "Powerful Haitian Mambo". The two helped runaway slaves to flee southwards into uninhabited islands in the Caribbean. Apparently, Randolph took to the Voudou practices, being called, "The White Houngan".

In 1880, in the northern Louisiana swamps, Randolph was arrested for the deaths of three people. Eyewitnesses claim it was a Voudou expulsion that went awry. Randolph was sentenced to life in prison, only to be released in 1894 for "age-related ailments".

"Woah.", Jason exclaimed. "I'm a descendant of a Voudou Priest?"

Randolph's father, John Delapore, the patriarch of the family, also had a uniquely exceptional life.

Born in 1795 to the Carfax estate, John fought against the British in the war of 1812, making quite a name for himself as a young commander. In 1816, John joined the First Board of Public Works in Virginia, building canals to the James river for the transportation of goods from West Virginia. This made John a very wealthy man and boosted his political career. Sadly, in 1852, the newly constructed railroads made river travel inefficient, and the Board began to lose money. Soon, the glamour of Carfax faded into ill-repair.

In 1865, John fought for the south in the defense of Richmond. Union soldiers broke through their defenses and set fire to the town and countryside. John desperately tried to save his estate, but ended up dying within the flaming timbers of Carfax.

Apparently the Carfax estate was a big deal. It was built in 1675 by a 'English nobleman' who moved to the Colonies under mysterious circumstances. For over a hundred years the Carfax estate of Virginia held the line of Delapores, only to be destroyed in flames.

Jason did the math, "From 1675 to 1865, that was almost two hundred years. That place must have been ancient."

Surviving the fires was a Howard Delapore, age 7, who escaped with his parents to Massachusetts.

Howard was a prodigy in manufacturing appliances, and made a small fortune for himself. Married in his early-thirties to a young Elizabeth Sullen in 1889, they had a child, Alfred, in 1896. Sadly, Elizabeth took ill and died in the winter of 1893.

"Damn", Jason muttered sympathetically.

With the outbreak of World War I, a 21 year-old Alfred volunteered for service in England as an Aviation Officer in 1917. Sadly, Alfred was grievously wounded in a sortie in the Battle of Le Charmel, discharged and returned home in 1918. Alfred died at his father's home in 1920.

"Jesus." Jason shakes his head in disbelief.

The site had little information of the remainder of Uncle Howard's life. Apparently in 1921 he claimed a parcel of land in South Western England and spend much of his amassed fortune to return the squalid castle there to its former splendor. Upon its completion in 1924, Uncle Howard moved to England to reside in the grand estate. Tragically, not long after moving in, he was overcome with a vague mental illness and confined to Hanwell Sanitarium, dying there in 1927. No diagnosis of his mental illness or cause of death were listed.

Jason sighed. "That was the end of the other Delapore line. That's just awful. Maybe we are cursed."

Clicking on a link, a black-and-white photo from a news article appears showing a portly middle-aged man standing with a younger man in a field, an ancient castle framed behind them. The caption reads, "Mr. Howard Delapore and Cpt. Edward Norrys, proprietors of Exham Priory, Anchester"

CHAPTER
4

That night, asleep on his couch in front of the TV, Jason

dreams. He is in a grove of shady trees, entering a clearing. In the clearing stands his portly great uncle, dressed in his early 1900s business suit. Behind him is a castle, perched on a precipice against towering limestone walls. The priory's stone towers shone bright white in the noon-day sun. His uncle waved to him, beckoning him to come forward.

Jason awoke from the pleasant dream with a drowsy smile. His contentment was interrupted by the flashing alarms of his phone. He had work. As he squinted at his screen, finger hovering over the "accept" button, he suddenly became overwhelmed with apathy. For the first time in a long while, Jason instead clicked the "Decline" button. Jason sat up incredulous. He couldn't believe he had just declined a job. He knew this could mean less money for food, or even problems with rent - but why did he feel so good inside?

After a quick shower, Jason was back on his bike, navigating traffic to the public library.

At his usual spot in front of the terminal, Jason spent hours poring over his newly discovered family. Each link showing obituaries, birth certificates, and news articles pertinent to each. So much information. He became absorbed with the stories behind each member of his family. To his shock, Jason had completely missed lunch, buying some snacks from the library vending machines.

As day moved into night, Jason discovered the tab labeled "Living Relatives". The page that appeared held seven names, each with their whereabouts listed as "Unknown". Bemused but ready to move on, Jason spied the button labeled "Widen Search". Worth a try. He clicked it, and the screen displayed a spinning "Wait" icon. After an impressively long time, a new page loaded. There were now dozens of names on the list. Some of their locations were known, showing cities from around the world: Lisbon, Buenos Ares, Bergen, Minsk. At the top of the list, there was one name on a gold background - a site member.

The name read "Katherine Porter" apparently living in Glasgow Scotland. He clicked on her info page. No picture. A member for a year. No comments. Jason clicked on a line of buttons, finding the "Next Page".

The screen went black. An icon spun in the center of the screen. The words "Connecting to Video Chat" appeared at the bottom of the screen.

"Wait, WHAT!?", Jason blurted. He frantically searched for a "Quit" button. "How the fuck do you...", he began, aggravated.

The screen suddenly filled with video. A woman with disheveled hair was squinting into the camera. "Hello?", she said groggily.

"Oh shit", Jason stammered, frantically hammering the escape key.

"If you're saying something, I can't hear you.", the woman said, pointing a finger at her ear.

Jason looked around the monitor for a microphone. Finding one, he switched it on. "Uh... hey.", he stuttered.

"Hey", she said back, rubbing her eyes. "What time is it?"

"Oh my god, I'm so sorry!" Everything came flooding out. "I'm on this web page, GeneticHeritage, and I saw that you were a member... It just went to video-chat. I didn't mean to call you!"

"No worries", she smiled, "It's only midnight. Barely even asleep."

She had a nice smile. "Katherine, look, I'm sorry I bothered you.", Jason smiled back. "I'm going to hang up now... as soon as I can find out how..."

"Not a worry. It's not a problem. And it's Katie", she said, slipping on a pair of glasses. "So where are you calling from?"

"Pittsburgh. From the public library".

"Really? Are public libraries open that late there?"

Jason laughed, "Time difference! It's actually just before 8pm here. Got a few minutes before closing time."

"So, if you're calling from that web site, you know my name... So who are you?"

"Oh, my name is Markus..." Jason mentally slapped his forehead. "...I mean, Jason. Jason Delapore."

Katie raised an eyebrow. "So, not Markus then?"

"I'm sorry. The name is... ah... new to me."

"Hmm...", Katie pauses. "Sounds like there's a story to that."

Normally a very guarded person, Jason finds himself launching into his life story. He was surprised at how easy it was to share. Katie listened until he finished.

"You spent your whole life in an orphanage!?", she said incredulously.

"Not one orphanage, it was usually foster homes... but yeah, until I aged out of the system a few years back."

"Unbelievable", she said sympathetically. "And you never knew your real name!?"

"The DNA tests I took as a kid came back as 'Inconclusive', or so they told me." He game a sardonic smile, "At least not knowing who your parents are let me imagine what they were like."

The emotions were in Katie's voice, "It must have been hard..."

"Life is life, you know. It just is what it is. I had some good times at foster homes - learned how to ride a bike, even celebrated a few birthdays." Markus grinned, "And, hey, Markus Smith is still better than John Doe."

Katie giggled. "After all the stuff you went through, to come out on the other side a decent person - you are strong, Jason Delapore."

Jason's cheeks burned with the warmth of a genuine smile.

"I got on that site over a year ago trying to find other distant family members. I had just about given up. But then, blam! You call out of the blue. Crazy", Katie says. "Have you found any more of our relatives?"

"Nope.", Jason admitted, "You're the first."

"You've taken a look at some of our family tree, I take it?", She asked. "Pretty flippin' weird, right?"

"Yeah...", Jason let out an long incredulous breath.

"I know, right?", Katie bolstered. "What the hell is up with our family? Everyone seems to die in strange ways. It's like we're really unlucky."

"...or cursed.", Jason interjected.

"Yeah. Kinda makes you believe in that sort of thing, doesn't it?"

They laugh together. Jason notices for the first time that someone has moved next to him. Startled, he looks at the librarian standing over him. The librarian silently glared at him and touched the watch on his wrist.

"Oh. Hey Katie, it looks like the library is shutting down now..."

"Wait!", Katie rushed. "Call me back tomorrow! Just at a more decent time."

"Sure. I will.", Jason stammered.

"Promise me.", Katie said sincerely. "You're the first family I've found outside of my own."

Jason felt a welling of feelings. "I promise. Tomorrow."

Katie smiled back at him, and with a "Good night Pittsburgh", the screen went blank.

Jason looked around, seeing that the library was empty except for a few janitors at work.

A librarian locked the heavy doors behind him as Jason lifted his bike down the stairs. It was dark and cold. The rain looked like it would return.

Jason was the happiest he had ever been.

CHAPTER 5

Jason was up early the next morning. The smile continued across his face.

His work flew by as he anxiously awaited for a proper time to call Katie again.

When should he call? His 7am was her noon. But what if she had a job? Maybe calling at noon, her 5pm would be better? What time does she eat dinner? These feelings of anxious anxiety were new to him.

He settled on noon.

Racing back to the Library and up the concrete stairs, he plopped in front of his computer terminal and nervously logged in. As he clicked on "Video Call", he realized he was holding his breath. The screen turned black. The waiting icon spun.

Katie answered with a great smile and a big, "Hello again!"

They chatted about one another, sometimes awkwardly, and sometimes intimately, doing the social dance of getting to know one another.

Katie was born in Livingston, just outside of Edinburgh in Christmas of 1999. She was the only daughter of Geoff and Sylvia Porter. She has lived there all her life. She was a self-professed "fat kid" as a child, always being criticized by her mum. When she was 16, she found a love for rock climbing, which she still does for fun.

She confessed to never having a good relationship with her parents, who always seemed disappointed in her, or disapproving of her choices. A tomboy at heart, her mother always wanted to make her into something she wasn't - glamorous. Her mother was obsessed with appearances, especially those that attracted men. Katie's teenage rebellion was to dress in normal clothes without the heavy make-up her mother pushed onto her.

At 20, she attended Glasgow College, and for the first time she realized she didn't know what she wanted to do with her life. After two years of misery, she decided that college wasn't for her and dropped out to "see the world". In the past year, she had backpacked to both Spain and Italy for climbing expeditions.

"Backpacking alone across Europe, huh?", Jason remarked. "You sound pretty brave."

"More like pretty broke", Katie jested. "I would have much rather taken a plane. However, if you ever need a good recommendation for a hostel, I'm the gal to talk to."

They laughed.

"So then what do you do for work?", Jason asked.

"Just odd jobs that I get from the internet that I can do from home. Nothing too interesting. But it does let me keep this old flat. What about you?"

"Bicycle delivery", Jason said, hefting his bike in front of the camera. "Basically, I get messages to pick up packages and where to deliver them. It's repetitive and a bit of a workout, but it does give me a chance to see lots of the 'Burgh."

"You spend all day on your bike?", Katie said incredulously. "I don't think I could do that. My butt would hurt too much."

Jason laughed. "There are days when sitting on ice is the only relief."

They laughed together.

"Ok, so you know how I got on GeneticHeritage.com, but how did you find it?", Jason inquired.

Katie paused, tilting her head, thinking.

"I've always wanted to find a new family.", she said honestly. "Maybe it was because I was an only child with no one to play with, or maybe it was the relationship with my mum, but I wanted to find others like me."

"We didn't ever go and visit relatives, we never got birthday cards in the post.", Katie continued. "No aunts, uncles, cousins, or even grandparents."

"I remember one time when I was a kid, talking to my dad, asking him about his family. He spun me this yarn about our ancestors being wild people - witches and druids who danced around ancient stone henges in the moonlight."

"That story changed me. Ever since, I would have fantastic dreams about singing around a fire under the stars.", She paused in memory. "So yeah, I've been interested in my family history ever since."

Noting that it was getting late, they promised to call again the next day.

And so they did. Each day. For a week.

It was all Jason could think about.

Back in the library, on another call.

Katie was talking about her research into their family lineage. "Here, take a look at his. It's my family tree. For those of us who are from the direct paternal line, our last name gets bastardized dozens of times. My name 'Porter' was originally 'La Porte' three generations ago. But six generations before that, the last name showed as 'De La Port'. Your name sounds pretty close to the original."

"Weird", Jason said. "Any reason for the name change?"

"None that I could find.", Katie shook her head. "At first I thought these were just clerical errors, you know? Like government misprints or something."

"Like Ellis Island", Jason commented.

"Yeah. But check this out. The website had signed historical documents from a few of them - landshare deeds and whatnot. Their own signature was written as 'La Porte'."

"Well maybe they just dropped the 'De' part...", Jason ventured.

"And added an 'e' at the end? I dunno. It seems sketchy - like they had intentionally changed their last name."

"Like they were on the run from the law or something?", Jason joked.

"With our family? Who knows."

Jason was spending much of his time in the library. He was arriving earlier and earlier doing internet searches on his various relatives. He was neglecting work messages and knew this month's rent was going to be tight, but didn't care. He was driven.

Jason spent hours researching the antebellum Carfax estate in Virginia, as that was the origin of his family line. According to archived newsprint, the Carfax estate had finished construction in 1675, when the Virginia colony was still new. The sprawling estate along the James river was one of the largest plantations at that time, harvesting both corn and tobacco as cash crops. In several articles, nothing was said about the owner of the estate, only that he had come from English nobility with a sizable bankroll.

Who was this mysterious ancestor of his? He was determined to find out.

He stumbled across a cargo manifest, digitized from a shipping log from 1681. In the flowing cursive writing, it showed the bushels of corn and tobacco being loaded for transport back to Europe. The owner's name was clearly written: Walter De La Poer.

"Got you!", Jason grinned. Moving deftly through the internet, he muttered, "So, you came from England to the colonies in 1670-something... you were nobility of some kind...lets see..."

Jason found a website of old English heraldry and peerages. He searched for "De La Poer". And what he found astonished him.

"Katie! You're not going to believe this!", Jason said excitedly. "I think I found our common ancestor."

"Whaa... I've been looking for years... How...", Katie stammered.

"My Internet-foo is strong.", Jason smirked. "Check this out. The Carfax estate in Virginia where my entire line of Delapores come from, was built in 1675 by a 'Walter De La Poer'."

"De La Poer?", Katie echoed.

"Apparently, he was a English nobleman who fled to the colonies under 'mysterious circumstances', right? Well, it turns out - are you ready for this? - Turns out he was wanted for the murder of his ENTIRE FAMILY."

"Woah.", Katie said shocked.

"Right!?", Jason continued unabashedly. "So get this: he was a Baron. The 11th Baron in succession for a place called Exham

Priory. After doing a little digging, I found that the De La Poer line had ruled there for centuries, since the castle was built in 1277."

"That's like...", Katie stared upwards, doing the math, "...750 years ago."

"So, the guy who built the priory was named Gilbert de la Poer. He was presented with the title Baron of Exham by no other than Henry the Third! Apparently he had saved the king's life in 'The Second Baron's War' - whatever that was. This is the first De La Poer entered into English nobility, it is the origin of our last names."

"That...", Katie began, "...is friggin' amazing!"

They laughed and joked about being from nobility. Maybe they should get a castle of their own sometime.

Their conversations carried into the night.

CHAPTER

6

The next day, Jason woke with the sun.

Leaving the shower, with a toothbrush in his mouth, he checked the mail that came in last night. Junk... Junk... Bill... A plain business envelope. Tearing it open, he found a new credit card adhered to the paperwork. His breath caught when he saw the name on the card: Jason Delapore. Finally. The world knew his real name. He felt changed, renewed. Taking out the card with reverence, he was overcome with emotions. Today was the first day of his new life.

Jason reached the Library early, eager to share his small triumph with Katie. He was surprised at her excitement when she answered.

"Jason!", she shouted with barely contained energy. "You won't believe what just happened!"

Jason, surprised, could only fumble, "Wh..what happened?"

"I found Exham Priory!" Before Jason could comment, Katie continued, "It's still standing, as a matter of fact it's been refurbished! A guy by the name of Mazhar Sadik purchased it awhile back and restored it. SO I called him."

"Wow", was all Jason could say, as he tried to process everything. "Wait, you what?"

"I know! Impulsive! But I found the contact number and thought: what the hell!", Katie was beaming. "Turns out, he's a Turkish historian who studies the families that once lived in that region. When I told him about our ancestors, he was giddy with questions."

Katie trembled with anticipation, "Jason - he invited us to stay there! He said as long as we want. A week! A Month!"

Jason tried to say something, but nothing came out.

"We could meet up in England and then get to Anchester and actually stay in a castle! Our castle!"

Jason still paused.

Katie sobered a bit on Jason's non-response. "Oh, I mean, I get it. I know you have a job. A life. You can't just drop everything and run off to England on a whim..."

"Let's do it.", Jason said, surprising himself.

"Really?", Katie looked surprised but elated.

Something deep within him felt right somehow...

"Yeah", Jason said more firmly. "There's absolutely nothing holding me here. I've always wanted to see the world... yeah, screw it. Let's go!"

Katie was overwhelmed, bursting with laughter. "Oh my god! I can't believe you said yes! We are going to have so much fun!" She took a deep smiling breath. "Ok! There's a lot of planning to do. Phone calls to make, plane tickets to buy... I'll start making plans!" She gave a cute little shriek. "I'm so excited! I can't wait to see you in person!"

"Me too.", Jason laughed.

Katie ended the call with a quick, "Love ya!"

Jason swelled with happiness and anticipation.

CHAPTER

7

$\mathcal{P}$lans were made and tickets were purchased.

The morning of his flight to Bristol, Jason stood at his doorway observing his apartment. The dime-store couch, the ancient TV, the garage sale end tables - they were the first pieces of furniture he ever acquired. Before he thought it was a sign of being an adult, but now he could see it for what it was: baggage weighing him down.

Backpack over his shoulder, he closed his apartment door leaving his furnishings and his life behind him.

In the entrance, he dropped his keys in the mailbox and propped up his bike near the stairway with an attached note reading "To a good home". On the street, he hailed a taxi and slid into the back. As the car drove off, Jason's thoughts were only on the impulsiveness of his decision, and the excitement of a drastic change in life.

Jason had never seen an airport in person. It took him awhile to navigate the crowds and the confusing signs to finally reach the ticketing kiosk. One-way flight to Bristol Airport, England. No luggage.

Jason thought the plane was luxurious, even in coach. Even though this flight had cost him most of his amassed savings, he was thrilled at the first-time experience. Once the excitement of take off had passed, and the reality of an eleven hour flight settled in, the drifting landscape out the window lulled him into a quiet sleep.

And Jason dreamed. Rolling green hills becoming tall forests of white-barked trees. A wall led to a garden of fountains and topiary surrounding a towering stone fortress. The drawbridge was down. Standing with arms outspread was a woman in a slender white dress and a crown of flowers woven into her hair. Her smile was achingly beautiful as she beckoned to him.

"Come to me, my Love."

Jason awoke with the dream words still fresh in his mind. Outside his window, the long rays of dusk played over the sea far below. Swirling low fog crept over the ocean, swelling around the cliff shores of England.

Jason waited in plain view of the exit from the Glasgow flight. He barely noticed that he had been standing for twenty minutes with his backpack over his shoulder, waiting with giddy anticipation. How long did it take this plane to disembark? A stream of passengers began trickling into the terminal. Jason was on his toes, surveying the crowd, not realizing he was holding his breath.

She came through the passage, her blue eyes surveying the terminal, and found his. With an audible gasp of excitement, she exclaimed, "Jason!". She ran at him like a luggage dragging missile, colliding with him in a fiercely awkward embrace.

"Well, hi", was all Jason could stammer as he regained his breath.

Grinning, she looked up at him. "You're taller than I'd pictured." She then hugged him even tighter.

Eventually parting, the two looked at one another in person for the first time.

"I can't believe we're doing this!", Katie remarked. "And here I thought I was out of my impulsive teenager phase."

"I think we might actually be a little insane", Jason quipped.

They laughed together, making their way out of the airport.

"So what do we do, get a taxi, or...", Jason looked up the busy airport terminal.

"Mazhar said he would have a driver waiting for us.", Katie said in a pretentious voice.

Jason let out an impressive whistle.

"I know! Fancy, right?", Katie smiled.

"So, what is this Mazhar like? Do we know anything about him?", Jason inquired.

"I just spoke to him over the phone", Katie said, "I mean, he seemed like a really nice guy. Said he was a philanthropist - which I guess means he's rich."

"Well, he does own a castle...", Jason commented.

Katie stopped, suddenly remembering. "Oh my god! You won't believe this!" She paused dramatically. "We're not the only ones staying at the priory. Mazhar has others of our family staying there! Cousins! It's going to be a family reunion!"

Jason thought that this Mazhar must be wealthy to put up so many guests on a whim.

"I think that's him", Katie exclaimed.

A large man with tanned skin and a short dark beard wearing a tie and jacket stood near the exit doors. He held up a card which simply read, "Delapore".

"Hello!", Katie said with alacrity. "I think we're who you're waiting for."

The man took a few moments to process them, then outstretched a hand. "Come", he said in heavily accented English.

He led them out of the airport and to a luxury sedan parked on the street. He opened the trunk and gestured for their bags. As he placed the luggage into the car, Jason noticed the gold necklace he was wearing. At first he thought it was a cross, but the top had a hook on it - like a question mark.

Both Katie and Jason thanked him, as their belongings were sealed shut. He then opened the rear doors to let the two slide into the comfy leather seats. Jason and Katie shot each other impressed looks.

The chauffeur got into the driver's seat and pulled out onto the busy roadway.

To Jason's initial panic, he thought they were driving on the wrong side of the road. He and Katie had a laugh over it. Jason had never been out of Pittsburgh, let alone the United States. This was all new to him.

The two made nonsensical small-talk, as they were both overwhelmed with a child-like sense of adventure.

Katie asked the driver a few questions about Mazhar and the priory.

He responded with "My English, eh, not so good", incorporating a hand gesture and a forced smile.

"Well, we have a few hours until we reach Anchester", Jason noted.

"I am so excited!", Katie exclaimed in exuberance. "I'm going to be talking the whole way there!"

Katie was sleeping on Jason's arm as the sedan rolled through the lush English countryside. It was a clear night, illuminated by an almost full moon. Outside the sedan window passed vast rolling green hills, only to be swallowed by thick tree lines. Jason watched the scenery in wonder, actually seeing the world for the first time.

Another split off the highway showed a road sign declaring, "Welcome to Anchester".

Jason nudged Katie awake, pointing at the sign. She awoke with a yawn. Noticing how close she was to Jason, she took an embarrassed shift away from him. They both peered out their windows.

A few old cottages and dilapidated farms were scattered throughout the woods. It went on this way for a few miles.

Then, the forest broke. The town looked like something out of an old Gothic tale; an arrangement of wood and plaster walls, dark pitched roofs, and glowing yellowed windows. The buildings were built on top of one another, haphazardly, with only narrow alleys between them, lit by dim streetlights.

And just like that, it they were past.

"Not much of a town", Katie remarked.

"More like a gas-stop", Jason joked.

The sedan turned down an unkempt side-road, leading deeper into the woods. The outlines of bleak mountains stood in their direction.

Wondering how much further they need to go, Jason looked at his phone's Maps app. A pop-up chimed, stating, "GPS not found. No Signal."

The winding road led upwards through tree-lined hills overlooking a desolate valley. Rounding a curve, the driver slammed on his breaks, cursing loudly.

"What is it?" Katie asked, as she and Jason craned their necks to see.

The driver grumbled to himself. "A dog", he finally coughed before driving again.

As they continued, Jason thought he saw an animal in the woods, lit white in the moonlight.

After a slow drive up an elevated path, the priory came into view from around a cliff face. The ancient stone towers and imposing gatehouse were fully illuminated by strategically placed powerful exterior lights, casting an ethereal glow on the weathered walls and making the place look more like a luxurious resort than a medieval fortress.

As they approached the gatehouse, they passed an odd looking car on the side of the road. Inside were two men, sitting with the light off in the dark. As the sedan passed, they lowered into their seats suspiciously and made no gestures to them.

Passing through the gatehouse, meticulously maintained stone gardens and intricate statuary filled the expansive estate courtyard, all bathed in the warm light emanating from countless hidden fixtures.

The car ground to a stop in the gravel-lined courtyard. Jason and Katie stepped out in awe, craning their necks to take in the towering walls and stained glass windows decorating the soaring towers of the priory, lit as if it were high noon. The driver barked orders in Turkish to several servants, who slinked to the trunk of the car, efficiently gathering Katie's luggage and Jason's lone backpack.

They followed the servants along the garden-lined path to the massive, intricately carved entrance doors. The courtyard was a marvel of landscaping, with perfectly manicured topiary and burbling fountains, the soft light illuminating the dark ivy that clung to the ancient stone walls.

A tall, Oxford-dressed young man approached them, carrying a large rifle in the crook of his arm. He was devilishly handsome, and appeared surprised to see them.

"Mazhar?" Katie asked politely.

He laughed, shaking his head. "No, I'm Caleb." He eyed them both up and down with a smirk. "I forgot you two were arriving today." He casually extended a hand towards the priory, bidding them to follow him. "Let me show you around."

Jason waved his phone around, trying to get a signal. "There are no cell towers within miles of here," Caleb mentioned, "And, we're in the shadow of those cliffs. This whole place is a dead zone."

As they walked, Katie eyed the rifle. "Were you going hunting?"

Caleb nodded, "Pheasants. The moors around the priory are lousy with them."

"At night?", Jason asked.

Caleb's grin widened. "Never know what you'll get at night. Makes it more exciting."

"Do you hunt on horseback?" Katie asked excitedly, "Are there horses here!? I love horses."

Caleb replied, "Afraid not. Historically, they've never been able to keep horses here." He shrugged at Katie's playful pouting, "Temperamental animals, I guess."

Servants swept open the main doors into the grand foyer of the priory. The interior was a stunning display of history, with ancient tapestries covering the walls, priceless paintings hung in ornate frames, and museum-quality displays of artifacts and weaponry. Partially hiding herself behind the foyer doors, a meek looking girl looked on. She was dressed in black, had dyed hair, and wore too much eye-liner. "This is Kylie," Caleb introduced. She clumsily waved a greeting before moving out of their way. "She's... shy", Caleb continued.

A throaty female voice soared from the stairs, "Well who is this that graces these halls?" The young woman was wearing a long satin dress and had her hair done up like a 20's flapper. She glided effortlessly down the stairs, her eyes fixed on Jason.

"And this is Alexia" Caleb announced.

She stopped uncomfortably close to Jason, extending a delicate hand, "Charmed, I'm sure." Jason awkwardly took her outstretched fingers and gave them a shake. "You must be Jason", she said in a sultry tone.

"Yeah", Jason stammered. "And this is Katie."

Katie took a step forward, smiling. Alexia, not taking her attention from Jason said breathily, "I'm sure."

"Come! Let me show you around!", Alexia announced, grabbing Jason's arm and leading him up the stairs. Katie's smile faded, shocked at the audacity of the woman.

As they ascended the stairs, Alexia moved in close to Jason. He turned to shoot Katie a pleading look with his eyes.

Caleb snickered as he began climbing the stairs, "Now Alexia, play nice with your cousins."

Kylie slowly moved past the stunned Katie. Katie whispered to her, "Is she always this way?"

"No," Kylie whispered, "She's usually more of a bitch." They shared a smile as they followed up the stairs.

The five walked through stone halls lined with ancient tapestries and exquisite paintings. "This is amazing," Jason shared in awe.

Alexia chided him, "You get used to it, darling. It's like living in a museum."

The doors at the other end of the room burst open, and a tall, modernly dressed man entered like royalty. He threw his arms open and flashed an inviting smile. "My friends! Merhaba!"

Striding towards them, he hugged and kissed his greetings. "Mazhar.", Katie smiled.

"Please, call me Maz! I take it your journey here went well?"

Jason nodded, "It was my first plane trip."

"Really?", Maz said incredulously. "Never travelled anywhere except to your homeland? The pull of your ancestors must be strong in you."

They made small talk for a while. Maz appeared extremely gracious and apparently overjoyed to have more company staying with him.

"Well", Maz clapped his hands, "It is late. You must be tired from your travels," He made a quick gesture to some servants. "Please make up the tower guest rooms for them, and prepare some food. They must be hungry from their travels." He turned to Jason and Katie, "Please, make yourself at home! Tomorrow we can talk about everything!"

Giving a noble bow, Maz turned to leave. Katie said sincerely, "Thank you, Maz! For all the hospitality!"

He waved a hand as he walked away, "Think nothing of it! This is your family home. I am merely the curator."

Ascending the stone stairway, a short hall opened before them. Two wooden doors on either side were framed by tapestries and exquisite paintings.

The servant motioned them to the last door on the left and opened it with a flourish.

Katie giggled with excitement as she saw the lavish medieval bedroom that she would be staying in, complete with a four-poster bed and antique furnishings.

"It's like a dream!", she said taking in the ambience.

"Sir", the servant said to Jason in clipped English, "Your bed is in the tower. At the end of the hall."

He turned to follow the servant out, glimpsing Katie's look, he instead said, "I'll find it. Thank you."

The servant bowed and asked, "Is there anything you need?" Katie thanked him profusely as he left.

Katie made a girlish cry and leapt on the bed, laughing. She turned to Jason, "I can't believe this. It's like a dream."

Jason, sitting on the edge of the bed, nodded. "I know. Going from a studio apartment to... a castle! It's unreal."

"It's more than that, though", Jason began thoughtfully. Katie rolled onto her stomach and looked at him seriously. "It's not the castle or the servants - it's like something I've always wanted but couldn't quite put my finger on..."

"It's like fulfillment", Katie said, "Like belonging."

"Exactly!", Jason sighed. "I never know I wanted or even needed it, but now... I feel like I have it."

Katie reached out and put her hand on his. "I feel the same."

Jason and Katie both blushed and quickly changed the tone.

They laughed at how small their lives seemed before all this.

"I'm too excited to sleep," Katie giggled, "I'll probably stay up all night talking."

Before long, Katie was snoring softly in her bed. Jason slid the blankets up over her, and quietly left the room.

At the end of the hall, a spiral stairway ascended. Climbing up the stairs and past the narrow stained glass windows, he opened the heavy wooden door at the top of the stair. The circular bedchamber was stunning. A low-orange fire glowed in the hearth, its light mingling with the moonlight from the shuttered window panes. Tapestries, paintings, dressers, and wardrobes lined the stone walls. Thick rugs lay on the floors leading to the magnificent bed in the center of the chamber.

Jason, taking the experience in, sat on the edge of his bed, looking out over the moon-lit gardens behind the priory. There was a knock on the door.

Maz was there, holding a lidded bowl. "I thought you might be hungry." He lifted the lid and the exotic scent made Jason realize that he was famished. "It's Tava - lamb stew - a family recipe." Maz handed the bowl to him. "Careful. It's hot."

Jason thanked him and began to dig in. Smiling, Maz looked around. "I hope everything is to your liking."

Jason, with his mouth full, grunted and nodded his affirmative. The stew was warm, rich, and spicy - a perfect comfort food.

"Good! Good," Maz exclaimed. "It makes me happy to see so many De La Poers back in their ancestral home."

Jason, chewing on a lamb chunk, asked, "Are you a De La Poer too?"

Maz laughed. "No! No, I'm afraid not. I am from old Turkish blood."

"If you don't mind me asking," Jason wiped his lip, "Why are you so interested in the De La Poer family?"

Maz clapped him on the shoulder. "Historical genealogy is my life. I've spent years tracking various genetic lines from all over the world. However, you De La Poers are unique. You have one of the oldest lineages in the modern world."

"Really?" Jason said incredulously.

"It is a fact," Maz held up a finger. "This castle has been in the De La Poer family line since 1277. For four hundred years the De La Poers ruled over these lands, until 1673."

Jason asked, "1673? That was Walter De La Poer."

Maz raised his eyebrows, "Very good! Yes, Walter was the last in the line of the English De La Poers."

Jason hesitated before asking, "Is it true that he murdered his whole family?"

Maz frowned, "There was a great fire in the priory. Walter and a few servants were the only survivors. It is hard to believe that the ruling

Baron would murder his entire family. I believe the fire claimed their lives."

Maz continued, "The priory sat as a vacant ruin until 1920, when your great uncle Howard purchased it and reconstructed it to its former beauty."

"The article I read said that Uncle Howard was overcome by a mental disorder shortly after rebuilding this place."

Maz looked sympathetic. "True. Tragedy has a way of following your family line. I think he was still grieving from the loss of his son. He must have thought that the priory would change that, but in the end, he was still just a lonely man."

Maz got a far-off stare, "Some places in this world form connections with families. With their bloodlines. The longer they live there, the more powerful the connections. The stronger the pull back to their homes..."

Maz and Jason sat silently for a long moment. Abruptly, Maz announced, "Well! It is late." He took the dishes and said kindly, "Please, get some rest. Tomorrow we will have much to talk about!" And, just as fast as he entered, he disappeared out the door.

$\mathcal{J}$t did not take Jason long to fall asleep on that plush bed, as all the leagues of travel suddenly weighed down on him. Like most nights, Jason dreamed.

He dreamt of an older man in a 1920's suit, holding blueprints and pointing to workers, overseeing the re-construction of the priory. Standing in the gatehouse door, a woman in a white dress with a crown of flowers beckoned to him. The man dropped his paperwork and followed her into the castle, as if entranced by her ethereal presence. Drifting through the doorway and into the rocky floor, he followed her, never quite reaching her. She wound down a rough-hewn stairway, through moldering catacombs, and down further into glistening subterranean tunnels.

"I see you, my love," her voice echoed, sending chills down his spine.

Darkness closed around him, suffocating and oppressive. The tunnel walls transformed into stacks of decayed bones and skulls, a macabre tapestry of death. The man screamed as the darkness flooded around him, engulfing him from the legs up, its icy tendrils clawing at his flesh. In his last moments, he clawed at his face, babbling incoherent words as the weight of history crashed down into his mind, driving him to the brink of insanity. The darkness swallowed him whole, accompanied by the sound of scraping, chittering shrieks that echoed through the void.

Jason startled awake, his heart pounding in his chest. He shook his head, but the ominous scraping sounds persisted, now invading his waking world. As the terrible noise grew louder, he noticed the paintings on the walls begin to vibrate and buck on their nails, as if possessed by an unseen force. His eyes were drawn to the large tapestry opposite his bed, where the fabric twisted and moved behind it, like squirming serpents writhing beneath the surface.

The scraping and screeching reached a deafening crescendo. Jason rose out of bed, drawn towards the undulating tapestry, his curiosity overpowering his fear. As he reached towards it, the sound suddenly stopped, plunging the room into an eerie silence. Startled, he quickly moved aside the tapestry, his heart in his throat. Behind it was only a stone wall, cold and unyielding. He looked around incredulously, his mind struggling to reconcile the nightmare with reality. Running his hands over the stones, he felt a clammy dampness with his fingers, but nothing more.

A knock on the door caused him to jump, his nerves frayed to the breaking point.

"Yes," Jason said, his voice trembling.

A servant opened the door just enough to look in, concern etched on their face. "Is everything all right, sir?"

"Did you hear that?" Jason asked, still examining the wall, desperate for validation. "That noise?"

The servant paused, an unsettling silence filling the room. "All I heard was your fitful sleeping, sir. Can I get you anything?"

Shaking his head, Jason apologized, his mind reeling with doubt and confusion. "No, I'm good."

Completely exhausted and now questioning his own sanity, he returned to bed, the remnants of his nightmare still clinging to his thoughts like a dark shroud.

The next morning, the sun shone through the tower window, casting a warm glow on Jason's sleeping form, curled up in an uncomfortable ball of blankets. A knock at the door stirred him from his slumber. Katie opened it a crack, saying, "You missed breakfast."

Jason groaned and pulled the covers up over his head, trying to block out the intrusion. Katie slid into the room, her footsteps soft on the stone floor. "It's 10 am, and the day is beautiful."

Jason croaked, "Just five more minutes..." his voice muffled by the blankets.

Katie plopped on his bed, the mattress dipping under her weight. "Bad night sleep, huh?"

Realizing he wasn't going to get any more rest, Jason sat up and rubbed his eyes, the remnants of sleep still clinging to him. "Had a nightmare," he murmured. "It was a waking nightmare, you know? Kept going on after I thought I was awake."

"Woah," intoned Katie, her eyes widening. "That sounds intense."

Jason sat up and yawned, stretching his arms above his head. "I haven't had one of those in a long time."

Noticing that Jason had no shirt on, Katie blushed and turned away, her cheeks turning a delicate shade of pink. "Alright, you have five minutes to get dressed. Then I'm coming back. With an air horn."

Jason smiled as Katie closed the door behind her, the click of the latch echoing in the quiet room.

A few minutes later, Katie and Jason descended the stairs into the priory's Great Chamber. Couches and over-stuffed chairs stood on heavy rugs on the stone floor, their rich fabrics and intricate patterns adding warmth to the space. A mighty fireplace, large enough for someone to stand in, yawned darkly along the central wall, its charred bricks hinting at countless stories shared around its hearth. More tapestries, paintings, and cabinets lined the walls, giving the room an ancient, yet regal decor. Windows looked out into the sunlit gardens beyond, their leaded glass casting intricate patterns on the floor.

Jason let out a whistle of admiration. "This place is amazing."

As the two took in the vast room, they were startled by a robed figure emerging from the shadows. He bowed to them and stated, "Mazhar regrets that he is occupied. He bids you to look about the priory as you wish."

"Thank you..." Katie began, but the man turned to leave before she could finish, his robes swishing softly as he disappeared through a side door.

Heading to the large double doors, Jason swung them open to reveal the gardens within the priory walls. Both Jason and Katie caught their breath at the beautiful sight that greeted them. Hedges and topiaries wound between blossoming trees and lush grass, their carefully manicured shapes creating an enchanting labyrinth of greenery. Fountains and reflecting pools housed marble statues from myth and legend, their serene faces gazing out over the tranquil waters. The high priory walls encircled the gardens, ending into the high granite cliff face towering over the grounds, its rugged surface a stark contrast to the manicured beauty below. The air smelled of blossoms, their sweet fragrance carried on the gentle breeze. Small insects flitted between the sun beams, their delicate wings catching the light. Croaking toads could be heard within the ponds, their deep calls adding to the symphony of nature.

Everything was immaculate, as if the gardens had been plucked straight from a fairy tale.

Jason and Katie wandered through the gardens, pointing out the amazing sights or trying to identify the various Grecian statues, their laughter ringing out in the peaceful surroundings. After sight-seeing for hours, they were amazed at how extensive these gardens were, each turn revealing new wonders to behold.

Occasionally they spied men in grey-blue robes tending to the grounds - pruning, watering, fertilizing. Most of the robed men had shaved heads, some with dark bushy beards, their faces etched with lines of concentration as they went about their tasks. Their medieval attire did not look out of place in the priory gardens, giving them the impression of secular monks, dedicated to the upkeep of this enchanting place. They utterly ignored the two as they went about their chores, their focus unwavering.

Jason and Katie talked and laughed as they explored the gardens, their conversation flowing easily as they shared stories and dreams. They spoke about their pasts, their likes and dislikes, and their outlooks for the future, each revelation bringing them closer together.

"I want to see the world!" Katie said as she swung around a statue, her eyes sparkling with excitement. "It is such a vast and interesting place, full of amazing things to experience." She lost her balance, but Jason caught her, his arms encircling her waist. Katie clung to him and continued, "I hoped that college would open up my life, but it made me realize that if I wanted to see the world - I should just do it."

"I've never really felt like a part of the world," Jason said truthfully, his voice tinged with a hint of sadness. "Living place to place like I did, I always felt like an outcast."

Katie looked at him with sympathetic eyes, her heart aching for the loneliness he must have felt. She gave him a quick hug, her arms offering silent comfort. "One thing about this world," she said, "anyone can find their place in it."

Approaching the towering cliffs at the back of the priory, Katie became excited, her eyes lighting up with anticipation. "Oh! I would love to climb that!" Katie gasped, her gaze tracing the rugged surface. "Look at all those holes in the granite face. That would make for an excellent free climb."

The two moved to the very base of the cliffs, surveying them, their necks craning to take in the sheer height. "My parents never got why I loved to climb. They were all like 'Why would you want to do that?', and 'looks dangerous', and 'girls don't climb mountains'." She smiled at Jason, her expression a mix of defiance and pride. "So, it became my thing. My personal retreat from life."

In one of the granite holes, something shuffled, catching their attention. A large black rat squirmed within the fissure, its oily fur glistening in the sunlight. As it eyed them, its beady gaze unsettling, the two began to notice that other holes in the cliff were occupied by dark, oily rats with glittery eyes, their presence a discordant note in the tranquil gardens. The more they looked, the more rats they noticed, their numbers seemingly endless.

Jason says, "Looks like they have a rat problem," his voice tinged with disgust.

Returning to the priory for lunch, they wrapped their sandwiches to go and headed back out into the gardens - this time headed to the topiary maze, its twisting paths beckoning them to explore.

As they wandered through the twisting green walls of the maze, they laughed and talked, choosing directions randomly in hopes of getting lost, the thrill of adventure coursing through their veins. At times, the maze would open up into small secluded areas with benches and a statue fountain, offering a moment of respite from the winding paths. In these, they would sit and talk some more, sometimes picking at their lunches, the day bright and warm around them.

After a long journey, they reached the end of the maze, which opened into a large grassy clearing. At its center, a circle of monolithic standing stones and menhirs towered over the topiary walls, their ancient presence commanding respect.

Katie let out an exclamation of awe, her eyes wide with wonder. Grinning at Jason, she ran into the circle and laid down in the grass, giggling and bidding him to join her, her joy infectious.

As they stared up into the blue cloud-filled sky between the shadows of the stones, Katie said, "I told you my dad would tell me about our pagan ancestors who danced around stones like these. Of course, he would call them all witches fornicating on Devil Stones. Very protestant, my da. Those stories just made me want to find out more about my real history, you know? Where I really came from."

She turned to look at Jason, her eyes soft with affection. "And that's how we found each other." The two smiled in the grass at one another, a moment of connection passing between them.

The crunch of gravel approached them, breaking the spell. They sat up to see two of the robed groundskeepers already entering the clearing, their faces impassive. Each wore a simple belt and the small golden 'crook' pendants, the metal glinting in the sunlight. They silently glanced at the two, not missing a stride, before turning towards another maze path, their robes swishing softly as they walked.

Jason and Katie looked at each other quizzically. "Are they gardeners or monks?" Jason ventured, his brow furrowed in confusion.

"What's with those pendants they all wear?" Katie wondered, her curiosity piqued.

Jason shrugged, "Maybe they're some sect of Christian? You know, like good shepherds?"

As the robed gardeners approached their exit path, they suddenly stopped, their bodies tensing. A black rat was sitting in the path before them, its gaze fixed on the men. One of the men clutched his pendant, and Jason could hear something like a quick prayer from the other, their voices low and urgent. They both made some kind of hand sign before slowly moving around the impeding rodent, their movements cautious and deliberate. The large vermin scurried into another topiary as they passed, its dark form disappearing into the greenery.

Katie and Jason looked at one another in confusion. "That was... weird." Katie said, her voice tinged with unease.

"Yeah," Jason agreed, "I guess they don't see the rats as a problem."

Being genuinely troubled, the two left the henge and made their way back into the maze for an exit, their minds buzzing with questions.

The sun approached the granite cliffs to the west, threatening to darken the gardens in short time. Jason and Katie made their way closer and closer to the priory towers, visible over the hedges, their steps quickening as the shadows lengthened.

The two entered another small private area, just as Kylie entered from another direction, her face flushed and breathless. A camera hanging around her neck. "There you are!" she said, her voice tinged with relief.

"Hey Kylie," Jason and Katie greeted her, their voices laced with concern. "You alright?" Katie ventured, taking in Kylie's disheveled appearance.

Kylie puffed a bit and sat hard on a bench, her chest heaving. "I'm just not used to... all this... outdoors." She held up her camera unexpectedly, "Let me get a picture of you two." Jason and Katie barely had a chance to pose when the click and flash of the camera triggered.

Kylie stared into the digital camera screen, inspecting her work, then announced, "Maz is preparing a celebration for your arrival tonight. I was supposed to find you and tell you to head back. So... head back."

On the statue an arm's length from Kylie's bench, a black rat suddenly scurried around its marble torso, its movements quick and erratic. Kylie shrieked, her camera dropping onto its lanyard, leaping to her feet away from the thing, her face contorted in terror. She backed away as far as she could, her body trembling.

Jason shooed the rat away, his voice stern. It gave a menacing hiss before scuttling off, disappearing into the undergrowth. Katie moved to Kylie, her voice soothing. "It's ok. Look, it's gone now." The tremors of panic slowly left Kylie with Katie's comforting words, her breathing returning to normal.

Jason said, disgusted, "This place is overrun with those little beasts."

"Come on, let's get back to the priory," Katie said, guiding Kylie, her arm around the other girl's shoulders.

As the three made their way through the maze, Katie tried to cheer Kylie, her voice light and reassuring. "It's OK to be terrified of rats. I don't do so well with bees, myself."

Jason heard Kylie mutter under her breath, her voice barely audible. "I'm not afraid of rats... just those things..."

The feast hall table was filled with food, a veritable

cornucopia of culinary delights. Jason and Katie couldn't help but be impressed with the presentation. Covered dishes, baskets of bread, and carafes of wine adorned the table, each item carefully arranged to create a stunning visual display. Richly dressed servants brought more trays from the kitchen, their movements graceful and efficient.

Katie and Jason stood, waiting for the servants to finish their work, their eyes taking in the opulent scene before them. Caleb strode in and plopped down in one of the high-backed chairs, as if this was a regular affair. He picked a piece of meat from a platter and licked the fat from his fingers, his actions lacking the refinement of the surroundings.

Alexia swept into the hall, her slender dinner gown flowing behind her, the fabric shimmering in the candlelight. She looked at Jason, her eyes sparkling with mischief. "Darling! I've missed you." She gave him a kiss on the cheek, her lips lingering for a moment, and pulled him down into a chair. Alexia seated herself next to Jason before Katie could move, a triumphant smile on her face. Annoyed, Katie took a chair across from Jason, her eyes narrowing slightly.

No one noticed Kylie silently entering the room and taking a seat, her presence overshadowed by the more dominant personalities.

The main doors burst open as Mazhar entered like a royal presence, his stance confident and commanding. The servants stopped their duties to give him a low bow, their respect for him evident in their actions. Four blue-gray robed men entered behind him, their faces impassive.

"Wonderful!" Maz exclaimed, his voice booming through the hall. "You have outdone yourselves this time!" He took a seat at the head of the table, his movements regal. A servant immediately filled his wine glass, the dark liquid swirling in the crystal. The four robed men silently took up corners of the room, standing at attention, their presence a silent reminder of Maz's authority.

Maz gave a grand gesture, his arms sweeping wide. "Thank you all for joining me! I am so happy to see so many of the true De La Poers in their ancestral home once again." He raised his glass in toast, the light catching the wine and casting a ruby glow on his face.

As Jason reached for some bread, Alexia put her hand on his, her fingers trailing lightly over his skin. "We're so glad you wanted to stay with us." Jason fumbled nervously, his cheeks reddening slightly.

Katie, visibly annoyed, asked, "So how did the rest of you come to be here?" Her tone was polite, but there was an underlying edge to her words.

Caleb, chewing loudly, piped up. "I found most of them. Doing lots of searches for variations of the 'De La Poer' name. Right lengthy business, that." He spoke with his mouth full, crumbs falling onto his shirt.

Alexia pointed to herself and said "LaPorte", then pointed to Kylie, "Delop", and to Caleb, "De'Poor". Her tone was matter-of-fact, as if she was listing off items on a grocery list.

Katie raised her hand, "Porter". Her voice was clear and confident.

Jason said "Delapore", his voice quiet compared to the others.

Alexia cooed and said, "Ooh! You've got the best one - or at least the closest". She giggled, her laughter tinkling like bells. Gingerly eying Katie, she added, "Porter, huh? Are you sure you're related?" She laughed dismissively, her tone dripping with condescension.

Katie gave an obsequious smile, her eyes flashing with anger. "As far as I know, we're all related." Under her breath, she intoned "Bitch", the word barely audible.

Kylie blurted out, "Alexia used to live in a trailer park." The room went silent, the tension palpable. Caleb broke into laughter as Alexia shot daggers with her eyes, her face contorted with rage.

Alexia replied, her voice sickly sweet, "That's still better than a rehab center, darling." She smirked, her eyes glinting with malice. Kellie averted her eyes, her cheeks burning with shame.

Maz chimed in, his voice firm but gentle. "Now come come! We're all family! Do not squabble in front of our guests!" He turned to Jason, his expression apologetic. "No one can bicker like family."

Jason cleared his throat, trying to diffuse the tension. "So Caleb, how did you get here?" He asked, his tone friendly.

Caleb, his mouth full, replied, "That was all Maz." He gestured towards Maz with his fork, a piece of meat dangling from the tines.

Maz replied, his voice smooth and practiced. "It is true. But mere luck, really. I spent years searching for a true heir of Exham Priory. But, your family was scattered to the winds! And just when I thought I would be alone in this castle, I found Caleb while on a trip to France. He in turn found Kylie, and then Alexia. And now we are all one big happy family." He held up a wine glass, the light glinting off the crystal. Caleb swigged from his, the wine sloshing over the rim.

Katie asked, her curiosity piqued. "How long have you all been here?" She leaned forward slightly, her eyes intent on Maz.

Maz answered, his voice measured. "Just a few years. Fairly soon after I purchased the priory." He took a sip of wine, his eyes distant.

Kylie said under her breath, her voice barely audible. "Feels like forever." Her words were heavy with unspoken meaning.

Looking about, Katie asked inquisitively, her eyes taking in the opulent surroundings. "This place must have cost a fortune." Her tone was impressed, but there was an underlying question in her words.

Maz smiled, his expression enigmatic. "I have done... well for myself." He took a long sip of wine, his eyes never leaving Katie's face.

Jason, trying to make conversation while eying the strange platter of meats, asked, "You mentioned that you were a 'genetic historian'? What does that entail?" His voice was curious, but there was a hint of unease in his tone.

Maz waved dismissively at the question, his hand fluttering like a bird. "I trace the bloodlines of prominent families, ensuring their lineage is pure. Many royal families across the globe seek my services." His tone was proud, almost boastful.

Maz puffed up a bit, his chest expanding. "However, my real passion is in ancient religions. Well, one religion, specifically." His eyes gleamed with fervor, his voice taking on a zealous quality.

Katie asked, her interest piqued. "What religion is that?" She leaned forward, her elbows resting on the table.

Caleb rolled his eyes sarcastically, his voice dripping with disdain. "Oh, here he goes..." He slouched back in his chair, his posture one of boredom.

Maz began a familiar soliloquy, his voice rising and falling with the cadence of a practiced orator. "It is the oldest religion of the world. The worship of The Goddess. The Romans called her Magna Mater. The Greeks called her Cybele. The ancient Anatolians called her Matar Kubileya - the Mountain Mother. She has been called Gaia, Rhea, and Demeter. You see that statue?" He pointed to a seated, obese fertility statue, its curves exaggerated and its belly swollen. "I excavated that statue in Turkey. It carbon dates to over eight thousand years ago." His voice was reverent, almost awed.

Maz continued, his words flowing like a river. "She survived the invasion of the Hittites. She became the protector of Athens, giving mystic vision to those who would willingly castrate themselves."

His eyes shone with a fanatical light, his voice rising with each word.

Caleb cringed comically, his face contorting in an exaggerated grimace. Alexia whispered breathily to Jason, her voice husky. "What a shame that would be." Her eyes raked over his body, her intentions clear.

Maz continued, his voice growing louder. "It is said that Rome won the Second Punic War by listening to the word of the Sybiline Oracle. She became one of the primary Roman gods during the Imperial era." His words were like a sermon, his conviction unshakable.

Alexia said, her voice sultry. "And don't forget about her Atys." She smiled at Jason, her eyes smoldering. "Her consort." Her words were heavy with innuendo, her intentions unmistakable.

Maz continued, his voice softening. "Cybele is commonly pictured with Atys. Her servant, caretaker, and yes, consort. Their love for one another is unbreakable." His words were almost reverent, his eyes distant.

Katie said, her voice cutting through the silence. "Ok, but why have you been searching for De La Poers? What do you hope to find with us?" Her words were direct, her gaze unwavering.

Maz got a far-off look, his eyes unfocused. "I believe that the Cybele religion spread to the far corners of the earth. Including here in ancient Briton. I believe it was your ancestors, the De La Poers who practiced her religion well over a thousand years ago - maybe longer. I believe your family has a deep connection to these beliefs - and to this place." His voice was almost dreamlike, his words heavy with meaning.

Jason, trying to get away from the attentions of Alexia, asked, "Some of your, ah, servants around here..." He gestured towards the robed figures, his movements awkward. "I gotta ask: What's with the robes?" His voice was hesitant, as if he was unsure of how his question would be received.

Maz laughed loudly, gesturing to the robed men. "My 'servants' as you call them are my comrades. I brought them from Turkey with me. We have seen a lot of action together, right my brothers?" He said something in Turkish, holding up his glass. The robed men gave a militaristic salute before continuing their sentry stance, their movements precise and disciplined.

Maz continued, his voice proud. "They are all respectful of me. Their robes simply show their dedication to this priory." His words were final, brooking no argument.

Suddenly, a tremendous howl echoed through the hall. It was almost animal - and almost human. Everyone stopped in mid-bite as the pitiful sound reverberated through the walls, the hair on the back of their necks standing up. The four robed men shifted uneasily, their faces betraying their discomfort.

Maz's face turned dark and sad, his eyes clouding over. A servant whispered to Maz in Turkish, his voice urgent.

Jason, his voice concerned, asked, "Is everything alright?" Katie exclaimed, her voice rising with worry. "What was that?" Her eyes were wide, her face pale.

Maz said, his voice heavy with emotion. "That was... my son, Ehren. He has... physical and mental disabilities." His words were halting, as if each one caused him pain.

Katie sincerely said, her voice soft with sympathy. "Oh, I'm so sorry..." Her words were heartfelt, her eyes shining with compassion.

Maz motioned to a robed man and said, his voice firm. "See that he gets his dinner early." He gave an order in Turkish, his words sharp and commanding. The caretaker left, his robes swishing softly behind him.

The dinner continued quietly, the earlier revelry subdued by the haunting cry. As the servants began removing the dishes, Caleb exclaimed, his voice loud in the silence. "Well, I'm headed to bed." He pushed back his chair, the legs scraping against the stone floor.

Alexia touched Jason's arm, her fingers lingering on his skin. "Good idea." Her voice was sultry, her intentions clear.

Maz, his voice calm and measured, said, "Yes, let's get a good night's sleep. There is much to do tomorrow." His words were a dismissal, a clear indication that the evening was over.

As a swarm of servants cleared the table, their movements efficient and practiced, Kylie and Caleb were the first to leave, their footsteps echoing in the empty hall. Jason and Katie thanked Maz before walking down a hall and up the stairs to their rooms, their minds reeling with the events of the evening.

Entering the hall to the guest rooms, Jason felt a hand on his arm. Alexia stopped him as Katie continued to her room, her eyes glinting with mischief.

Alexia, looking up at Jason with longing eyes, whispered in his ear, her breath hot against his skin. "You know, these rooms can be big and lonely. It can sure be nice to have company. Nice... warm... company." Her words were heavy with innuendo, her intentions unmistakable.

Jason pulled back and stammered, his face flushing. "Ah... I'm kinda tired after so much food. I think sleep sounds good... by myself." His words were awkward, his discomfort evident.

Alexia looked ice-cold for a second, her eyes flashing with anger. She then smiled, her expression too bright to be genuine. "Suit yourself." Her words were clipped, her tone frosty.

She walked down the hall and knocked on a door, her movements precise and deliberate. Caleb was there, shirtless, his chest glistening with sweat. She entered and put her arms around him, her hands roaming over his skin. Still staring at Jason, they kissed, their mouths moving hungrily against each other as the door closed. Jason shook his head incredulously, his mind reeling with disbelief.

Jason got to Katie's room and knocked on her door, his heart pounding in his chest. She answered by opening it a crack, her face curious. "I thought you'd be staying with Alexia..." Her voice was hesitant, her eyes searching his face.

Jason stammered again, his words tumbling out in a rush. "What!? Alexia... GOD no. I just, um, wanted to say goodnight." His face was red, his embarrassment evident.

Katie was all sincere smiles, her eyes shining with warmth. "You want to come in... and talk a little?" Her voice was soft, her invitation clear.

Jason, his stomach churning, said, "Actually, that dinner isn't really sitting so well." His words were apologetic, his face slightly green.

Katie, her face scrunching up in sympathy, said, "I know, right?" She made a face, her nose wrinkling. "That was a lot of meat. And what's with all that cumin?" They both smiled, the tension between them broken.

Jason paused briefly, his eyes searching her face. "Alright. Goodnight, Katie." He turned to leave, his footsteps heavy on the stone floor.

Katie dashed from her doorway and kissed him on the cheek, her lips soft against his skin. She hurried back into her room, shutting the door, all smiles, her heart racing with happiness.

Jn a torch-lit cave, a man dressed in heavy white robes walks

with authority, his steps echoing through the damp, musty air. He wears a metal mask of a grinning Green Man, complete with leafy laurels and stag antlers, the grotesque visage casting twisted shadows on the rocky walls. He walks with a long wooden shepherd's crook into a twilit grotto, the darkness seeming to swallow him whole. Things in the grotto begin to stir, their movements sluggish and unnatural. White, flabby things lope on the filthy ground, mewling and grunting, their cries a mockery of humanity. The swineherd corrals one with his crook - a hunched, malformed thing with patches of cave fungus growing on its pallid skin, its eyes milky and unseeing. The Green Man raises his hand holding a primitive sickle, the blade glinting in the flickering torchlight, and chops it downward at the beast. A gout of blood sprays across the cave walls, and a human-like shriek of pain rends the air, the sound reverberating through the darkness. Dozens of black rats look on from the cave walls, their beady eyes glowing hungrily in the torchlight, their chittering echoing through the grotto like a sinister chorus...

Jason wakes from his fevered dream, his face covered in a sheen of cold sweat, his heart pounding in his chest. He looks about his room frantically, his eyes wide with terror, searching for any sign of the horrors that haunted his dreams. Realizing he is safe, he begins to relax, his breathing slowing as he tries to calm his racing thoughts.

But then, his ears pick up a sound - a scratching behind the dresser, the noise faint but unmistakable. It stops, the silence almost deafening. Then it returns again, more fervent, more insistent. It stops again, the quiet laden with a sense of dread. Jason listens pensively from the bed, watching the dresser in fear, his body tense with anticipation.

Suddenly, the scratching sounds are all around him, so strong it shakes the furniture, the room seeming to come alive with a malevolent presence. He feels the bed lurch as if something is pushing at it from beneath, the mattress bucking and heaving like a wild animal.

Panicked, he sits up and desperately looks for a weapon or something to defend himself, his eyes darting around the room in search of salvation. On a dressing stool, he sees it. A huge, oily rat perched on the stool, staring at him unflinchingly with milky eyes, its gaze boring into his soul. He blinks, hoping it's just a trick of the light, but the thing is still there, unfazed by the squealing shrieks and scraping around it, a silent sentinel of his torment.

This was no dream. This was real.

Jason grabs his glass of water from the dresser, his hand shaking with fear and rage. "Stop! STOP IT!" he screams, his voice raw with terror. He hurls the glass at the rat, the sound of shattering glass exploding across the wall and floor, the shards glittering like fallen stars in the moonlight.

Suddenly, the sounds stop, the silence almost as terrifying as the noise.

Jason pensively rises from the bed, his legs unsteady beneath him. He moves to where the rat stood, his steps slow and cautious. He crouches, and searches the floor around the tipped stool, but finds nothing but shattered glass, the remnants of his sanity scattered across the cold stone.

The door bangs open, and Caleb, Alexia, and Kylie stand in the doorway, their faces a mix of concern and annoyance.

"What's with the racket, cousin?" Caleb asks, his voice rough with sleep.

"You heard it too?" Jason asks, his voice hopeful, desperate for validation.

"Yeah, you screaming and breaking stuff," Caleb replies, his tone dismissive.

"You didn't hear the rats? They were everywhere...in the walls..." Jason's voice trails off, the realization that they didn't share his experience hitting him like a physical blow.

Caleb and Alexia give odd glances at one another, a silent communication passing between them. Alexia says mockingly, her voice dripping with condescension, "Darling, these walls are solid stone. There's nothing there."

Jason, still stunned, gestures to the broken glass, his voice desperate. "But there was one right there..."

Kylie quietly bends over and begins picking up the glass pieces, her movements methodical and precise, as if she's done this before.

Caleb began backing towards the hall, his eyes shifting nervously. "Well, you obviously...ah...scared it away, mate." His words are meant to be comforting, but they ring hollow in the face of Jason's terror.

Alexia, moving back with him, her voice saccharine sweet, "Yeah, try and get some rest, Sweetie. You're obviously just tired."

The two shut the door behind them, leaving Kylie still picking shards from the floor, her presence a small comfort in the face of Jason's mounting dread. Jason clearly hears Caleb say, his voice muffled by the heavy wooden door, "Sounds like he's going the way of Uncle Howard!"

Alexia's muffled voice replies, her tone mocking, "Off to the asylum with that one." Their footsteps drift down the hall, fading into the distance.

Kylie dumps the glass into a waste basket, the sound of the shards clinking together echoing in the quiet room. She begins closing the door behind her, then pauses, her hand on the knob. She whispers, her voice barely audible, "I hear them too." She shuts the door, leaving Jason alone with his thoughts.

Jason stands in his room, his hands on his temples as a massive headache begins to hammer in his head, the pain a physical manifestation of his mental anguish. He repeats to himself, his voice a desperate mantra, "I did hear them... I did hear them." But even as he says the words, doubt begins to creep in, insidious and unrelenting. Was he losing his mind? Or was there something more sinister at work in Exham Priory, something that only he and Kylie could sense? The questions swirl in his mind, tormenting him, as he stares into the darkness, searching for answers that may never come.

CHAPTER

14

The next day was overcast. A thick fog lingered over the priory grounds. Jason finally left his bed at noon as the fog began to dissipate with the dreary light of day.

He found Katie in the gardens. "Wow," she said, grimacing at his appearance, "You are not a morning person."

Jason attempted a smile, "Didn't get much sleep... again."

Katie looked sympathetic, "More vivid dreams?"

"A goddamn doozy," Jason exhaled, plopping down on an ornate bench.

"Well," Katie said, sitting next to him, "Tell me about it."

Jason gave a deep sigh. "The night before, I had a dream of Uncle Howard. I saw him building this place. Then, he followed some woman into the catacombs under the priory." He cleared his throat. "Then the whole place turned into skulls and bones and he was swallowed by darkness, screaming and clawing at his face."

"That's rather terrifying," Katie said. "Do you remember anything that could have triggered that dream?"

"Triggered..." Jason wondered. Thinking back earlier that evening. "Yeah, maybe. I did talk to Maz about Uncle Howard going insane after rebuilding the priory."

Katie smiled and bumped her shoulder against him, "Well, there you have it. You don't have anything wrong with you."

Jason paused. "Last night, I dreamt of a guy wearing a mask killing pigs, or maybe people, with a sickle."

"Oh. Clearly I was mistaken. You are insane," Katie said deadpan.

They laughed for a bit, then sat quietly.

Jason, breaking the silence with a sigh, "I didn't want to spoil our trip, but I do feel something about this place. I feel uneasy. Like something is... wrong."

Katie waved him off, "After those dreams, I'd be feeling uneasy too." She put an arm around his shoulder. "Maybe you're just feeling a little anxious, this being the first time you ever traveled anywhere. And this is a new, and somewhat strange place."

Katie stood. "Tell you what. We should get out - go see that town we passed... what was it called?"

"Anchester," Jason offered.

"We could go out see the countryside, do some touristy stuff. It'll be fun!"

"Yeah," Jason said. He actually felt better. "Yeah," he said with more conviction, standing with Katie.

They began walking through the gardens once again.

Heading in a direction they did not explore yesterday, they came to what at first looked like a miniature village. About a dozen small medieval hovels were clustered together. They appeared to be displaced in time, being made from woven sticks and clay. There were no windows, only a single bundled wood door was set into their earthen walls.

Jason and Katie stopped at a distance when first spying the huts. They both stared confused, trying to understand why the gardens would contain such archaic and out-of-place structures.

Just then, one of the doors swung open and two of the robed groundskeepers ducked to leave one of the hovels. The two wandered off silently into the gardens.

"Is this where the caretakers live?" Jason wondered out loud. "In these mud huts?"

They stared for a long while. Katie finally said, "So Maz lives in a castle, while his old buddies live in dirt and squalor?"

Jason murmured, "Maybe they should unionize."

Katie pushed against Jason's arm. "I'm serious! Why would they live like that?"

Jason ventured, "Maybe it's like a vow of poverty or something?"

The two stared a bit longer. Katie said, "I wonder what's inside."

"Probably all crucifixes and self-flagellation..." Jason joked.

Katie started for the cluster of huts. "I want to see."

Jason looked around cautiously, "What? You're not serious?"

"Come on," Katie whispered, "Just a peek inside."

The two crept across the open ground to the nearest hovel. Tracks of sandals were fresh in the damp earth around the hut.

Jason reached for the door. It had no lock and swung open, the gloomy daylight illuminating a small interior with a dirt floor.

Katie suddenly stopped. "Oh my god, I can't do it." Jason looked at her. "You go," she prompted. "I'll be on watch."

Jason's instincts told him to close the door and walk away. To his surprise, he found himself nodding to Katie and closing the door behind him.

With the door closed, darkness surrounded him. The fragrant smell of unusual incense hit his nose. His eyes slowly adjusted to the diffused candle light. The interior was all but empty. A thin mattress lay on the floor without pillow and only a thin wool blanket for comfort.

A small plain wooden dresser stood against the near wall. It had a mirror, a wash basin, a pitcher and glass, and a straight razor. In the upper edge of the mirror, stuck between the pane and frame, was a black and white photograph.

Jason leaned in to see the photo's details in the near darkness. Two dozen soldiers stood at attention in front of a large flag. They were dressed in uniforms and each carried a rifle. Jason could not identify the uniforms. They looked archaic, with belts, high boots, and tall hats. The rifles they were carrying also looked out of place. Instead of a modern military rifle, their rifles had wooden stocks and were bolt-action. The flag had three horizontal colors with an intricate symbol in the middle. There were characters surrounding the symbol in a middle-eastern script. Jason noticed that standing in the front of the men was a tall figure in a more opulent uniform - an officer of some sorts. Squinting, the man's face came into view. It looked like Maz, but with a thick mustache. He looked exactly the same as he did last night.

"No way..." Jason exhaled, running his hand over the photo. It felt very old, on a thick paper that had been warped by water or time.

Jason dug out his phone and snapped a picture of the photograph. The device played a loud shutter-snap sound.

"What do you see?" Katie's voice startled him.

Jason whispered loudly towards the door, "I don't know... I think they were all military or something. I think Maz was their leader."

With his eyes fully adjusted, Jason notices the dim candlelight is glowing from behind a standing partition against the far wall. The three-walled divider was built of lacquered wood; the flickering candle flame illuminating the wall behind it.

Jason crept towards it, moving back one of the walls. The divider was heavier than it looked. Hidden behind the partition was a small shrine ensconced within the wall. Candles burned with thick incense alongside a two-foot tall statue sitting on the wall shelf. The statue appeared to be of a Greek woman in a flowing toga, seated on a great throne. Two lions formed the armrests of the chair. In front of the statue was a small basin over a short wooden cabinet. A thick prayer rug lay on the floor before the statue.

Jason again snapped a picture, capturing the strange shrine.

Jason moved closer to the shrine statue, trying to get a better look. As he leans over the basin, he notices a dark stain around the bowl. At the bottom, a black, murky liquid glistens oily in the candle glow. "What the..." Jason questions quietly. Without thinking, he puts a finger into the liquid. It is greasy and strangely warm. Holding his finger to his nose, the substance had no smell, save a faint sour odor - like an old cheese left out in the day.

Wiping his hand on his pants, he bent down to look at the basin cabinet. It had a single small door on it. Against his better judgment, he opened it. The hinges squeaked. Inside were unlit candles, a mortar and pestle, and a brown glass jar. The jar looked like it was filled with a fluid, and something floated in it. Brushing past the candles, Jason reached in and withdrew the jar. Holding it to the candlelight, he looked through the brown glass and into the murky liquid. The thing suspended in the liquid looked fleshy and organic, like an organ of some sort. Jason turned the glass in his hand, trying to identify the clump of floating matter. Then his mind made sense of what he was looking at - and now he would never un-see it.

Drifting in the liquid was a pale severed penis and testicles of a full-grown man.

Jason jerked with such revulsion, he almost dropped the jar. "Are you fucking kidding me!?" Jason hissed, trying to keep his voice down. He gingerly placed the jar back in the basin cabinet and shut the door. He took a step back from the horrible little shrine, and heard a loud creak. The sound came from beneath the prayer rug

Jason was standing on. He looked down at the rug, noticing that it was not flush with the floor.

Jason pulled up the corner of the mat, uncovering wooden planks that formed a cover over the dirt floor. Through the slits in the planks, Jason could see a dark void beneath.

Jason pauses, weighing his decisions. "Oh man, don't be stupid..."

Curiosity again besting logic, he bent down and lifted the trap door. A narrow chute, lined in rough stone bricks led straight down into blackness. A sturdy looking wooden ladder was against one side. A billow of cold, damp air drifted up from the darkness.

"Don't do it..." Jason told himself.

Before he knew it, he had one foot on the ladder and was making his way down. "What are you doing?" he whispered to himself to fight back his fear.

Climbing down the ladder, he realized it was longer than he thought. After about 20 feet, he finally reached a rough floor. The only illumination was the faint candles shining through the chute above him. Jason again fished out his phone and turned on the flashlight.

He thought he would be in some sort of cellar or storeroom. Jason was surprised to find himself in a brick lined tunnel. The corridor reminded him of a sewer. It had a low ceiling and smelled of dirt and mildew. The bricks looked rough, like they were carved from the granite cliffs outside.

Hunched and walking slowly down the passage, Jason noticed that it was sloping downwards. He held one hand to the wall as he went, shining his light vigorously. His palm passed through something wet and slimy. Grimacing and looking at his palm, he saw a dark streak of thin but viscous liquid. As he wiped it on his pantleg, he ran his light over the bricks he had passed. He saw a hole in the stone, about an inch in diameter with a smear of that ooze around it. In his phone light, he noticed another hole - and then another. Now that he was looking for them, he noticed that all of the bricks had these holes bored into them. "They all have them..." he whispered to himself.

Jason took a step back from the wall, and took another picture with his phone. The loud shutter-click sound echoed down the tunnel.

Without warning, a black-furred rat squeezed out of one of the holes illuminated by Jason's phone. It hopped down the wall and plopped onto the floor next to Jason. He stepped back in surprise. The rat stood still, affixing him with pale glassy eyes. Jason did not move.

The two stood gazing at one another for seconds. Jason broke the standoff by taking a step back from the creature. Suddenly, it lowered its head and hissed at Jason. Its teeth gleamed and the fur on its wet back stood as the shriek became louder.

Jason's light caught another rat extruding from a hole in the brick. Then another. Waving his light around, Jason saw that rats were oozing from the pores in the walls, dropping wetly onto the tunnel floor. There were hundreds of them. And they were still pouring out.

Raw fear began to overtake Jason. The mass of rats were so thick, they crawled on top of each other, forming a flopping squirming mass. Then the mass began to slither towards him.

Jason turned and ran.

His bouncing light cast wild shadows around the ancient corridor. Jason heard the deafening scratching and screeching swelling behind him. The ladder was just up ahead.

He slipped on something, stumbled and crashed into the floor. His camera went spinning away from him. He scrambled to his feet, starting for the ladder. Stopping himself, a thought flashed in Jason's mind, "If you leave your phone, they'll know you were here..."

"Fuck!" Jason cursed, turning to race towards his dropped phone. He swept it from the ground just as several rats slid around his feet. He ran. Faster than he thought he ever could. Leaping onto the ladder, he frantically scrambled upwards.

Reaching the lip, he pulled himself up onto his knees. Rolling to the side, he slammed the trapdoor down and threw the prayer rug over it.

He laid on his back on the dry dirt floor, his heart hammering in his chest and his breath coming in ragged gasps. The shriek of the rats were gone. He slowly brought his breathing and wits back under control.

Muffled sounds suddenly came from outside. Voices. Deep voices. They were approaching.

Jason leapt to his feet and jumped towards the door. He quickly cracked it open and slipped out of the hovel. He lowered his head and began to walk away, back towards the gardens.

"Hey!" a loud voice cried from behind him. Jason lurched to a stop. "What are you doing?" Jason turned to see two robed groundskeepers rounding the hut and striding towards him. One barks, "You should not be here!"

The two looked visibly angry. They stopped close to him. They were both large men. Their frames were muscular, and they looked every bit the soldiers in that photo. Both had shaved heads. One had a trimmed beard that made him look even more intimidating. Jason could see the edges of thick tattoos peaking above the robe's collar.

The bearded one shouted into his face, "What were you doing?"

Jason could only stammer, "I... I was..."

"Oh there you are!" Katie's musical voice came from behind him. "I found the bathroom. It's back over this way." She moved up to Jason's side and slipped an arm around his shoulders. "Thank you for looking for me!" She smiled up at him, then the groundskeepers.

"Yeah... I was looking for bathrooms," Jason intoned. Jason followed Katie's smile at the two bewildered caretakers. They both stared incredulously, but did not make any accusation.

"Come along!" Katie said, turning Jason around and began moving towards the gardens. She turned to wave at the men, "Sorry for the intrusion!" Jason turned to see the two robed figures eyeing them suspiciously.

Jason whispered under his breath, "I hope you actually found a bathroom - because I think I need one now..."

Jason and Katie sat on marble benches in the secluded garden clearing. The fountain gurgled water behind them.

"I think you just saved my life," Jason admitted. "Seriously, did you see those guys?"

"I saw them coming and went to hide. I hoped they'd just walk past. Then you burst out the door..." Katie shrugged, "I just improvised."

"Thank god it worked," Jason sighed, still upset from the encounter.

Katie sat down next to him and gently punched his shoulder, "No worries. I got your back." Jason couldn't help but smile. The two sat quietly for a bit. Each of their presences reassuring the other.

"So what was in there?" Katie finally asked.

"You're not going to believe this," Jason began, taking out his scratched phone from his pocket. "This is some weird shit."

Jason flipped through his photos, telling her about the shrine, the preserved contents of the jar, the trapdoor, and the rats in the subterranean tunnel.

"Wait," Katie interrupted, "you found a... severed dick?"

"In a jar," Jason completed.

"What the actual fuck?" Katie said disbelieving.

"And all those bricks down in the tunnel. All riddled with holes." He shivered, "I mean, there must have been thousands of those rats..."

Jason looked around at the gardens, the cliffs, and the priory. "I think this whole place is just one giant rat hole."

"Alright," Katie nodded, "There is obviously some strange stuff going on around here." She paused, "Tomorrow, we're headed to Anchester. We can take a break from here - get a new perspective on things."

For a long time the two sat in the gardens, only the gurgling fountain breaking the silence.

CHAPTER 15

Once the sun moved behind the granite cliffs, the priory fell into premature darkness. The gloom of dusk wrapped across the ancient structure, the orange-red sky dimly illuminating the stone walls and gardens. Inside, the flickering light of candles danced on the faces of the old portraits and statues that lined the halls.

Jason and Katie stood before one of the paintings, studying the stern visage of a long-dead ancestor. Katie tilted her head, a mischievous grin playing on her lips. "This one looks like you," she teased, nudging Jason with her elbow.

They were startled by the sudden appearance of a groundskeeper, his robed figure emerging from the shadows like a specter. "Dinner is ready," he intoned, his deep voice echoing in the cavernous hall.

Entering the dining hall, they found the rest of the family already seated at the long table, the warm glow of the chandeliers casting golden light on their faces.

Maz, seated at the head of the table, spread his arms wide in welcome. "Ah! There they are! Dinner is served." His voice was jovial, but there was a hint of impatience in his tone.

Two robed men stood at attention on either side of the far door, their hands clasped behind their backs, their faces impassive.

Katie made a point to sit next to Jason, flashing a triumphant smile at Alexia, who narrowed her eyes in response.

"Come! Eat!" Maz urged, gesturing to the platters of steaming food that covered the table.

Jason, noticing an empty seat, furrowed his brow. "Caleb isn't joining us?"

Maz waved a dismissive hand. "No. Not tonight."

Alexia leaned forward, a wicked gleam in her eye. "He's out hunting," she purred, her voice dripping with innuendo.

Katie raised an eyebrow. "Hunting? At night again?"

Alexia smiled, her teeth flashing in the candlelight. "Hunting by the moonlight. It's when all the best game comes out."

Jason shifted uncomfortably in his seat. "Sounds kinda dangerous..."

Alexia laughed, a low, throaty sound. "Caleb lives for dangerous hunts," she said, her eyes glinting with a feral light.

Katie rolled her eyes. muttering "I bet he does..."

Kylie giggled nervously, her eyes darting between the others.

Maz cleared his throat, drawing their attention back to him. "Caleb's hunting skills do provide us with a variety of meats," he said, motioning to the table with a flourish, across the plates of roasts and carved meats.

Katie's face fell, her eyes widening in horror. "Not Bambi..." she whispered, her voice trembling.

Alexia grinned, a cruel twist of her lips. "Oh, this isn't Bambi, it's..."

Maz glared at her, his eyes flashing with warning.

Alexia caught herself, her smile turning sickly sweet. "...It's her mother!" she finished, taking an exaggerated bite of the meat, her eyes never leaving Katie's face.

Maz flashed a tight smile and continued to eat, his jaw clenched. "So, what have you and Katie been up to?" he asked, his voice too casual.

Alexia leaned back in her chair, a seductive smirk on her face. "Do tell..." she drawled, her eyes raking over Jason and Katie.

Jason shifted in his seat, his face flushing. "Just touring the grounds. The gardens are much larger than they first look."

Katie, her eyes narrowing, leaned forward. "What's with the rats?"

The table went still, the only sound the flickering of the candles.

Katie, not reading the room, pressed on. "Those big black oily things."

She noticed the two robed men staring at her. "The place is kind of infested with them," she continued, her voice growing stronger.

She looked around the table, taking in the nervous glances and tense postures. "They act like they have the run of the place." Alexia and Kylie exchanged anxious looks, their eyes darting to Maz.

Maz paused, his face unreadable. "The rats are our guests," he said finally, his voice low and measured.

Katie's brow furrowed, her confusion evident. "Guests?"

Maz leaned forward, his eyes boring into hers. "They have lived in these grounds far longer than we have. This is more their place than it is ours."

Katie shrugged, her appetite suddenly gone. "Still, you should really get an exterminator out here, you know, before the plague sets in."

Maz's face darkened, his eyes flashing with anger. "I believe they might be an endangered species. Besides, they lend an air of depth and mystery to the place, don't you think?" His voice was mirthless, his words clipped.

He paused, his eyes taking on a faraway look. "The foundations of this priory are very old. Beneath us are crypts built in the Gothic era holding the De la Poer line. It is said that the priory itself was built on Saxon graveyards and even roman catacombs beneath those." He let his words hang in the air, the silence heavy with unspoken meaning. "Those rats were probably there long before any of them."

Jason, sensing the tension, cleared his throat. "Katie and I are thinking of going into town tomorrow," he said, trying to change the subject.

Maz's eyes snapped to his, his gaze intense. "Unfortunate timing. The coach was just put into the shop today. We should have it back again in a few days."

Jason glanced at Katie, his brow furrowed. "No worries, we were planning on walking anyway."

Maz stared at them, his eyes unblinking. "You would do well to be cautious. Some in Anchester still believe the old superstitions about this place. 'An abode of witches and werewolves'." He forced a grating laugh.

Kylie hunched her shoulders, her voice small. "They're definitely not very nice to us."

Alexia slammed her glass down on the table, her eyes blazing with anger. "A bunch of unwashed backwoods sheep-shaggers," she spat, her words slurring slightly.

Katie lifted her chin, her eyes defiant. "I guess we'll have to see for ourselves."

Maz leaned back in his chair, his face an unreadable mask. "For years now, some thieves from the town have been stealing the supplies we buy. One time, they went so far as to set fire to the gardens."

Jason's eyes widened, his mouth falling open. "Damn. That's crazy."

Maz nodded, his expression grim. "Remember: the ignorant cannot be trusted and the superstitious cannot be reasoned with." He picked up his fork, his attention returning to his plate. "But, yes. Have a good time."

The rest of the dinner passed in tense silence, the only sounds the scraping of cutlery on plates and the occasional clink of a glass. The air was heavy with unspoken words and hidden meanings. Jason and Katie exchanged glances, their eyes speaking volumes.

Something was very wrong in this place, and they were determined to find out what it was.

Jason said goodnight to Katie, his eyes heavy with exhaustion. In his room, he laid his head on the pillow and closed his eyes, the weariness of the day washing over him like a tide.

The dream began in the darkness of his closed eyes, a void that seemed to stretch on forever. The sounds of far-off screams echoed in the distance, growing louder and more distinct with each passing moment. Then, the screams were closer, their anguish and terror palpable.

A young girl's eyes flashed open from sleep, wide and fearful. She was dressed in a simple bedshirt, the fabric worn and thin. She moved to the window of her 1600's house, her bare feet padding softly on the rough wooden floor.

Outside, she saw people with lanterns fleeing a black tide of SOMETHING, their faces contorted in horror as they were dragged down beneath the dark wave, their screams cut short by the churning mass.

She rushed from her corner into the main room, her heart pounding in her chest. The clawing and scraping sounds became thunderous, filling the air with a deafening cacophony.

Her mother was at the front door, her body pressed against the wood, her face a mask of terror as she struggled to hold it closed.

Suddenly, the windows shattered, and oily black rats began swarming in, their bodies glistening in the flickering light of the lanterns. They swarmed around her mother's feet, their gleaming white teeth sinking into her flesh, drawing blood.

Screaming, her mother fell as an avalanche of rats engulfed her, their writhing bodies obscuring her from view. The little girl shrieked, her voice raw with horror.

The churning rats began to flood towards her, their eyes glinting with a feral hunger. She scrambled to the back door, her fingers fumbling with the latch, desperate to escape. She flung it open and ran, her lungs burning with each ragged breath.

Outside, a sea of rats swarmed in from all sides, their bodies a writhing mass of fur and teeth. The only way open to her was towards the barn, its weathered wood a beacon of hope in the darkness.

As she stumbled inside, the livestock were squealing, their bodies covered with biting vermin, their eyes rolling in terror.

She reached a ladder as black rats flowed to where she once stood, their bodies surging forward like a dark tide. Climbing to the hayloft, the rats followed her up the ladder, their claws scrabbling on the rough wood.

Panicking, she moved out onto a scaffolding beam overhanging the barn, the floor below covered with a swirling mass of rats, their bodies a seething ocean of black.

She slipped and fell, her fingers grasping desperately at the beam, her body dangling over the undulating swarm.

A tendril of oily rats crawled out onto the wooden beam, their bodies slithering over her fingers, their touch cold and slimy.

Her hold gave way, and she fell, screaming, into the churning mass of black...

The girl slowly opened her eyes, her body aching and sore. She was lying on a pile of hay - an island in a black sea of rats, their bodies still and unmoving.

She got up timidly, her movements hesitant and unsure. The rats were staring at her with murky white eyes.

Eerily, the rats parted to form a path out of the barn, their bodies shifting and flowing like water. She heard a woman's voice faintly whisper, "Come to me, my love," its tone seductive and alluring.

The girl carefully walked forward, her steps hesitant and unsure, as the rats scurried out of the way, their bodies parting like a river.

As she moved through the town, there were no people, no animals, no sounds - just squirming rats, their bodies a living carpet burying the village.

The rats led her out of the town, through the hills, and towards a burned castle, its towers rising like jagged teeth against the sky.

The rats led her to the gates of the ruined priory, its flame blackened walls crumbling and overgrown with ivy.

The doors opened, startling the girl, their hinges creaking from the past inferno. Again a voice whispered, "My Voice has come," its tone filled with longing and desire.

Jason woke up with a start, his body drenched in sweat, his heart racing in his chest. He rose from the bed, his breathing hard and ragged, and walked to the window, putting his hands on his face, trying to calm himself. "It was just a dream. It was just a dream," he repeated, his voice a desperate mantra.

Out the window, a great distance away at the edge of the rolling moors, he saw a light moving, its glow faint and flickering in the darkness. The tiny silhouettes of several people walked in the full moonlight towards the priory, their forms cast in shadow. Jason squinted to see a man with a shotgun slung over his shoulder, holding two long leashes with strange-looking white dogs at the end. Behind him were two robed figures wheeling a small tarp-covered wagon, its contents hidden from view.

Jason watched them with disturbed curiosity as they disappeared behind the edge of the gardens, their forms swallowed by the hedges.

"Hunting at midnight..." he whispered, his voice barely audible over the sound of his own heartbeat.

As he turned to go back to bed, he spied something moving along the garden edge, its form white and ghostly in the moonlight.

As he strained to understand what he was seeing, it suddenly reared up on its hind legs, sniffing the air - resembling a long-limbed man, its form twisted and grotesque.

Startled, Jason blinked and shook his head, his mind reeling. The thing dropped back down to all fours and darted to the next scrub, out of sight, its movements quick and furtive.

Jason stayed at the window, searching for the thing, but finding nothing, the moors empty and still in the moonlight.

Jason laid back in bed, his mind racing with questions and doubts. Staring upwards at the ceiling in the dark room, Jason feared he was losing his grip on reality, the lines between dream and waking blurring and shifting like the rats in his vision. He closed his eyes, trying to will himself back to sleep, but the image of the girl and the rats lingered in his mind, haunting him like a waking nightmare.

Jason's door burst open, the sudden noise startling him from his fitful sleep. Katie's voice rang out, far too cheerful for the early hour, "Rise and shine, sleepyhead!"

Jason sat up, his eyes bleary and his hair sticking up at odd angles. He squinted at Katie, his voice rough with sleep, "What time is it...?"

Katie grinned, her eyes sparkling with mischief. "Time to put on your walkin' shoes and take me to town!" She held up a pair of sneakers, dangling them by the laces like a trophy.

Jason groaned and fell back into the bed, the soft pillows enveloping him like a cocoon. He closed his eyes, willing sleep to take him once more.

After a moment of silence, Katie's voice broke through his haze, her tone playful but with an edge of warning, "I WILL dress you myself..."

He grabbed a pillow, throwing it at Katie with a half-hearted grunt.

Minutes later, Katie and Jason, with backpacks slung over their shoulders, left the doors of the priory behind them. They began walking down the road, the gravel crunching beneath their feet, the brisk morning sun casting long shadows across the countryside.

"Pretty much a straight shot down this road," Jason said, his voice still rough with sleep. "I don't think we made any turns getting here."

Katie nodded, her eyes taking in the rolling hills and everpresent forest. "What was with that reaction last night? 'You would do well to be cautious?' I mean, who speaks like that?" She put her elbow below her eyes, like drawing up a cape, and adopted a thick, vaguely Eastern European accent. "Except Dracula?"

They laughed, the sound echoing across the empty fields. Suddenly, Katie's laughter cut off, her face growing red. "Oh my god! Was that racist?"

Jason looked at her, his brow furrowed in confusion. "What, to vampires?"

"No, to elderly...Turkish gentlemen."

Jason thought for a second, his eyes distant. "Dracula was Romanian, not Turkish."

Katie gave him a deadpan stare, "You're not helping."

Jason held up his hands in mock surrender. "I think he was just warning us. The town looked sort of backwoods. Maybe it's full of bumpkins and a-holes."

"A-holes, huh?" Katie teased, her voice light and playful.

"You know what I mean," Jason continued, his tone growing serious. "If people there are that suspicious of the priory, we might want to be... alert."

"Maybe," Katie relented, her eyes scanning the horizon. "Still, that was an awfully convenient time for the car to break down."

"True," Jason admitted, his voice thoughtful. "That was... suspicious."

She continued, her voice growing more animated, "Seriously, he sounded like he was trying to talk us out of going."

As they walked, they noticed a parked car along the road in the distance, the outlines of two men barely visible through the windshield.

Jason squinted, his eyes straining to make out the details. "Hey, wasn't that car there when we arrived?"

Katie nodded, her eyes fixed on the vehicle. "Yeah, I think so."

As they got closer, Jason called out to the car, his voice friendly and open, "Hey, you guys need some help?"

Suddenly, the car's lights snapped on, the engine roared to life, and the car turned around swiftly, kicking up a cloud of dust and gravel as it sped back down the road towards town.

Jason watched the car disappear into the distance, his face a mix of confusion and annoyance. "Not social, apparently."

Katie snorted, her voice dripping with sarcasm, "Well, they definitely seemed like a-holes."

The two continued down the road, the sun climbing higher in the sky, the day growing warmer with each passing minute. The countryside stretched out before them, a patchwork of forests and hilly fields, the distant mountains a hazy blue on the horizon.

They walked on, the road stretching out before them like a ribbon, the town of Anchester a distant shape on the horizon.

CHAPTER
18

$\mathcal{A}$s Jason and Katie approached the outskirts of Anchester, the

countryside began to change. Old farmhouses lay abandoned, their windows broken and their paint peeling, the once well-tended fields now overgrown with weeds and brambles. But as they drew closer to the center of town, the dilapidated buildings and ancient roads gave way to paved streets and new buildings, a clear sign of past gentrification.

A sign above a corner shop advertised "Coffee House" in bold, cheerful letters. Katie's face lit up, her eyes sparkling with excitement. "See? They have a coffee shop. Civilization!"

The two made their way to the Coffee House, Katie entered, the bell above the door jingling merrily. Jason spied a strange old woman glaring at him from across the street, causing him to pause. She stood there, unmoving, her eyes boring into him with an intensity that made the hair on the back of his neck stand up. Jason gave a hesitant wave, trying to be friendly, but the woman's scowl only deepened, her face twisting with obvious disdain.

Entering the coffee shop, the air was warm and inviting, the rich aroma of freshly brewed coffee and baked goods filling the space. But despite the cozy atmosphere, the place was all but deserted. Two men sat in a booth, sipping their drinks in silence, their eyes darting towards the newcomers with a mix of suspicion and curiosity.

Katie was at the counter, studying the menu with a look of intense concentration. She turned to Jason, "How do you like it?"

Jason, still distracted by the old woman out the window, mumbled a vague "Yeah," his eyes never leaving the strange figure.

Katie pulled his arm, her voice taking on a playful edge. "Coffee? Hello?" She waved a hand in front of his face, trying to get his attention. Then, she noticed what had captured his focus so completely.

"She's just staring at us," Jason said, his voice low and uneasy.

Katie snorted, her voice dripping with sarcasm. "Huh. She's DEFINITELY an a-hole." They shared a smile, the tension broken for a moment.

The girl behind the counter, a pretty young thing with bright eyes and a friendly smile, leaned forward conspiratorially. "Hey. Are you two from the priory?"

Katie nodded, her voice light and casual. "Yeah. We just got there a couple of days ago."

The girl's eyes widened, her voice dropping to a whisper. "It must be cool living in a haunted house."

Katie laughed, her voice ringing out in the quiet space. "No ghosts or ghoulies there... well, except for Alexia..."

They made their orders and Jason handed the girl his new credit card, the plastic still shiny and unmarred. The girl glanced down at the card in her hand, and her face suddenly went pale. "De La Pore!" she gasped, her voice barely audible.

The two young men at the table suddenly stopped eating, their eyes fixed on Jason and Katie with an intensity that was almost palpable.

A rugged man with crossed arms stood behind the counter, his eyes narrowed and his jaw clenched. He made eye contact with the girl, shaking his head in silent admonition. The girl meekly quieted and handed the card back to Jason, her hands trembling slightly.

The girl leaned forward, her voice a harsh whisper. "They say the priory is cursed...and so is anyone who lives there."

The man behind the counter roughly placed their coffee on the counter, the liquid sloshing over the sides of the cups.

Katie backed away, her eyes wide and her face pale. Jason grabbed the drinks, his voice tight with forced politeness. "Thanks for the coffee." They left the shop, the bell jingling discordantly behind them.

Outside, the old woman was gone, the street empty and silent. Jason and Katie sipped their coffee, the hot liquid burning their tongues and throats.

"Okay, this place is giving me the creeps," Katie said, her voice shaky and unsure.

Jason nodded, his eyes scanning the street for any sign of trouble. "Maybe we should head back?"

Katie sighed, her shoulders slumping in defeat. "I didn't walk all the way here just to have some yokels chase us away."

The two began walking down the street, their footsteps echoing on the cobblestones. Katie commented on the old buildings lining the streets, their facades a mix of faded grandeur and neglect.

Behind them, the two men from the coffee shop emerged, following at a distance.

CHAPTER

19

Katie snapped pictures with her phone of the old, but renovated buildings that lined the streets of Anchester. The town had a quaint charm, the facades of the shops and houses a mix of faded grandeur and modern touches.

Looking in a storefront window, Katie commented on the clothes on display. "Vintage last year," she said with amusement.

Jason, however, was distracted. He had noticed two men across the street, keeping pace with them, their eyes fixed on the couple with an intensity that made his skin crawl. "Hey," he said, his voice low and uneasy. "Are those the two guys from the coffee shop?"

Katie glanced over, her brow furrowed. "Probably. It's a small town."

The two began walking, turning down another street, their footsteps echoing on the cobblestones. Katie rolled her eyes, her voice taking on a teasing edge. "So paranoid."

But Jason's unease only grew as he saw the two men turn down their street, joined now by a third man. Their faces were set in grim determination, their eyes never leaving them. Jason took Katie by the arm. "We might want to walk faster," Jason said, his voice tight with tension.

They strolled quickly down the street, their hearts pounding in their chests. Behind them, the three men were on their tail, their footsteps growing louder with each passing moment.

Suddenly, a car pulled up in the street ahead. It was the same car they had spied along the road, its engine idling and its windows tinted. Two large men got out, their faces hard and their eyes cold. They began moving towards Jason and Katie, their strides long and purposeful.

"Oh shit," Katie whispered, her eyes wide with fear.

Without a second thought, Jason and Katie moved quickly into a side-alley from the street, their breath coming in short, panicked gasps. They made their way down the narrow alley, the walls pressing in on them from either side, the air heavy with the stench of garbage and decay.

Ahead, two men rushed in from other alleys, their faces twisted with cruel smiles. Jason and Katie stopped short, their hearts pounding. They were cut off. Looking behind them, they saw the five men at the entrance to the alley, heading towards them with a menacing air.

Jason raised his hands in a gesture of surrender, his voice shaking slightly. "Hey guys, it's cool. We get the hint. We're leaving."

The lead thug, a large brute with a face like a slab of meat, said nothing as he approached. The seven men closed in on them, their eyes glinting with malice.

"De la Poer," the brute said, his voice a low growl. He sized Jason up, his eyes raking over his body with a sneer. "You don't look so scary to me." He gave Jason a push, sending him stumbling back a step. The others laughed, their voices harsh and mocking.

Jason held up his hands, his voice pleading. "Hey man. It doesn't need to be like this. We'll just go."

The brute's face twisted with a cruel smile. "You know what we do to witches?" He played it up for his buddies, his voice rising with each word. "Stone them! Burn them!" He leaned into Jason's face, spittle hitting him. "Right after beating the shit out of them."

One of the men grabbed for Katie, but she pushed him away, her face contorted with anger. Jason shouted, his voice raw with fear and rage. "Don't touch her!"

The men surrounded them, their fists clenched and their faces twisted with hatred. The brute punched Jason in the gut, sending him doubling over in pain. Katie was grabbed from behind, screaming "Get the fuck off me!" as she struggled against her assailant's grip.

Jason, his vision blurring with pain, grabbed a wooden plank from the street and swung it with all his might at the brute, hitting him square in the face. There was a sickening crunch, and blood poured from the brute's broken nose, his eyes wide with shock and agony.

The thugs were stunned, their mouths hanging open in disbelief. Katie, seizing the moment, splashed her hot coffee in her assailant's face, sending him reeling back with a howl of pain. Jason grabbed her hand, and they ran, their feet pounding on the pavement as they fled down the alley.

Behind them, the brute spat blood, his face contorted with rage. "Kill these cunts!" he roared, his voice echoing off the walls.

Jason and Katie fled down back alleys, their breath coming in ragged gasps. The seven men were close behind, their footsteps growing louder with each passing moment.

They ducked behind a wall as two men searched an adjacent alley, their voices low and menacing. They narrowly avoided another group by moving through an abandoned building, avoiding the broken glass on the ground.

Finally, the alley opened into an open clearing, an ancient barn standing dark and brooding at the far end. "There!" Katie said, pointing at it, her voice trembling with fear and exhaustion.

As Jason moved towards the barn, he was slowly overcome, transfixed by the scene before him. His vision flashed to the dream, a small girl chased by a swarm of rats running into the same barn, her screams echoing in his mind.

Katie, concerned, tugged at his hand. "Jason! Come on!" She led him into the old structure. The air was thick with dust and the stench of decay.

Entering the barn, Katie closed the doors behind them, her hands shaking. She looked around frantically, "Shit. We can't bar it from this side."

Jason stared up at the rafters, his mind lost in the dream. Again, his vision took over, showing the girl climbing out across the beam, only to fall into the mass of rats, her screams echoing in his ears.

Katie, spying thugs from the window, hissed urgently. "They're here. Get down!"

In a daze, Jason moved with Katie behind some stacks of mildewed hay, his mind still reeling from the visions.

"This is it," Jason babbled, his voice barely above a whisper. "This is the place. The girl..."

Katie, her face inches from his, whispered fiercely. "Snap out of it, Jason."

Jason stammered, his eyes wide and unfocused. "In my dreams. It was here."

Katie took his face in her hands, her eyes boring into his. "Please. I need you, Jason."

He sobered instantly, his eyes clearing, and nodded at her, his jaw set with determination.

From outside the barn, they heard the thugs' voices, low and menacing. "Check around back. I'll check in here."

The barn doors rattled and creaked open, the sound sending shivers down their spines.

Jason looked around frantically and found a weather-beaten shovel. He took it in his hand, gripping it tightly to his chest.

Heavy footfalls in the dirt came closer, the sound growing louder with each passing moment. The brute came around the hay bales, his face twisted with rage. "There you are..."

Jason lunged, cracking the brute in his bloody face with the shovel. He howled in pain, his hands flying to his shattered nose.

Jason and Katie raced out of the barn into the clearing in desperation. But they were quickly surrounded by the other thugs, their faces twisted with hatred. Jason kept them back with the rusty shovel, his eyes darting from one face to another.

From the barn, the brute emerged, blood pouring from his nose, his face contorted with rage. "You filthy witch-blood! You broke my fucking nose!"

The men ringed them, their fists clenched and their eyes glinting with malice. The brute slid on brass knuckles, the metal glinting in the sunlight. "We was just gonna rough you up. But now..."

A shrill voice cut through the throng, stopping the brute mid-sentence. "Put it down, Butch." The old lady they had seen before was standing at the edge of the clearing, her face set in a scowl.

The brute, Butch, looked at her in confusion. "Ain't we supposed to beat witches?"

Entering the circle of thugs, the old woman said, her voice sharp and commanding. "Do these two look like witches to you? Any of you!?"

Another thug, his voice hesitant, said, "But Gam, they're De La Poers."

The old lady straightened, her eyes narrowing. "Oh? Is that so?"

She eyed Jason and Katie up and down, her gaze intense and searching. Finally, she said to them, "Then you should come with me."

Butch suddenly whined like a child, his voice petulant. "Aw, but Gam! They hit me in the face! TWICE! They broke my nose!"

The old lady turned to leave, her voice dismissive. "Serves you right, chasing them down like that."

Jason and Katie stayed in place, unsure of what to do, their eyes darting from one face to another.

The old lady turned back, her face softening slightly. "You don't have anything to fear from me, children." Suddenly, she glowered at them, her eyes narrowing. "Unless you really are witches..." Her face cracked a wide grin, her eyes sparkling with mischief. "Come on! I'll make some tea."

The old lady turned and walked away, her steps slow but sure. The crowd began following the old lady, their faces sullen and defeated.

Jason and Katie hesitated for a moment, hearts still pounding, their eyes locked onto each other. What choice did they have? Their hands clasped tightly together, they followed the old lady and the thugs.

Jason, Katie, and the group of men followed the old woman down streets and alleys, their footsteps echoing in the quiet of the town. Eventually, they reached an old wooden building with a sign reading, "Antiques, Curios, and Whatnot."

The shop door opened with a tinkling of a bell, and as the men began filing into the store, Jason turned to the old lady, his voice sincere. "Thank you for intervening, ma'am."

The old lady fixed him with a piercing stare, her eyes narrowing. "If you're from the priory, you'd best not be thanking me yet."

Inside, the shop was filled with antiques, boxes, and garbage from across the decades, the air thick with the musty scent of old things. Several more young men lounged around the store, but they jumped to their feet when the old lady walked in, their eyes wary and suspicious as they eyed the two strangers.

The old lady barked orders, her voice sharp and commanding. "Don't any of you hooligans have work to do? Josh, why aren't those boxes packed!? Kennith! Alex! Get yer damn drinks off the merchandise! Hooligans the lot of ye!" As she spoke, the men scrambled to obey, their movements hurried and frantic. "Brennan, start some tea for our guests."

A man with an eye-patch snapped to attention, his voice gruff as he turned to another. "You heard 'gam! get to it!"

The old lady waved her hand towards a row of ornate dining table chairs, her voice softening slightly. "Have a seat."

Katie hesitated for a moment before sitting down, her voice uncertain. "Thanks."

The old lady plopped down on a crate, pulling out a big cigar. "Call me Old Alice. All my grandkids do." She turned to one of the men, her voice commanding. "Benny, give your gam a light..."

As a man approached with a lighter, Jason's eyes caught sight of red wording stamped on the side of the crate. He leaned forward to read it, his brow furrowing. "Explosive Material."

Alice puffed on her cigar, her eyes twinkling with satisfaction, "...there's a good boy."

Jason's voice was hesitant, his eyes wide. "Those aren't real explosives, right?"

Alice looked down at the crate and began to laugh, the sound loud and jarring in the warehouse of a shop. The hooligans joined in, their laughter nervous and forced.

Suddenly, Alice's face grew serious, her eyes boring into Jason's. "Yup. But that's not what you wanted to ask me."

Jason stammered, his face flushing. "Um, uh..."

Alice leaned forward, flicking her cigar at him, her voice low and intense. "You wanted to ask me about that barn you found yourself in. About the girl."

Jason's mouth fell open, his eyes wide with shock. "H-how...did you..."

Alice sat back, a knowing smirk on her face. "Psychic! I can see it all over your aura. That, and you looked like you had seen a ghost."

Katie turned to Jason, her voice confused. "What is she talking about?"

Alice's voice rose, her eyes distant, her voice orating. "1674! A year after the priory was burnt to the ground! Legend says, a horde of rats descended upon the town, devouring man and beast alike!"

Jason's voice was barely above a whisper, his eyes unfocused. "Yes... I saw it."

Alice continued, her voice growing more animated with each word. "The survivors tell of a child being led away by the rats - a bastard girl of the De la Poer line - led back to the priory to become its witch-queen!"

Katie turned to Jason, her voice rising with confusion and concern. "Wait, what do you mean, 'you saw it'?"

Jason's voice was distant, his eyes still lost in the memory. "...a dream I had... More than a dream."

Alice's voice was low and intense, her eyes glinting with a strange light. "Baron Walter thought he ended the evil of that place. He killed his entire family and burned the priory to the ground! But after four hundred years, it still needed their blood, and another De la Poer was summoned to reign over that cursed place."

Jason's voice was barely audible, his mind racing. "Walter... the last of the De la Poer line..."

Alice nodded, her voice matter-of-fact. "Yep! His brothers, his sisters, his mother...every De la Poer in the priory got the knife that night." She thumbed at her neck for added drama.

Butch, who was being tended to by the thug with the eye patch, blood staining the front of his shirt, shouted angrily, his voice nasal and distorted. "They're De la Poers, Gam! Ain't they the ones responsible for all our problems!?"

Alice whirled on him, her voice rising to a shout. "Now Butch, if you can't say anything nice to our guests GET THE HELL OUT."

Butch angrily put on his cap and stormed out, his footsteps stomping petulantly across the wooden floor.

Katie's voice was confused, her brow furrowed. "We haven't caused any problems, why is he so pissed?"

Alice's voice was somber. "He's got good reason to be. His gal Terra has gone missing. Her whole family too."

Jason leaned forward, his voice wavering. "Missing?"

Alice nodded, her voice anxious. "There one morning, the next - poof - gone. Good lass, too. Too good for ol' Butchie."

She took a deep breath, growing more serious. "They're not the only ones, neither. Over the past few years, many families have gone missing. The old families. The ones that still believe in the old tales. The ones that were outspoken about restoring the priory a second time..."

Katie's voice was skeptical, her eyebrows raised. "Are you sure they're not just moving away? Hate to break it to you, but this town's kinda skeevy."

Alice shook her head, insistent. "Gone in the middle of the night, without a word? Cars in the garage, closets full of clothes? And only the families that hated the priory..."

Jason's voice was hesitant, his eyes searching Alice's face. "Are you saying that Maz had something to do with this?"

Katie's voice was incredulous. "He's seems eccentric, not some sort of madman."

Alice sighed, putting out her cigar with a decisive motion. With a billowing exhale of smoke, she said, "There is an evil in that place. I've felt its presence for a long time."

She leaned back, her voice growing distant. "When Howard Delapore rebuilt the priory, almost a hundred years ago, he found something beneath the place. Something so bizarre and ancient he hired an anthropologist, a famous explorer, and a psychic to help him investigate. Of the seven men that entered the recesses below the priory, only six returned - and none were ever the same afterwards."

Jason's voice was quiet. "Howard was my great uncle."

Alice nodded, her voice growing more intense. "Howard Delapore was locked away in Hanwell sanitarium that very night. Mr. Thornton, the psychic investigator, couldn't handle the horror he had witnesses and was soon taken to Hanwell alongside him."

She leaned forward for emphasis. "Thornton was my grandfather. I inherited my psychic gifts from him. On his death bed, he made me promise to never let the priory return to power. I was six years old."

Alice's face grew somber. "They both died in that madhouse, within a few years of one another. I believe they simply could not go on living with the memories of what they found down there."

Suddenly, Alice's mood switched, shouting impatiently. "Brennan! Where's that tea!"

A man came in with petite porcelain tea cups, distributing them to the guests with a nervous smile.

Alice's voice was matter-of-fact, her eyes fixed on Jason and Katie. "The famous explorer, Sir William Brinton wrote a book on his experience under the place, just before committing suicide. I think it was this book that led that Turk, Mazhar, to the priory. He bought it in 1945."

Jason stopped mid-sip, his eyes wide with shock. "Wait - you mean, like 2000 or something..."

Alice shook her head, her voice insistent. "No, sweetie, I remember it well. It was only a year after the second war ended. Outta the blue, here comes this foreigner with money, buying up the place." She produced a flask out of her jacket, her movements practiced and smooth.

Katie's voice was confused. "But wait, that would make Maz, like..."

Alice nodded, her voice amused. "Older than me? Yeah! A bit! If you ever figure it out, let me know how he does it!" She wrenched the cap off with her teeth and added a healthy pour into her tea.

Jason and Katie glanced at one another in disbelief. Old Alice took a long drag from the tea cup.

Brennan sat on a crate, idly flicking a knife between his fingers, his eyes fixed on Jason and Katie with a cold, calculating stare.

Alice's voice was casual, but her eyes were intense. "Any-hoo. I've been trying to keep my word to my grandpappy Thornton. Me and my boys have been keepin' an eye on the priory, sabotaging them when we can, stealing their supplies when we can't. Gotta prevent whatever evil plans are afoot."

She leaned in conspiratorially. "You two wouldn't happen to know what those plans are, would ya?"

Jason's flashed a nervous smile. "No. No evil conspiracies going on here."

Alice's face smiled, but not her eyes. "Good. That's good. I'd hate to have to kill ya." After a pause, she began laughing. A little too long and loudly.

She pulled in even closer, fervor in her words. "There is something stirring in the bowels of that cursed place, I can feel it."

Katie's smiled and nodded, but her eyes darted towards the door. "Ok. Well, we should be going."

Alice leaned back on her crate and chuckled. "Nonsense! You just got here!"

Jason and Katie looked nervously at one another, their eyes speaking volumes. Katie's voice was hesitant, "We don't want Mazhar to become suspicious, right?"

Alice squinted at her, her wrinkled eyes narrowing, then blurted out. "Good thinking! Off with you then!"

Jason and Katie stood and began backing towards the door, their movements slow and cautious.

Alice's voice was grave. "If I were you, I'd run from that place as fast as my legs can carry me." Her tone abruptly changed, her voice bright and cheerful. "Nice meeting you two!"

The eye-patched hooligan closed the door behind them, the sound of the bell tinkling in the quiet of the street.

Jason and Katie began to walk away from the curio shop. Katie said rather shakily, "Was it just me, or was Old Alice just a crazy lady?"

Jason spied more hooligans glaring at them from the shop windows, their faces twisted with suspicion. His voice was low and urgent, his eyes fixed straight ahead. "Walk now, talk later..."

The afternoon sun hung low in the sky as Jason and Katie made their way back to the priory, the road rolling over hills and through copses of trees. Katie kicked a pebble, sending it skittering across the path. "Okay, so Maz was right, the town is full of crazy people."

Jason nodded, his brow furrowed in thought. "They seemed so... angry... at us." His shoulders unconsciously hunched against the weight of their hostility.

Katie shrugged, her ponytail bobbing with her stride. "Thugs looking for an excuse to beat the crap out of outsiders. Probably to take out their frustrations of living in such a crap town." She scuffed her shoe against the ground, sending up a small cloud of dust.

"Thank goodness that old lady showed up when she did," Jason said, his voice tinged with relief.

Katie snorted, rolling her eyes. "She's nuttier than all of them! Blaming everything wrong in her life on the priory? Getting her whole family in on it? That's just a sad way to live." She shook her head, her lips pursed in disapproval.

Jason glanced at her, his voice hesitant. "What about the disappearances?"

Katie waved a dismissive hand. "I still say they're just moving away, like any sane person would. The crazies are just trying to spin it into something sinister so, once again, they can blame the priory." She kicked another pebble, sending it flying into the grass.

Jason's voice was quiet, almost to himself. "Still, there's something weird about the priory."

Katie moved closer to him, slipping her arm around his waist. "Weird? Definitely. Snatching people in the night? I don't think so." She gave him a reassuring squeeze, her touch warm and comforting.

They walked in silence for a moment, the only sound the crunch of their footsteps on the gravel and breeze through the arbors. Jason's voice broke the stillness. "I think I want to go to Hanwell Asylum tomorrow."

Katie stopped short, her eyes quizzical. "What?"

"The sanitarium where my great uncle was taken," Jason began to explain.

Katie's voice was incredulous. "Yeah, I remember the old lady saying that, but WHY would you want to do that?"

Jason's mind flashed back to his dream, the image of his uncle scratching at his face in terror. "Something about the priory drove him mad..." He trailed off.

Katie's voice was gentle. "Or maybe it was the grief from losing his son in the war..."

Jason shook his head, his eyes determined. "I'm feeling it too. Something. I don't know what. The dreams I'm having. Maybe Hanwell has some answers."

Katie shook her head, exasperated. "After a hundred years? What are you hoping to find?"

Jason ran a hand through his hair. "I dunno. Records or something. Anything that can tell me what he saw - what he was suffering from..."

Katie's voice was firm, her eyes locked on his. "Jason, you're not going crazy. You said it yourself, you have always had vivid dreams. You're just dreaming of the old stories you heard."

Jason tried to make her understand. "But, the barn - that girl. I never heard that story before."

Katie's eyes sparkled with mischief, a grin tugging at the corners of her mouth. "Well, obviously you did, somewhere. Unless..." She stared at him with mock intensity. "Unless YOU'RE PSYCHIC TOO!"

Jason couldn't help but smile, a chuckle escaping his lips. "Come on..."

Katie giggled, dancing away from him, her arms outstretched. "Ooh! Don't get too close! Your mind powers might overwhelm me! I see it all over your aura now!" She spun in a circle, her laughter ringing out across the empty road.

Jason shook his head, his smile widening as he watched her twirl. The tension of the day seemed to melt away in the face of her playful antics, the weight of his thoughts lifting like a fog in the sunlight.

They continued up the road, the castle looming in the distance, its towers reaching towards the afternoon sun. The air was warm and sweet, the scent of wildflowers drifting on the breeze. For a moment, the world seemed brighter, the shadows of the priory and the town falling away behind them.

The sun dipped behind the granite cliffs as Jason and Katie reached the castle, casting long shadows across the grounds. As they reached the gatehouse, the intense lights came to life around the grounds, making the priory seem almost welcoming.

Entering the Great Hall, the two unslung their backpacks, the bags thumping against the flagstone floor. Katie stretched, her face twisting in a grimace. "That's it. I'm done with walking... forever." She rubbed her lower back, her fingers digging into the sore muscles.

Jason chuckled, his own legs aching from the long trek. "It sure seemed closer on the way here."

Katie brushed stray strands of hair from her face, her nose wrinkling. "...and less dusty. I'm gonna go change." She headed towards the stairs, her footsteps echoing in the cavernous space.

As Katie disappeared upstairs, Jason wandered through the hall, his eyes drawn to the pictures and portraits that lined the walls. He stopped in front of one large piece of framed scrollwork, the intricate design catching his eye. A man and woman were drawn in an illuminated style, their faces serene and regal. A man in a red tunic with a short trimmed beard and a circlet on his head, and a pale woman in a long green dress.

"Gilbert and Milicent De La Poer." Maz's voice came from behind, startling Jason. He spun around, his heart leaping into his throat.

"Jesus...You startled me." Jason placed a hand on his chest, feeling his pulse slowly return to normal.

Maz continued, his eyes fixed on the portrait. "The first Baron and Baroness of Exham Priory. They were granted the title and these lands by King Henry the Third for their support in the Second Barons War in 1266."

Jason whistled softly, his mind trying to grasp the enormity of the history before him. "That was..." He trailed off, searching for the right words. "Ancient."

Maz turned to him, his eyes questioning. "How was your trip today? Uneventful, I hope."

Jason hesitated, his mind flashing back to the confrontation in the alley, the old woman's dire warnings. Uneventful was the last thing he would call it. "I don't understand," he said eventually, his voice hesitant. "Why do the people of Anchester still hate the De La Poers?"

Maz's expression darkened, his voice low. "Fear of your family's pagan beliefs."

He pointed at the portrait, his finger hovering over the necklace the lady in green wore. "Do you see it? There. In the picture."

Jason squinted, his eyes searching the intricate design. "I'm not sure I..." He trailed off, his gaze settling on the intricate drawing. The pendant around the woman's neck was a round stone figure, its breasts and hips greatly exaggerated, but with no head. "What is that?"

Maz's voice was almost proud. "It is a carving of the Corpulent Mother. Another symbol of Cybele. An ancient symbol. That figure is the oldest symbol of religion known to man."

He continued, his voice growing more animated. "This picture shows the link between your family and the Cybeline religion. That your family's history revolves around it."

Maz gestured to the portrait, his voice taking on a lecturing tone. "To openly worship such a pagan goddess, the good Christian folk of Anchester created elaborate stories to frighten their children and shun your family."

He extended an arm, inviting Jason to walk with him. Jason hesitated for a moment before falling into step beside the older man.

"In 1307, the De la Poer line was chronicled as 'cursed by God'," Maz continued, his voice low and intense. "They were painted as a coven of witches who steal children in the night and feast on their blood. The more terrible the story, the more it was repeated. Such is the way of ignorant peasants."

Jason's brow furrowed, his mind trying to make sense of the information. "But, what about Walter? Baron Walter? He wasn't a peasant listening to stories. What compelled him to kill his whole family and burn the priory down?"

Maz sighed, his expression growing somber. "As I said, insanity and tragedy runs in your family. Walter, your great uncle Howard - they seemed to rebel against their family - against their very nature. Much like my Ehren."

He reached out to a picture of a twenty-something man, his fingers brushing the glass with a tender touch.

Jason studied the portrait, his eyes taking in the young man's features. "Your son. He looks..."

"Normal?" Maz supplied, his voice tinged with bitterness.

Jason shook his head. "I was going to say 'like his father'."

Maz's lips twisted in a sad smile. "He tried very hard to be that."

Jason had to ask. "What...ah...is he afflicted with? If you don't mind me asking."

Maz's expression grew distant. "Nothing that can be cured."

Jason's heart ached for the man, his voice soft with sympathy. "I'm sorry."

Maz waved a dismissive hand, his voice growing callous. "Impatience always does harm." He sighed. "Sometimes a life serves as a warning to others", he said bluntly. "Excuse me."

He abruptly turned and walked away, his footsteps echoing in the empty hall. Jason watched him go, his mind reeling with the revelations of the day. As he began walking back to his room, he turned back to the illuminated portrait. His eyes tracing the lines of the ancient couple, the symbol of the Corpulent Mother now seeming to be the only thing he could focus on.

He suddenly snapped out of his trance. He did not know how long he was staring at that portrait. At that ancient symbol of fertility.

"Where are you, my love?" The haunting voice echoed through Walter's mind as he jolted awake from his nightmare, his bedsheets soaked in cold sweat.

With a sense of dread, Walter descended the stone stairway towards the dining hall. Laughter and the clink of silverware drifted up from the red-glowing room. As the light fell across his face, a look of fear and revulsion overwhelmed him, the blood pounding in his ears.

The scene that greeted him in the dining hall was one of debauchery and horror. A dozen family members of all ages lounged around the table, engaged in incestuous flirting and debauchery. They glutinously consumed plates of raw pale flesh of disturbingly familiar shapes.

Walter was overcome with horror, his mind reeling at the sight before him. His body continued to function, but his mind had gone, retreating into a place of numbness and disbelief.

A man with a greasy beard finally noticed him, his voice booming across the room. "Ah! Walter! Finally you grace us with your presence!"

A woman with her blouse barely fastened leered at him, her voice dripping with suggestion. "Come cousin! Sit with us!"

Another man chimed in, his voice mocking. "Yes Baron! Take your seat at the table!"

Several people pulled back the large chair at the head of the table, their eyes glinting with drunken mirth. Walter, dream-like, walked to the chair, his movements stiff and mechanical.

He heard his family whispering conspiratorially under their smiles and toasts, their words like poison in his ears.

One woman gossiped, her voice low and cruel. "Mother has finally shown him everything! The little lamb!"

"He is to be the Atys," one man said, his voice thick with implication.

A woman whispered darkly to another, her eyes narrowing. "At least he's Baron - for NOW." The two chuckled menacingly, holding their knives closely.

The bearded man continued, his voice thundering. "Come! Eat cousin!" He stabbed a large knife into an enormous rib-cage, the flesh glistening in the candlelight.

Walter stood from his chair, looking at the scene of depravity around him, his mind reeling with disgust and horror.

The man's voice was insistent, his eyes gleaming with a feverish light. "Claim your birthright, Walter!" Several others raised glasses and jeered him on, their voices rising in a cacophony of madness.

Walter reached out and took hold of the knife, his hand shaking. As his laughing cousin tore flesh from a femur, Walter snapped out of his delirium, overcome with revulsion.

In a flash of rage, he stabbed the man through the neck, causing his eyes to bulge in surprise as he coughed blood and meat. Only a few at the table noticed, some beginning to drunkenly laugh and point at the spectacle.

Walter made a gesture with his hand, and his four loyal servants removed their knives from their sleeves, setting upon the dining family with a fury born of righteousness.

Walter watched with a pale complexion as his cousins and siblings were murdered before him, their blood staining the tablecloth and pooling on the floor.

As the last of his cursed brethren fell bloodied into their chairs, the servants looked to him for guidance, their faces grim and determined.

Walter removed his knife from his cousin's throat, his hand steady and sure. He took a cutlass from the nearby wall, as his four loyal servants gathered to him. "It is time," he said, his voice cold and resolute.

Walter and his trusted servants moved through the towers, slaying family members as they slept. Those that woke were given no quarter, their screams echoing through the ancient halls.

"What are you doing, my love?" The voice was back, taunting him, mocking him.

Walter reached his mother's room, the matriarch of the family. She pleaded with him at first, then became a fury of strength and rage. She overwhelmed three of Walter's servants and almost strangled him, her hands like claws around his throat. Walter was able to beat her to death before setting her bedchamber on fire, the flames licking at the walls and consuming the evil within.

As the fire spread, he and his three remaining servants fled the priory, the heat of the flames at their backs. Something dark flowed after them, filling the halls and enveloping a terrified servant, dragging him back into the inferno.

Finally escaping Exham, Walter stood and watched the place burn, the flames reflecting in his haunted eyes.

A lone woman's voice spoke once again, the sound chilling him to the bone. "Oh, my Love. Don't you understand? We cannot die."

Jason's eyes flashed open in bed to the sound of a digital alarm, the dream still clear in his mind. He gasped for air, his heart racing as he switched off his phone's alarm and slid out of bed. Dawn had yet to break as he made his plans for Hanwell Sanitarium.

Arriving at the priory's gatehouse in the cloudy pre-dawn, Jason

searched for the bicycle he had seen there earlier. It was old and appeared to be used only for emergencies, but it was still in good working order.

As he rode out of the main gates, Caleb was returning from a hunt, his rifle slung over his shoulder. They glanced at one another as they passed, a moment of silent acknowledgment.

Moving fast down the road, Jason passed the same parked car he had seen before. He glanced behind him several times, but it remained stationary, a silent sentinel watching the priory.

Jason pedaled through the wooded road, his eyes flicking between the path ahead and the maps app on his phone. The GPS was useless, but the map still provided some guidance.

After a few hours of hard riding, Jason finally passed an old and rusted metal sign bearing the words "Hanwell Sanitarium." He stopped at a chain-link gate barring his way down a concrete driveway.

Jason propped his bike against the fence and moved to the locked gate. A weather-worn sign read "Condemned - Unsafe, Do Not Enter." Beyond the gate, the brown brick building loomed, its better days long past. Cracked concrete sidewalks were overrun with weeds, windows boarded up, and graffiti marred the walls. The darkening skies cast an ominous pall over the abandoned institution.

Undaunted, Jason opened the chained gate just wide enough to duck and squeeze himself through.

Entering the sanitarium through the front doors, which were surprisingly unlocked, Jason cautiously inspected the waiting room. Old chairs stood in a pile in the corner, a broken coffee table in the middle of the room. Testing the main doors to the institution, he found them locked. He slid under the counter of the receptionist desk, and moved to the employee door behind. It opened with little resistance from its rusted hinges.

Now in the dark, he switched on his phone's flashlight. The hallway lay before him, dusty and foreboding. Ceiling tiles had caved in due to roof leaks, rust and mold creeping down the walls like a sickness.

Moving through another set of doors, he came into a room filled with abandoned stretchers and wheelchairs, their presence a haunting reminder of the building's past. He flicked his light around, coming to rest on a wall where an embedded sign read "Administration."

Climbing the stairs, he entered a room filled with old desks and stacks of chairs, the air heavy with the scent of decay.

He froze as he heard a squeaking sound, followed by a thump and rustle behind an overturned desk. Trembling, he approached the desk, reaching out with a shaking hand… and flung it aside. A small brown mouse, stunned by the sudden light, squeaked loudly and raced off along the wall. Jason sighed in relief, his pulse pounding in his ears.

A sign above a doorframe read "Records". The door was partially off its hinges from water damage. Jason pushed the door, and it creaked loudly before falling to the floor with a resounding crash that reverberated through the building. Jason paused for a moment, listening intently. "Smooth..." he chided himself. Hearing nothing, he continued cautiously.

Entering the claustrophobic room filled with shelves of boxes, Jason coughed as dust motes sparkled in the phone's light.

Jason scanned the faces of the boxes, searching for dates. "1970s...1960s..." He moved down a different row, where the boxes were visibly older. "1930s...Ah! 1920s..."

Moving along a wall of boxes labeled "1924," he slid one out and searched through the names on the files - no good. He pulled out another box and searched through the file names - still nothing.

On the third box, fingering through the stained manila file folders, he reached a name: "Thornton, Hugo".

Jason stopped, his eyes widening. "Thornton... Old Alice's Grandfather..."

Sliding the folder out of the box, he examined the various papers inside: A Mental Evaluation form containing the clear text "Paranoid Delusional," another medical form reading "violently phobic of rats". Several hand-scribbled pictures of black rats baring their teeth, devil-men with shepherds' crooks, and emaciated, ghoulish humans with black claws and fangs. Finally, a Death Certificate, with the cause of death listed as "Asphyxiation, self-inflicted".

Continuing through water-stained boxes, he finally came across a folder labeled "Delapore, Howard."

Looking through the folder, much of the paperwork was moldy, ink-run, and stuck together. Only a single paper remained legible. It said, "Personal effects moved to Storage Box 8-11-24."

Jason whispered to himself, "Storage Box?" He looked about, "Where's the Storage Room?"

As he left the records room and re-entered the administration area, he heard the scratching and squeaking of the mouse again.

He ignored the sound, but as he got halfway through the room, the mouse suddenly screeched in a death-cry. Jason stopped, shining his light around. He jerked when he thought he saw a black rat scamper across a table, its form barely visible in the darkness.

Moving quickly from the room, he hurried down a daylit hallway. Suddenly, he heard something from outside - the sound of a loud car engine. Stopping at a window, he saw the same car from the road pull up with a squeal of tires, outside of the gate. Three men carrying cricket bats made their way to the chain-linked fence. Butch, medical tape across his nose, pulled down his cap as he moved to the gate. Inserting his bat into the locking chains, he made a forceful twist, and the rusty lock broke open.

Jason muttered to himself, "You've gotta be shitting me..."

Coming down the stairs, he heard the breaking of glass and splintering of wood as the hooligans made their way roughly through the main doors.

The men shouted tauntingly into the halls, their voices echoing off the walls. "Come out, witch-blood! We gotta score to settle."

Jason pulled up against a wall as the two men laughed and called out menacingly. "What's wrong? Don't want to play like before? That's OK, we'll come to you..."

Jason waited for their flashlights to sweep past and the heavy footsteps to move away.

He crouched and quietly headed for the exit.

He slid through the reception window and ducked behind the desk as a thug walked past, his voice low and threatening. "We know you're here, witch-blood. The longer we look for ya, the more of a beating you're gonna get."

Waiting for his chance, Jason suddenly saw a sign on the wall: "Storage".

Glancing between the front door and the passage labeled Storage, Jason grit his teeth and made his decision - moving quietly towards the storage area.

He turned his phone light back on, moving down the dilapidated corridor.

Reaching the doors at the hall's end, he found them wedged shut.

He pushed as softly as he could, but the wood made a loud cracking sound as the door opened.

Jason darted into the room as, down the corridor, a hooligan said, "What was that?"

Another dusty area with box-lined shelves greeted him. Jason quickly moved down the rows, his heart racing. "Come on... come on... come on..."

The voices were louder now, closer. "Is that you, witch-blood?" "We're gonna do to you what your family done to our town."

Jason's eyes fell on a box at eye-height. Amazingly, it read "eight eleven twenty-four."

As the room doors were pushed open loudly, Jason grabbed the box and crouched behind the shelves.

"That tosser is in here," one of the thugs said, his voice thick with menace.

Quietly lifting the lid from the box, Jason looked through the clothes and shoes. He came across a small leather-bound notebook. He quickly grabbed it, but dropped the cardboard box lid in his haste.

"That I heard." The thugs started walking towards Jason, their bootsteps heavy on the dusty floor.

He slid the book into his waistband, quietly darting behind another shelf as their lights shone about.

Jason held his breath. The hooligans moved down the shelves next to him, their presence a palpable threat.

Jason was suddenly caught in a flashlight beam, his heart stopping in his chest. "There 'e is!"

Jason pushed on the shelf with all his strength, sending the boxes toppling onto the two thugs on the other side.

Jason made a run for it, a loud clatter and heavy footsteps signaling that the thugs were close behind.

The hooligans were right on his tail as he raced back into the entrance.

He had to slow to get between the broken doors. Almost out, hands from behind roughly grabbed him and pulled him back into the building.

Two of the thugs grabbed at him. Jason dodged fists and a swinging cricket bat, but was grabbed from behind and hit deep in the ribs. As he doubled over, the bat hit him solidly in the side of his head, knocking him to the ground.

His vision blurry, Butch stood over him, his nasal words hissed in anger. "You cursed my home! You took my Terra away from me!"

One of the other men said with some importance, "Butch..."

Butch, consumed with hatred for Jason, spat, "All you devils deserve to go to hell!" Butch raised his bat to deliver a massive blow.

The other thug shouted excitedly, "Oy! Butch, there's someone..."

A flash and a thunderclap sent the thug spinning backwards.

At the entrance, Caleb stood with a leveled shotgun and smoking barrel, two robed figures behind him.

The groundskeepers sprang forward, one grabbing Butch, wrenching the bat from his hands. Before the other hooligan could react, the second robed man was on him, bending and contorting him like a wrestler would a child. With one muscled arm around the thug's throat, there was a sickening wet crunching sound, and the body went limp. Immediately both groundskeepers were holding Butch. Though he was built like an ox, his struggles did nothing to slow the robed men's beatings.

Caleb smiled down at Jason, his voice casual. "Be thankful I kept an eye on you, cousin."

The groundskeepers held up the battered Butch as Caleb examined him, his eyes cold and calculating.

Butch, spitting blood, snarled, "You Bastards! You killed him... Devil-spawned bastards, the lot of ye!"

Caleb returned his glare with a wry smile, his expression unreadable.

Butch focused on Caleb, his eyes burning with hatred. "I seen you... at night. Stalking 'round the town, with your 'dogs'."

Caleb drew towards him, his voice low and dangerous. "Have you now?"

Butch gave a bloody grin, his teeth stained red. "We see what you have done. We'll end your whole family."

Caleb smirked, his eyes glinting with a dark amusement. "Not likely."

The shotgun roared deafeningly. Jason's ears rang. Butch jerked in a cloud of smoke. The emotionless groundskeepers dropped his body, the thud of flesh on concrete echoing in the sudden silence.

Jason weakly tried to rise from the floor, rage welling up in him. "What the fuck?"

Caleb flicked at the splattered blood on his clothes and sighed heavily, his expression one of mild annoyance.

"Get him up," Caleb said, his voice cold and commanding. Jason was roughly lifted by the groundskeepers and dragged through the front door.

The daylight blinded him as his head still swam from the cricket bat blow. He was thrust into the back seat of a sedan, too dizzy to move.

Caleb shouted to the groundskeepers, his voice carrying across the empty lot. "Well, bring them too!"

The burly groundskeepers returned to the door, dragging the bloody bodies of the hooligans.

Jason heard the trunk open. Felt the thuds and bouncing of the car. Then a final slam of the trunk.

Opening the car door, Caleb pointed, his voice bemused. "Ditch the bike..."

Caleb slid into the passenger seat, his voice almost jovial. "Well, that was exciting."

Jason stammered, his voice thick with horror and disbelief. "You...fucking killed them!"

Caleb shrugged dismissively. "More like scraping shit from a shoe, really. Besides, I couldn't let them harm my family, right?" He offered a rag to Jason, who placed it on his bleeding temple, the rough fabric stinging against the wound. "Hope you didn't get roughed up too much. I mean, sneaking out of the priory - even when we warned you about the locals - not a brilliant move, mate."

A groundskeeper moved into the driver's seat, the second dropping heavily into the back.

Caleb gestured towards Jason, and snapped his fingers in annoyance. The groundskeeper began roughly patting down Jason, his hands invasive and unwelcome.

Jason struggled weakly, his voice hoarse. "Get... get the fuck off me!"

Caleb's voice was calm, almost soothing. "Easy, just checking for wounds."

The large groundskeeper wrenched the book from Jason's waistband. Jason tried to grab for it, but he grimaced from the pain, his body betraying him.

The groundskeeper held it up for Caleb. He thumbed through the diary casually, growing more interested with each turn of the page. "Is this... from great uncle Howard? You actually found this?" He chuckled, the sound dark and unsettling. "You are a tenacious one."

Jason, blood running into his eye and head pounding, began to swoon. He reached out for the book, his movements weak and uncoordinated.

Caleb pulled it away, his voice taunting. "I think I'll be keeping this. You wouldn't want any spoilers, now would you?" He grinned to himself, absorbed in the book, his eyes scanning the pages with a curious intensity.

Jason's eyes fluttered as he crumpled into the seat, his consciousness fading.

Caleb, with an unconcerned glance, said, "You alright there, cousin? Don't go and die on me..." His voice trailed off, and Jason thought he heard him murmur, "...not just yet..."

Jason blacked out as the car pulled out of the abandoned sanitarium, the darkness claiming him as the tires crunched on the concrete drive.

CHAPTER
25

Jn the snow-draped forest outside of the priory, five children in rough-spun tunics played, their laughter ringing through the stillness of the winter landscape. The trees stood tall and silent, their branches heavy with a thick blanket of pristine white. The boys' breath misted in the frigid air as they tossed a worn, red ball back and forth, their cheeks rosy from the cold and their eyes bright with merriment.

As they played, they sang a haunting nursery rhyme, their voices high and clear in the crisp air:

"La-dy Mar-garet De La Poer,

once a witch but now no more!

Children close to Exham parts,

chopped them up and ate their hearts!"

Unknown to the children, something in the treeline moved closer, its presence dark and malevolent. The shadows seemed to deepen, the forest growing colder and more foreboding with each passing moment.

The boys continued their game, oblivious to the danger that lurked just beyond the edge of the clearing. They sang the second verse of the rhyme, their voices taking on a more ominous tone:

"La-dy Mar-garet De La Poer,

once a witch but now no more!

Mar-ried Sa-tan, now she's dead,

took three ax-es to the head!"

Suddenly, the sound of a breaking branch caused the children to stop, frozen in fright. Their eyes wide with fear, they huddled together, their scarves fluttering in the icy breeze.

A shadow descended through the trees, dark and oppressive. A pale face appeared, hovering in stark contrast against the shadowy woods. Its features were beautiful, pure white skin and perfectly painted red lips. The children stared in horror, their mouths agape, as the face drifted towards them, its eyes black and soulless.

"It's her!" one child shrieked, his voice high and terrified.

Like a spell being broken, all the children screamed and began to flee, their feet slipping on the icy ground. They ran in different directions, their tunics flapping behind them like the wings of frightened birds.

One child remained, standing transfixed by the beautiful face hovering in the darkness at the edge of the forest. His eyes were wide with a mix of wonder and terror.

Another boy turned back and stumbled to a stop, his voice hoarse with fear. "Tommund! TOMMUND!"

The beautiful porcelain white face floated majestically and silently to the treeline. From its blood-red lips, a smile began to curl.

Like the crack of a whip, a dozen oily black tendrils lashed out of the darkness towards the boy, their movements lightning-fast and grotesquely unnatural. They wrapped around his arms and legs, lifting him off the ground with a sickening ease.

The other boys screamed and raced away, their hearts pounding in their chests and their lungs burning with the cold. They ran as fast as their legs could carry them over the icy ground.

The forest was silent once more, the only sound the whisper of the wind through the trees. Nothing was left in the clearing except for the red ball, lying forgotten in the snow.

Jason stirred from his slumber, his eyelids heavy and his mind groggy. As he attempted to rise from the bed, a sharp pain shot through his body, forcing him to move slowly and deliberately. He gingerly touched the bandages wrapped around his head and side, wincing at the sharp ache that pulsed beneath them.

Katie was at his side, her hands gentle as she eased him back onto the pillows. "It's all right. It's all right," she soothed, her voice soft and comforting, yet concerned. "What happened?"

Jason grimaced, his words coming out in a hoarse whisper. "It was Alice's thugs. They must have followed me... I don't think he liked having his nose broken..."

Suddenly, the memories of the incident came rushing back, and Jason's eyes widened in horror. He bolted upright, ignoring the pain that tore through his body. "Caleb! H-he shot them!" he exclaimed, his voice tinged with panic.

Katie's brow furrowed in disbelief, her mouth falling open in shock. "What?"

Before she could say anything more, the door swung open, and Maz strode into the room, his expression a mix of concern and disapproval. "Ah good. He's awake," he said, his voice imperious.

Maz approached the bed, his eyes scanning Jason's injuries with a critical gaze. "Look what they have done to you," he tutted, shaking his head. "I told you those people were dangerous. Superstitious fools."

Jason's voice was insistent, his words tumbling out in a rush. "Caleb shot them. I think he killed them."

Maz's expression hardened, his lips pressing into a thin line. "Caleb said that he saved you from being beaten to death. I think you owe him your life."

Jason struggled to sit up, his face contorted in pain and frustration. "But those men... we need to call the police." He held his head as another wave of pain crashed over him, his vision blurring.

Maz waved a dismissive hand, his voice calm and assured. "Caleb has taken care of it. You were all trespassing, and this was clearly self-defense. I doubt any charges will be filed."

He rose from the bed, his movements smooth and deliberate. As he opened the door to leave, he paused, turning back to face Jason. "I wouldn't advise you to leave the priory any time soon...

For your health." With that, he shut the door, the sound echoing in the sudden silence.

Katie turned to Jason, her eyes wide with disbelief and concern. "What the hell happened out there?"

Jason's mind raced, his thoughts jumbled and hazy. Suddenly, he remembered the diary. He reached behind his back, his fingers scrabbling at the empty space where the book should have been. Panicking, he patted himself down, his gaze darting about the room in desperation. "Wait...Where did it... no... The diary! It's gone..." he mumbled, his voice thick with disappointment. Swooning, he slumped back onto the bed, his face contorted in pain.

Katie's lips quirked into a mischievous smile, her eyes sparkling with triumph. She reached into her back pocket, her movements slow and deliberate. "You mean - this diary?" she asked, withdrawing the small book with a dramatic flourish.

Jason's face lit up, his eyes widening in surprise. "Yes! How did..."

Katie grinned, tossing the book onto his lap. "When they were dragging you out of the car, I saw it on the passenger seat. It looked important and out of place, so I grabbed it. Good thing I did. Caleb and those men tore apart the car looking for it."

Katie's expression darkened. "They told us the car was in the shop. Were they lying just to keep us from Anchester?"

Jason picked up the diary, his fingers running over the worn leather cover with reverence. "So what is it?", Katie asked.

"A diary. Great uncle Howard's diary." He thumbed through the small book, his eyes scanning the pages with intense concentration. "It might explain... how he wound up in that place."

Katie's voice tinged with skepticism. "In the asylum? You do know you're trying to get explanations from a crazy person's diary, right?"

Jason shook his head, his expression determined. "I don't think he was crazy." He glanced at Katie, catching her worried glare. "Or at least not completely crazy," he amended, wincing as another bolt of pain shot through his skull.

Katie sighed, her expression softening. She reached out, her hand resting gently on his arm. "Rest. You just got clocked by a cricket bat. You're lucky to be alive." Quickly, she leaned in, pressing a soft kiss to his forehead before rising from the bed and moving towards the door.

As she reached for the handle, Katie paused, turning back to face him. "I don't think you're crazy, either," she said, her voice barely above a whisper. With a small smile, she slipped out of the room, closing the door quietly behind her.

Jason lay back on the pillows, the diary clutched tightly in his hands. His mind raced with questions and possibilities. He knew that the answers he sought lay within the pages of the small book, and he was determined to uncover them, no matter the cost.

Jason flipped through the diary, straining to read the scrawling

handwriting. Vivid images of his uncle in the asylum and his venture beneath the priory flash into his mind with each sentence.

The diary began with the death of his son, Alfred. He wrote of his loneliness and sorrow before meeting with Captain Norrys. He wrote of the reconstruction of the priory, and his moving into Exham. He described the feelings of returning home from a long absence. Then the rats came to him.

The final paragraph was just before his death in the sanitarium. The script was almost illegible with the speed it had been scrawled.

August 11th, 1924

It came to me again. That demon Swineherd tending his unholy flock in that cavernous abyss. Even as I wake from those gulfs of darkness, I can hear the rats - clawing and screeching within the very boards of my cell. I hear them calling my name - drawing my mind deeper into the infernal catacombs under the priory.

Oh that day! That cursed day! Sir Brinton, Trask, Thornton, and poor Norrys - we thought ourselves immune to the horror - evolved beyond that antediluvian madness! But the rats - that beautiful voice from the rats - it called to me, yearned for me. Made me remember who I was - where I came from.

I did not kill Norrys! Norrys was a casualty of my heredity - to the horrors beneath the priory!

Even as I write this, I can hear her voice calling me back to Exham. I find that I want nothing more than to dwell in that evil place - to be the Atys she desires!

But no! I will not succumb to the curse of my ancestors! I will be free! The rats will not claim my soul!

Evening had fallen, the flood lights from the gardens spilling into the room where Jason lay asleep, the book resting on his chest like a fragile treasure.

A sudden knock snapped Jason awake, knocking the diary to the floor. With a quick, panicked movement, he snatched the book from the floor and shoved it behind his pillow, his eyes darting to the door. "Come in," he called, his voice rough with sleep.

The door creaked open, and Katie's face appeared. "It's just me," she said softly, slipping into the room and closing the door behind her.

Jason let out a deep breath, his body sagging back against the pillows in relief. He ran a hand over his face, wincing as his fingers brushed against the tender bandaged lump on his head.

Katie moved to the side of the bed, her eyes scanning his face with a sympathetic gaze. "So? Did you find anything?" she asked, her voice low and conspiratorial.

Jason shrugged, his expression wry. "Well, my uncle and I seem to have a few things in common - crazy hallucinations. Disturbing dreams. An irrational fear of rats."

Katie perched on the edge of the bed, her hand resting gently on his arm. "So what did it say?"

Jason's mind wandered back to the pages of the diary. "There's something about the priory - or what's beneath the priory," he said, his voice barely above a whisper.

Katie nodded, her expression thoughtful. "Maz said the priory was built on top of catacombs and stuff."

Jason shook his head, his eyes intense. "It's gotta be more than that. Uncle Howard keeps raving about our ancestry - about how the De la Poer line is... cursed."

Katie's eyebrows raised skeptically. "Yup - sounds like classic paranoia to me. I probably would have locked him away too."

Jason sat up, his expression earnest. "Katie, I'm serious. I don't think Walter De la Poer was a madman at all."

Katie's cocked her head, trying to remember. "Walter... He was the one that killed his whole family and fled? That's pretty much the definition of crazy, isn't it?"

Jason's voice was insistent, his words tumbling out in a rush. "I think he had a good reason. Whatever terrible things they were into, he was justified in doing it."

Katie held up her hands, her expression growing serious. "Okay, now I'm being serious. Anyone saying stuff that fucked up needs to get some sleep," she grimaced, her gaze flickering to the lump on his head. "Give that lump some time to heal."

Jason lay back, his body sinking into the pillows as Katie pulled the covers up around him, her movements gentle and soothing.

"Whatever is going on… the rats, our ancestors, the Cult of Cybele… it's all connected. And so is Maz somehow. I don't trust anyone here," Jason murmured, his eyes growing heavy with exhaustion.

Katie's expression softened with a smile. "You realize you're starting to sound paranoid too."

She leaned in, pressing a soft kiss to his forehead before rising from the bed and walking towards the door.

Jason's hand slipped beneath the pillow, retrieving the diary. He began to crack it open and read.

Katie paused at the door, her hand on the knob. She turned back, pointing at the bed. "Sleep. You. Now." Her voice brooking no argument.

Jason sighed, his shoulders slumping in defeat. He slid the book back under his pillow, his fingers lingering on the cover for a moment before he settled back against the pillows, his eyes drifting closed.

Katie watched him for a moment, her expression a mix of affection and worry. Then, with a soft sigh, she slipped out of the room, closing the door behind her with a gentle click.

CHAPTER 27

$\mathcal{A}$ young noble on horseback, accompanied by a small retinue

of followers, rode into a small, dirty village of thatch-roofed hovels. As he surveyed the squalid surroundings, his eyes were drawn to a beautiful woman emerging from one of the huts. She caught his gaze, her smile seductive and alluring.

The noble dismounted, drawn to her like a moth to a flame. As he approached, she leaned close, her breath hot against his ear. "I have seen you," she whispered, her voice a siren's call. With a beckoning gesture, she led him into the hut.

The scene shifted, and the two were suddenly inside the house, laying in bed, their bodies glistening with the sweat of their lovemaking. The noble's fingers traced the pagan charm she wore - the corpulent mother symbol of Cybele.

"The Great Mother," she purred, her eyes glinting in the dim light. "She bestows power to those who worship." She rolled onto him, her body pressing against his. "I will show you," she promised, her voice a seductive whisper.

The vision blurred, and the woods came into view. The noble and the woman stood amidst a copse of standing stones, the flickering firelight casting eerie shadows across their faces. On a squat stone altar, the woman carefully lifted a bowl filled with a dark liquid.

The nobleman took the bowl from her, bringing it to his lips and drinking deeply. As the liquid coursed through his veins, he looked down at his hands, overcome with a surge of energy. Drawing his sword, he struck at a nearby tree, cleaving it in half with an explosion of splinters.

"This is only a taste," she said, her eyes glinting with promise. "The world can be ours." They embraced passionately, huge black rats scurrying around their feet.

The vision shifted, plunging into darkness. Illuminated by the dancing flames, the woman's eyes were inky black, her voice a haunting chant. "The son of the king will fall," she intoned, her body swaying back and forth. Her eyes slowly cleared, and she smiled at the kneeling noble. "Unless you are there..."

Suddenly, the brightness of day filled the vision, accompanied by the thunder of horse hooves, the clang of steel, and the screams of men. On a battlefield, the soldiers of Simon de Montfort clashed with the royal forces of Edward Longshanks.

King Edward, surrounded by Montfort spear-men, was knocked from his horse. As the enemy closed in for the killing blow, a deafening battle-cry rang out, drawing their attention. The nobleman, clad in shining armor, rode into their midst, his sword falling like a reaper's scythe.

The enemy was cleaved like butchered meat, bodies and limbs flying in all directions. As the last spear-man fell, Edward looked up at his savior, surprise and gratitude etched on his face. The noble rode to his side, offering his hand to the fallen king.

Another battle flashed into view, the armored nobleman sweeping through the enemy ranks like a titan. Simon de Montfort, his retinue shattered, fled for his life. His chest exploded in a spray of gore as a spear jutted through his back. The noble, holding the spear from atop his horse, drove the impaled man into the ground.

The vision shifted to the King's camp, where Edward looked down at the bloodied severed head of Montfort, dropped at his feet. He smiled at the noble, the burning banners of the usurper billowing in the fields behind them.

The scene changed once more, the opulence of a royal palace coming into view. A large procession stood before the seated King Henry III. The young noble rose from his bow on the carpeted court floor, his eyes meeting those of his sovereign.

"For your deeds, I bestow the title of First Baron of Exham," the king declared, his voice ringing through the hall. In the crowd, the noble's beautiful wife smiled, her fingers caressing her pagan charm.

The vision shifted a final time, revealing a large clearing before towering granite cliffs. The foundations of a priory were being laid by workers, the stones rising from the earth like the bones of a great beast.

Hand in hand, the noble and his wife oversaw the construction of the priory, the ancient standing stones replaced by the walls of their new home. As the dream faded, the image of the Corpulent Mother charm glinted in the sunlight, a promise of the dynasty to come.

$\mathcal{A}$fternoon light streamed through the windows, casting a warm glow across the room. The quiet knock at the door sounded like a gong in the silence. Jason bolted upright in bed, then groaned in pain. Katie, seeing the distress she had caused, winced and whispered apologetically, "Sorry..."

She glanced around the room, her look troubled. "Have... you seen my purse? Did I leave it here?"

Jason rose from the bed, his movements slow and careful. "I don't think so..."

Katie's eyes narrowed with confusion. "I had it when we got back from Anchester..."

Jason, acting on a hunch, rummaged through his dresser drawer. "Wait... my wallet's gone."

Katie's voice was tinged with disbelief. "Are you sure?"

Jason nodded, his expression grim. "It was here before I left for Hanwell."

His tone turned serious. "Someone took it."

Katie's eyes opened wide, the implications sinking in. "Why would anybody take our stuff?" Her voice dropped to a whisper. "Unless..."

Jason finished her thought. "...they didn't want us going anywhere."

Determined, Jason began getting dressed, ignoring the throbbing pain that rolled through his sore head, causing him to sway unsteadily.

Katie rushed to his side, propping him up. "Woah! Easy there! You're in no condition."

Jason, stubborn and restless, continued putting on his clothes. "I've felt worse. Besides, I'm going kinda stir-crazy in this room."

They explored the priory, slipping into unoccupied rooms and giving them a cursory inspection. Opening yet another door, they found themselves in another bedchamber. After a cautious glance to ensure they weren't being watched, they crept inside, closing the door behind them.

Jason looked around, bewildered. "Another bedroom? How many does this place have?" The room appeared to have been cleaned long ago, a thin layer of dust covering the immaculately arranged furniture and bedsheets.

Katie, her frustration mounting, sighed. "Are we really going to search through every room?"

Jason, determined, continued his search. "What choice do we have?" He rummaged through a dusty nightstand drawer. "They could have hidden our stuff anywhere."

Katie, crooked her head in thought and pondered aloud. "Let's think about it. Who would have taken our stuff?"

Jason looked up at her, his eyes narrowing. "Maz. One of his groundskeepers. A servant..."

"Or..." Katie deduced, "Someone that could watch our doors. See us coming and going. Someone like..."

Jason finished, his tone ominous. "Caleb and Alexia," Katie confirmed, nodding.

They peered down the hallway at the closed door to Alexia's room, their hearts pounding in anticipation.

Suddenly, the door swung open, and they ducked around the corner, holding their breath. Alexia glided out of her room, continuing down the hall, away from them.

Seizing the opportunity, they snuck cautiously down the stone hallway and up to the door, their footsteps muffled by the thick carpet.

They exchanged a glance before trying the door. It was unlocked.

Quickly, they swept into the room and shut the door behind them, their hearts racing.

Alexia's room was a cacophony of sensations - the musky scent of perfume, stacks of shoeboxes, a closet overflowing with dresses, an unmade bed with a fluffy pink comforter, and a large vanity covered in an array of makeups, lotions, sprays, and perfumes.

Jason and Katie began searching the cluttered space, but after a few minutes, they found nothing of consequence.

Suddenly, the approaching voices of Caleb and Alexia sent a jolt of panic through them.

With barely a moment to spare, Jason darted behind a privacy screen while Katie dived down, attempting to squeeze under the bed. To her dismay, the space was too low. She cursed under her breath as the door opened. She held her breath.

Alexia's voice drifted into the room. "Yes, but do we have enough?"

Caleb's response was dismissive. "We have plenty. I've gathered enough - even for her."

Alexia moved to the vanity, applying perfume. "It's just - when she's full, she's happy."

Caleb, his reflection in the mirror reassuring, spoke confidently. "And when she's fat and happy, we'll present ourselves."

Alexia smiled, her eyes gleaming. "We'll be chosen, and we'll live happily ever after, forever and ever."

Caleb, his gaze wandering the room, shrugged. "That's the plan."

Alexia, moving around the bed, suddenly frowned. "But what if she doesn't choose us?"

Caleb, unconcerned, replied, "We still have the other two, just in case."

Alexia turned to him, somehow not noticing Katie's prone form on the floor. "But then, won't most of the power go to them...?"

Caleb grinned seductively, his voice smooth. "We'll just make sure our offering is... irresistible."

He pulled Alexia close, his smile cool and confident. "We've been waiting years for this, getting her familiar with us day by day. She'll choose us."

Alexia, her voice tinged with desperation, whispered, "She'd better..." She leaned in, kissing him, but his response seemed less than passionate.

The two left the room, and Jason and Katie exhaled loudly, their bodies sagging with relief.

Katie stood up, her face a mask of confusion. "What was all that about?"

Jason emerged from behind the partition, his brow furrowed. "Who is 'She'?"

They continued searching the room, their minds reeling with questions.

Katie, her voice low and urgent, wondered aloud, "And being 'chosen'? What the hell is going on in this place?"

Jason, closing a drawer, shook his head. "I'm not finding anything."

Katie, her search equally fruitless, sighed. "Me either."

Stealthily, they moved down the hall again, approaching another door.

Jason, his voice a whisper, questioned, "Kylie's room?"

Katie, her expression determined, nodded. "Worth a look."

They tried the door. Unlocked. With a quick glance, they slipped inside.

Kylie's room was a stark contrast to Alexia's - unkempt, haphazard, and randomly mismatched, with boxes and clothes strewn everywhere.

Jason, taking in the chaos, remarked, "Definitely Kylie's room."

They began searching, careful not to disturb the disarray too much.

On a shelf, Jason noticed a digital camera - the same one Kylie had used to take their picture in the garden days ago.

He picked it up, bringing up the storage memory and scrolling through the pictures. In the small digital screen, he saw himself and Katie talking among the standing stones.

Advancing the pictures, he came across images of Caleb and Alexia. Another click revealed a smiling stranger in the gardens. Then another two in the same spot.

Jason, his voice laced with confusion, muttered, "What the..." He continued scrolling, revealing more pictures of unfamiliar people - singles, couples, and small groups - all posing in the gardens.

He moved to Katie, holding out the camera. "Check this out."

Katie took the device, staring at the screen as Jason advanced through the images. "Who are all these people?"

Jason, drawn to a closed box at the edge of a dresser, lifted the lid, revealing a pile of belongings - purses, wallets, jewelry, IDs. "Son of a..."

Rummaging through the contents, he held up his wallet, his voice a mix of relief and anger. "Found it."

Katie, reaching into the box, exclaimed, "That's my purse!"

They stared at the other items, their minds racing.

Katie took a wallet, opening it and reading the name. "Robert LaPoor..."

Jason, examining the contents of a small clutch, found a driver's license. "Michelle Delpoor..."

Katie, her eyes widening as she looked at a passport, whispered, "Ernesto Del Pobre..."

Jason, his gaze sweeping over the box, muttered incredulously, "All De La Poers..."

The door opened, and Kylie walked in, stopping short as she saw them, a gasp escaping her lips.

Her eyes fell on the box in their hands, and she tried to speak, but terror seized her tongue.

Jason, his voice gentle, attempted to explain. "Sorry we're in your room... We were just looking for..."

Katie, her eyes flashing with anger, demanded, "What the fuck, Kylie? Who are all these people?"

Kylie stammered, her voice barely above a whisper. "Guests... relatives..."

Katie pressed further, her tone accusatory. "Why do you have all their stuff?"

Kylie, tears welling up in her eyes as she reached for the box, choked out, "It's... it's proof."

Katie, her voice rising, shouted, "Proof of what!?"

Kylie, clutching the box like a lifeline, whispered, "Proof that they existed."

Katie's next words caught in her throat, the gravity of the situation sinking in.

Kylie's hands trembled as she held the box. "Some tried to leave. But they all ended up... staying."

She rocked back and forth, her voice a haunted whisper. "I tried to show them... Tried to tell them..."

Jason, his brow furrowed, asked softly, "Tell them what?"

Kylie's eyes locked with his, a desperate intensity in her gaze. "About the dreams. About the rats. About HER."

Caleb and Alexia pushed open the door, their presence a looming threat.

Caleb, his smile cold and calculating, asked, "What's happening in here?"

A wave of anger washed over Jason as he saw Caleb, his fists clenching at his sides.

Katie, trying to diffuse the situation, stammered, "We were just... looking for our stuff."

Alexia, her rage sudden and fierce, turned on Kylie, her voice dripping with venom. "You took their stuff too?"

She advanced on the cowering girl, her words a barrage of insults. "How many times do I have to tell you not to fuck with other people's stuff, you crazy fucking klepto!"

Kylie rocked back and forth, her words desperate. "They're still here... They're still here..."

Alexia, towering over her, spat, "They're all gone now, you stupid bitch!"

Katie, trying to intervene, stepped between them. "Hey! Back off."

Alexia, undeterred, continued her tirade. "This crazy act is just bullshit. You're just mad you didn't get chosen."

Jason, his voice rising, tried to intervene. "Hey! Come on!"

Caleb, his tone nonchalant, remarked, "Hey cuz - you're bleeding."

Jason reached up to his bandaged temple, his fingers coming away stained with blood.

Katie, overwhelmed with concern, took Jason by the shoulders and began leading him out of the room.

Caleb smirked, his voice dripping with condescension. "Off to bed with you two."

Katie glared at him as she guided Jason through the door, her jaw clenched in anger.

Alexia slammed the door shut, leaving Kylie whimpering, clutching her box of memories.

Katie helped Jason up the stairs and into his bed, her touch gentle but firm.

Jason, his voice heavy with exhaustion and frustration, muttered, "Fuck all of this. I don't know what the hell's going on around here." He cringed in agony, his head wound throbbing. "We need to leave."

Katie, changing the bloody bandage around his head, grimaced. "Not like this, you're not."

Jason, taking her hand, his voice urgent. "I'm serious. There's too much fucked up weird stuff going on in this place. All those people in that box. Relatives?"

Katie, her voice uncertain, offered, "Kylie probably just stole their IDs before they left, just like she stole ours."

Jason, his eyes searching hers, whispered, "Yeah...but what if they really didn't leave?"

Katie paused, considering his words. "I think your paranoia might be rubbing off on me," she said, securing the last of the bandages.

Jason held her hand, his gaze intense. "Katie, we need to go. Tomorrow."

Katie, her expression one of fierce determination, nodded. "Yeah. Fuck this place. Just get some sleep."

She squeezed his hand and kissed his forehead before leaving the room.

Once again, Jason lay in bed, willing sleep to come to his aching mind.

Under an overcast sky, a dense, dark forest stretches endlessly over green rolling hills. Mist clings to the tangled undergrowth, veiling the primeval forest floor in a shroud of billowing uncertainty.

A group of a dozen leather-clad Danes, their breaths forming ghostly clouds in the chill air, march slowly through the labyrinthine maze of trees. Their armor clinks softly with each purposeful step, shields ready, spears and axes gripped tightly in weathered hands, wary of the silent wilderness they have found themselves in.

Their leader, a tall man in gilded scaled mail and white fur cloak, surveys the towering forest with a furrowed brow, a sense of unease gnawing at his gut. His hand instinctively goes to the hilt of his magnificent broadsword, whose wolf-head pommel glints in the dim daylight.

A long-bearded man, clutching a worn parchment map, gazes around with a mixture of confusion and apprehension. A low growl rumbles from one of the warriors, prompting the map holder to gesture frantically, attempting to convey their surroundings. Before he can speak, the warrior's patience snaps, and with a sharp bark, he slaps the map from the man's trembling hands.

A sudden movement catches the leader's eye, and he hisses a command. The group froze, tension thick in the air as they strained to catch any sign of danger.

Hearing a buzzing, the leader points to a gnarled oak ahead of them. A Dane at the forefront cautiously approaches the tree. Parting the overgrown branches with his spear, he reveals a gruesome sight. Bones and antlers hang from long strands of woven hair amongst the branches. A carcass of a ram, long since disemboweled, hangs from the tree trunk, flies covering its carcass.

"Magna Mater!" he exclaims, his voice exploding through the silent forest, a chorus of fearful murmurs rising from his companions as they clutch their weapons tighter.

Suddenly, the forest comes alive with the sound of rustling foliage. Long wooden spears strike out of the undergrowth with deadly precision, catching the Danes off guard. Shadowy figures clad in black furs leap into the group of Norsemen, axes and clubs crashing onto shields.

Drawing his ancestral sword, the leader defends himself with ferocious determination. But the onslaught is relentless, and one by one, his comrades fall, their cries drowned out by the clash of steel and screams of battle.

As their ranks crumble, some Vikings flee into the gloom, while others are ensnared by shadowy assailants, dragged screaming into the depths of the forest.

The leader stands alone, surrounded by savages adorned with black face paint and bone ornaments. He swings his glimmering blade with immense fury, but the primitives are swift, striking at his legs with deadly accuracy - not to kill, but to incapacitate.

The leader is overwhelmed, held fast by many warriors, and forced to the ground. He is dragged against his will deeper into the heart of the forest. His cries of defiance muffled by the misty fog, his body battered and broken by the unforgiving terrain.

Through pain-blurred vision, he glimpses an ancient henge of standing stones looming in a gloomy clearing. He is forced to his knees, amongst the savages.

Amidst the chaos, a figure cloaked in robes emerges from the mist, wearing a grotesque Green Man mask that seems to twist and contort with malevolent intent. He wields a shepherd's crook with an air of sinister authority, his presence radiating an aura of ancient evil.

One of the black clad warriors presents the Viking's sword to the Green Man. He nods with appreciation and gestures to the side. The sword is thrown onto a pile of metal scraps.

Approaching the prostate Dane, the Green Man reaches down and grasps his face with a powerful hand, shifting his head side to side, observing the captive. The leader spits defiantly at the Green Man; foaming saliva dripping from his mask. The crook strikes him on the side of his head, bringing blood to his eye.

The Dane is dragged once again, out of the standing stones and towards a gaping cavernous amphitheater hewn into the side of a sheer cliff. Descending stone steps into the dark abyss, terror seizes the warrior's features as he beholds the horrors that await below.

30

Jason woke from the dream with a start, the sound of rain tapping against his window in the night, accompanied by the distant echo of rolling thunder. These dreams were more vivid than any he had ever experienced, feeling more like memories than mere visions.

He stood, still wearing the clothes from earlier, and made his way to the mirror to check his head, gingerly undoing the sticky bandages. As he glanced out the window, something caught his eye in the glare of the garden lights - a white, humanoid shape.

Straining to see it more clearly from his window, Jason watched as the figure darted behind the bushes near the garden wall. Determined to prove to himself that he wasn't going crazy, he raced out of the bedroom door.

Heading downstairs, Jason made his way to the doors leading to the gardens. He pulled on the handles, only to find them locked. Rattling the handles, he searched for a latch, but the lock required a key.

A robed caretaker, alerted by the commotion, approached from a nearby hall. Somewhat startled, Jason explained, "I think I saw something...out there. Can you unlock this?"

The groundskeeper moved to intercept him, his voice low and cautionary. "The gardens can be dangerous at night."

Jason glared at him, but the robed man motioned away mechanically. "Please..."

Frustrated, Jason darted away, following the windows that looked out into the garden. Rain thumped against the glass as the wind began to pick up.

He moved slowly, alert and intent, his eyes scanning the lit topiary through the window panes. As he passed several portraits on the wall, one caught his eye...

Suddenly, a flash of lightning illuminated the portrait of Lady Margaret De La Poer, her sallow white face leering ghoulishly, her pale complexion and red lips silhouetted by her black hair.

Jason started and backed away, flashes of his nightmares returning with vivid clarity. "Shit..."

He turned to the window, his heart in his throat.

A second flash of lightning revealed a face staring back at him from the other side of the glass. An emaciated, naked human with impossible features crouched in the grass not more than 20 feet away. Beneath its claws lay a small deer, its body limp and lifeless.

Paralyzed with fear, Jason and the creature stared at each other in the pulsing light of the lightning, their eyes locked in a terrifying moment of recognition.

Jason's scream was muffled by the oncoming thunderclap, the sound lost in the roar of the storm. The thing darted away with preternatural swiftness, clutching the deer in its jaws, its movements a blur of unnatural speed and agility.

Trying to follow its path as it darted through the topiary, Jason ran loudly up a stairway to the balcony overlooking the gardens, his footsteps echoing in the empty halls.

Throwing open the doors, wind and rain bursting into the hallway, Jason clutched the balcony railing, his knuckles white with tension. He scanned the hedges below, but could see nothing moving among the manicured greenery.

The sound of footsteps on the stairs alerted him to the presence of others. A swift grating sound, like metal scraping across concrete, caught his attention. Jason craned his neck to see out a window the metal lid of a cistern sliding closed, the movement almost too quick to follow.

A groundskeeper grabbed him jarringly, forcing him back inside as another shut the doors behind him.

Maz was there, his face a mixture of anger and concern. "What are you doing?"

Jason, his voice shaking, stammered, "I... saw something. A man... but it wasn't a man..."

Maz, turning to a robed caretaker, ordered, "Take him downstairs." He barked something in Turkish to the other, who walked quickly away.

As the robed man led Jason downstairs, he kept looking out the windows, desperate to catch another glimpse of the creature.

Thomas, Alexia, Kylie, and Katie thumped downstairs in their bedclothes, their faces etched with questions. "Who was screaming?"

Katie rushed to Jason's side, pushing the groundskeeper's hands off him.

Jason, stammering and pointing out the window, tried to explain. "It was right there."

Katie, holding him close, her voice soft with concern, asked, "Who was?"

Maz, having collected himself, descended the stairs, his voice calm and soothing. "A groundskeeper - locked out in the rain."

Jason, hissing angrily, his eyes flashing with frustration, retorted, "It wasn't any groundskeeper."

Maz, put his hands on Jason's shoulders, his tone obsequious tone countered, "My boy. What else could it have been?"

Jason stared at him, silently fuming, his mind racing with the implications of what he had seen.

Maz smiled, placing a hand on Jason's cheek, his voice gentle but firm. "With your head injury and the storm - you were just imagining things."

Several more caretakers strode into the room, their faces impassive and their movements precise.

Maz, his voice commanding, addressed the group. "We'll find whoever is out in the rain." He waved at the rest of them, his tone dismissive. "The rest of you! Go back to your beds."

They glanced at each other uncertainty, before reluctantly heading back up the stairs.

Katie held Jason close, leading him towards the stairs. They paused around the corner to hear what transpired behind them.

Maz barked orders to the assembled caretakers, his voice urgent and insistent.

Two of the men slung rifles over their shoulders, threw open the doors, and dashed into the rain-soaked gardens, their footsteps splashing through the puddles.

As they made their way up the stairs, Jason, his voice low and desperate, insisted, "I know what I saw." He stared pleadingly at Katie, his eyes searching hers for understanding. "Why would they need guns to find a lost groundskeeper?"

Katie, whispering, squeezed his hand, "I believe you." She looked up determined, "Come on. We're leaving tomorrow."

Darkness enveloped the cave, the sounds of slurping, wet tearing, and scraping echoing off the damp walls. A torch was held aloft, its flickering light illuminating the glistening stone, casting eerie shadows that danced and writhed.

Ahead, three gaunt, naked figures hunched over a flabby white body, their movements jerky and unnatural. As the light approached, they hissed, skittering away with impossible speed, vanishing into the shadows like albino cockroaches.

The flabby thing on the ground breathed raggedly, blood foaming beneath it, the sound wet and labored.

From the edge of the light, a shriek pierced the darkness, and a pale, emaciated thing leaped onto him, its movements a blur of unnatural speed and agility.

Its black eyes stared vacantly, sharp gray teeth snapping repeatedly at his face, the sound of flesh tearing filling the air.

Jason's eyes blinked open, the grey light of an overcast morning filtering into the room. Dark sleep-rings stained his cheeks, a clean bandage adorning his head.

Looking down, he found Katie in bed with him, both fully clothed, her head resting on his chest, her arm draped protectively around his waist.

He smiled, tenderly running his hand down her hair. "Morning," he whispered, his voice rough with sleep.

Katie stirred, slowly, making content murmuring noises. "Morning. How's the head?" she asked, her voice soft with concern.

Jason reached up to touch his forehead, wincing slightly. "Still seems to be attached."

Katie rose, staring at him, her eyes searching his face. They shared a moment, a silent understanding passing between them. "You look like hell," she said, a hint of a smile tugging at her lips.

Jason grinned widely, his eyes sparkling despite the exhaustion. "I dunno. I haven't felt this good in a while..."

The two drew closer, their faces inches apart, looking longingly into each other's eyes.

Suddenly, the door burst open, Caleb and Alexia standing in the doorway. Alexia, in a loud sing-song voice, announced, "Morning sleepy-head!"

She noticed the two of them in bed, her eyes widening in mock surprise. Alexia laughed, her voice dripping with innuendo. "Oh! I mean sleepy-HEADS!"

Katie, flustered, began to get out of bed, her cheeks flushing red.

Alexia, teasing, waved a dismissive hand. "No need to be embarrassed, darling! You two get your freak on. Don't mind us."

Jason, sitting up, his voice tinged with annoyance, asked, "Something we can help you with, Alexia?"

Alexia pouted, her lower lip jutting out. "You two prudes are no fun."

Caleb, his voice smooth and calculating, chimed in, "We just came to see how you were doing, cousin. You seemed a little...jumpy last night."

Jason, the memory of a shotgun blast still ringing in his ears, growled at him, his voice low and dangerous. "I'm fine."

Caleb pressed, his eyebrow raised, a smile playing at the corners of his mouth. "Are you sure? All that screaming and seeing things?"

Jason barked angrily, "It was just a groundskeeper, like Maz said."

Caleb's smile widened, his eyes glinting with a private joke. "That's all it was, was it?"

Alexia, plopping herself on the corner of the bed, ignoring any sense of privacy, asked, "So what are the two of you up to today?"

Jason, his hand on his head, his voice weary, replied, "Think I'm going to stay in bed today. Take some time and heal up."

Alexia's face lit up, her eyes sparkling with excitement. "Well, just make sure you're feeling better by tonight. We have a special event planned," she grinned. "Fun for the whole family."

Katie, barely containing her rage, her voice tight with forced politeness, said, "Wouldn't miss it."

Alexia, reading the room, her voice saccharine sweet, chirped, "Well then. We'll just leave you two love-birds in peace."

Caleb and Alexia closed the door behind them, the sound echoing in the sudden silence. The second it shut, Jason bounded out of bed, his movements quick and purposeful.

"That was no goddamn groundskeeper," he muttered, getting dressed, his voice low and intense.

Katie, her voice urgent, said, "I packed our bags last night. Let's just get the hell out of this place."

Jason paused, taking a long deep breath. "I... can't," he said, his voice heavy with resignation.

Katie stared at him, her eyes wide with disbelief. "What?"

Jason sighed, his shoulders slumping. "Not... just yet."

Katie stared, her mouth open, unable to find the words.

Jason, his voice earnest, explained, "I gotta know what's going on here. What was that THING I saw? All those IDs in Kylie's room... What is Maz hiding?"

Katie, her voice rising with incredulity, exclaimed, "That's what the fucking police are for!"

Jason shook his head, his voice low and insistent. "Where? In Anchester? No one is going to believe us! We have no proof!"

Katie stammered, searching for words, for rebuttals, for sanity.

Jason put his hands on her shoulders, his eyes locking with hers. "Katie..." He looked at her, his expression softening. "I gotta know."

Katie stared, then sighed in resignation. "Goddamnit." She got up, moving to the door.

Jason put on fresh clothes, his voice determined. "I just need a photo. Just one good picture of it. Proof."

Katie left the room, returning immediately in her own jacket, her face set resolutely. "Like hell you're doing this alone."

The gardens were wet from the storm, the overcast clouds casting everything in shades of gray. Jason and Katie snuck their way through the topiary.

Hearing footsteps approaching, they ducked down behind a hedge. Two groundskeepers carrying high-powered rifles walked past, patrolling the grounds, their faces impassive but scanning the area.

Jason and Katie reached the cistern, the lid firmly closed over it. Looking for a handle, Katie noticed long indentations on the lid. "Scratches," she whispered, her voice barely audible.

Jason held his hand over the lid, his splayed fingers tracing the long scratches, making them appear to be fingernail marks, the implication sending a shiver down his spine.

The two gazed at each other, gathering their resolve, then pushed the heavy lid to the side, the sound of stone scraping against stone echoing in the stillness. The deep well descended into shadow, metal rungs embedded into the stone walls forming a ladder leading downwards, the darkness seeming to swallow the light.

Jason gave a quick glance around, then moved onto the ladder, his movements careful and deliberate. Engulfed in damp shadow, Jason made his way down the old brick well, Katie descending above him, the only sound the drip of water and the creak of metal.

Jason paused to glance at the finger-sized holes riddling the stonework, his mind reeling with the implications.

A rung gave way, tumbling into the shadows with a distant splash. Katie whispered from above, her voice tight with concern, "You OK?"

Jason, his voice low and reassuring, replied, "Yeah. Just be careful of these rusted rungs."

Jason reached the bottom, stepping off the ladder and into ice-cold knee-deep water, the shock of the cold making him gasp. He switched on his phone flashlight as Katie hopped off the ladder with a splash, her teeth chattering. "Well, that's freezing," she said, her voice shaking with the cold.

The eroded bottom formed a small chamber, Jason's phone light illuminating a narrow opening in the wall, the darkness beyond seeming to beckon them forward.

The two exchanged nervous glances, then crouched down into the water, making their way through the ragged tunnel, the cold seeping into their bones.

"Holy shit, this water is freezing," Katie muttered, her teeth chattering uncontrollably, the sound echoing off the damp walls.

CHAPTER
32

The claustrophobic natural tunnel opened into a narrow, winding cavern, cut by a trickling stream. Jason and Katie swept their cellphone flashlights across the smooth granite walls as they waded through the water, the light reflecting with rippling caustics, creating an eerie, otherworldly atmosphere.

Ahead, the stream parted into a shallow pool. Beyond, a narrow tunnel moved up and away, its depths shrouded in darkness.

The two sloshed slowly out of the icy water, their legs soaked to their waists. "Glad I brought a jacket," Katie growled sarcastically, her teeth chattering from the cold.

Following the dry tunnel, the sound of flowing water slowly faded into the distance, replaced by the ominous guttural rumble of wind and the echoing drips of water, each sound amplified by the oppressive silence.

Jason's light shone on something piled on the ground. As they approached, they realized they weren't sticks, but bones. More bone piles were strewn about the tunnel. The sight sent a chill down their spines.

Jason bent down to examine the pile, his light revealing that many of the bones were broken, as if they had been crushed. Short, deep scratches could be seen in the larger long bones, the marks jagged and unsettling.

Katie gasped, her light illuminating a human skull in a wall crack. As Jason walked to inspect the skull, Katie said, her voice trembling with horror, "Are these human remains we're standing in?"

Jason looked down at the skull, its shape disturbingly warped. It was like starting with a wax human skull and melting it under a heat lamp. The top of the skull was compressed, almost flattened. The brow ridge was thick, and the nasal opening small and high. The most disturbing feature was the eye sockets - they were extremely wide apart and seemed smaller and somehow atrophied, as if they had adapted to a life in perpetual darkness.

"I'm not sure..." Jason trailed off, his voice barely above a whisper.

Jason rose, seeing movement from the corner of his eye and flashing his light down the passage. Something lithe and white darted from the light, disappearing into the dark tunnel ahead before Jason could react, leaving only a fleeting impression of something unnatural and terrifying.

Jason began moving toward the tunnel when he finally began to think about what he was doing. If this was the thing he saw in the gardens, they were woefully unprepared to be chasing it. They had no way to defend themselves if it attacked. He stopped, fear beginning to take over, hyperventilating with the rising panic.

Katie moved next to him. "Just one picture," she reminded him, her voice steady despite the fear in her eyes, "and then we're gone." She touched his shoulder reassuringly. "We'll put an end to this place." Jason clenched his jaw and continued forward, drawing strength from her presence.

Searching down the sloping tunnel, Jason was somewhat relieved not to see anything. The tunnel continued to wind, ever downward, the darkness seeming to press in on them from all sides.

After some time, the tunnel began to widen into a large, dim cavern. A string of electric lights against a far wall of the cavern gave a small amount of respite from the darkness. A strange, echoing noise filled the cave that could not be identified. Jason and Katie moved cautiously towards the lights, their footsteps echoing in the vast space.

Sweeping their footing with his phone light, Jason noticed that the otherwise smooth cave floor had ragged cracks splitting through it - like tiny chasms, narrow and jagged. Jason moved next to a fissure, seeing only darkness below. He shined his light down it and found only a gnarled wall leading straight into abyssal depths beyond his light's reach. He realized he stood on a precipice over an impossibly deep pit - a void that led to oblivion, its depths seeming to beckon him forward.

Vertigo began to overcome his senses. Staring into that blackness, he felt his body begin to swoon. Something down there, far below, stirred. Something that hungered. He felt the black pit suddenly moving up towards him, and he felt himself pitching forward into the abyss, his mind reeling with terror.

Katie leapt towards him, grabbing Jason as he fell towards the fissure. With a fierce jolt, she pulled him back to safety. Jason was breathing hard and trying to clear his head. "You OK?" Katie asked, her voice tight with concern.

Jason coughed, his voice rough. "How did you...? You saved me."

Katie gave him a reassuring smile, her eyes shining in the darkness. "Climber's reflexes."

After a moment to collect themselves, they continued towards the lights against the wall. The noises began to get louder and more distinct. Mewling sounds like pigs or sheep. They began to notice a rank and musty smell - like livestock, the stench growing stronger with each step.

Finally reaching the lights, they illuminated a steep tunnel leading up to a wide opening. The cavern sloped downwards out of the light's range, so they followed the lights upwards and into yet another tunnel.

This tunnel was different than their previous one, with obvious signs of human excavation. The slope quickly became a level floor lit by electric lights strung down the center of the tunnel. They passed several heavy wooden doors inset into the tunnel walls, imagined dark secrets behind each one.

In short order, the tunnel opened into a large dimly lit room. Standing at the threshold, Jason and Katie stood in disgust at the sight. It was an abattoir. The pervasive smell of blood and rot filled their nostrils, making them gag. Heavy hooked chains hung from the ceiling, their metal gleaming dully in the light. Stained wooden tables held an array of saws and cleavers, the blades crusted with dried blood. Dried rust-colored grime lay thick on the floor, though none of the hooks were holding any meat. The room ended in a tremendous industrial door almost the width of the room, its surface pitted and scarred.

They walked slowly into the room, arms covering their noses, staying away from the rows of suspended hooks, trying to ignore their gruesome purpose.

Just then, they heard a loud noise coming from the corridor behind them. A repeated squeal of metal. They looked at each other, panicked. Voices could be heard over the squeal, heading towards them, the sound growing louder with each passing second.

They darted behind a large wooden chopping block, just as a light entered the room. Two robed men were pulling a metal cart, its wheels squealing as they turned, grinding over the rough floor.

"All I'm saying," one of the groundskeepers was saying to the other in a husky voice, "is that Liverpool has a better lineup this year."

From behind the table where they crouched, Jason could see that both men carried rifles slung on their backs. "Fine," the other man growled at him, "I'll give you that. But Man United has just hired Bremmer as their Head Coach. That bloke knows how to whip his team into shape."

As the cart rolled by, Jason noticed that it was full of carcasses, the sight making his stomach churn. It was difficult to see from their vantage point, but Jason thought they looked like pigs. Pale skinned pigs, their flesh a sickly white in the dim light.

"Yeah," the first robed man said, "But the coach don't take to the field, now does he?" The two lifted the cart handles, spilling the contents onto the floor before the massive metal doors, the bodies landing with a sickening thud.

Trying to see, Jason realized that the pigs were quite large, curled in fetal positions. The more he saw, the more he thought that their limbs were altogether too long for swine, the proportions wrong in a way that made his skin crawl.

The groundskeeper continued, "Face it, mate, the Reds just have a better team this year." The second one snorted out loud but held his tongue.

"We ready?" the first groundskeeper asked. The second nodded slowly. The first walked towards the industrial door, to what looked like a panel. The two simultaneously bowed their heads, lifting their arms before them. They began to sing in deep, prayer-like intonations and made sharp signs with their hands. They quickly lifted their crook-pendants and kissed them. Then the first took a deep breath and pressed a button on the panel.

The doors began to pull apart with the thunderous sound of shearing metal. The two men hurried back from the doors, as if in fear of what might wait behind. Jason realized that he was closer to the door than the robed men and felt an ominous sense of danger.

As the doors slowly ground open, only pure darkness lay beyond. As the heavy doors began to stop, there was a long hydraulic hiss before a pervasive silence. Jason could see that behind the open doors, the room continued into a natural cave. Just beyond the threshold, the floor disappeared into a vast pit, its depths seeming to swallow the light.

Jason became aware of a distant sound, like sloshing and thumping. Every moment, the sound became louder and louder. Then, pouring over the lip of the pit, a flood of black rats began to well up and spill into the room. There must be thousands of the creatures, slithering on top of each other, moving like a single thick mass, flowing across the floor. When the edge of the flood touched the carcasses, it suddenly surged forward like a wave as the hungry rats tore into the corpse flesh. Within a second, the bodies were covered in a mound of writhing rats, pulsing and undulating, the sound of tearing flesh filling the air.

Katie pressed her hand to her mouth, trying to avoid gagging. Jason held her close, his eyes wide with horror. After an eternity, the pool of rats began to recede, pulling back from where the carcasses once lay, and slithering back through the metal doors and into the cavernous pit. One of the carcasses remained - partially devoured and covered in a viscous black slime.

A groundskeeper moved back to the panel with trepidation and quickly hammered a button. The doors began grinding closed. The second robed man, looking over the slime-covered, gnawed carcass, said, "Looks like she's full."

The two men rolled the cart to the lump of meat and hauled it onto the wagon. The first groundskeeper said, "Better tell the kitchen we have leftovers." The two burly men guided the squeaking metal cart down another passage, out of the room, their footsteps fading into the distance.

Jason and Katie were awestruck - dumbfounded at the impossibly horrible sight they had witnessed, their minds reeling with the implications.

Katie muttered, her voice trembling with terror, "We need to go. We need to go. We need to go."

Jason babbled, waves of understanding crashing into his mind, "That thing... that half-eaten thing. It wasn't a pig... Covered in slime... leftovers?" Suddenly, he had flashes of their dinners, Maz's stew. "It's... It's being served... WAS served... TO US!" Jason was hit with a stomach-lurching wave of nausea, retching uncontrollably and loudly, the sound echoing off the walls.

Katie held him as he coughed and spat, her voice urgent. "We need to go..." She lifted her head, hearing something. Jason began to hear it too. The faint sounds of a woman sobbing, coming from beyond a nearby thick wooden door.

The thick wooden door opened with shrieks of its ancient iron hinges, revealing a dark corridor. On both sides were ground-to-ceiling bars with intermittent cell doors. The smell of sweat and feces overwhelmed them, making their eyes water.

The weeping suddenly stopped as shadowy shapes shuffled back from the bars. On a stone floor covered in straw and filth, several people huddled together. Some were dressed in street clothes, others in bedroom clothes, but all were filthy, their faces gaunt and haunted. "Oh my god..." Katie gasped in shock, her hand flying to her mouth.

Realizing the two were not their captors, the captives rushed towards the bars. They whispered frantically, their voices hoarse with desperation. "Get us out of here!" "Please!" "You have to help us!"

Jason saw the old and rusted lock and chain around the cell door and lit his phone, looking for something to pry it with, his mind racing.

Katie shut the door to the corridor and lit her phone, shining it on the prisoners, her face etched with concern. "We'll get you out," she said, her voice steady despite the fear in her eyes.

The one girl with tearful eyes came to the bars. "Thank you," she sobbed, her tears making clean streaks down her dirty cheeks.

"It's all right," Katie soothed, holding the girl through the bars. "It's all right..."

Jason scoured the other cells, his heart pounding. A wooden bowl. A femur. Rusted iron shackles. Nothing with any leverage.

"Are you from Anchester?" one captive asked, their voice trembling with hope. "Are you police?" "Are there more of you?"

Katie just shook her head, her expression grim.

Jason considered a chunk of rock broken from the mortar of the wall. It would be loud, but it would work.

He raised the brick with both hands and slammed it down onto the old iron padlock. There was a tremendous clatter, but the loose chain seemed to absorb most of the blow.

Jason raised the rock again. Suddenly, the door swung open, and a robed groundskeeper strode into the room. He stopped, and the two locked surprised eyes, the moment stretching out like an eternity.

The groundskeeper moved to draw his rifle. Jason launched at him, running down the hall as the guard brought his rifle to bear. Jason swung his rock like a hammer at the side of the robed man's bald head. There was a burst of dust and stone as the old brick shattered against the groundskeeper's face, the impact sending shards flying.

Jason stared in horror as the man seemed to simply shake his head and glare in rage, his eyes burning with a terrifying intensity.

In a blur, the groundskeeper struck the befuddled Jason. The force of the blow staggered him back, his vision swimming.

The groundskeeper lowered the rifle at Jason, but Katie grabbed it by the barrel. The rifle fired, just missing Jason. The thunder rang through the stone halls, the sound deafening in the enclosed space.

Jason and Katie both leaped onto the groundskeeper, grappling frantically at his limbs. Impossibly strong, the man tossed the two around like children as they struggled to keep their grip, their bodies slamming against the cold stone.

Jason pushed with all his might, and the man staggered against the cell bars. Immediately, several of the Anchester prisoners grabbed him through the openings, piling on fast, barely holding the groundskeeper in place, their faces contorted with desperation and rage.

Frantically trying to keep the man's body against the bars, Jason saw a sheath along the groundskeeper's belt. "His knife..." Jason spat through his teeth, his voice strained with effort. Hearing that, the robed man thrashed violently, loudly breaking a captive's arm between the bars with a wet snap.

A slender hand from the cell grabbed the hilt of the knife and plunged it upwards into the groundskeeper's chest. His eyes bulged, but his struggle continued, his strength superhuman.

With a shriek, the weeping girl stabbed over and over, each blow ebbing the might of the groundskeeper. Finally, blood pouring from his side and his mouth, the robed man sputtered a gout of blood and went limp, his body sagging against the bars. The young woman with the knife continued to stab at the corpse, her face twisted with a feral rage. A voice from the cell said, "Terra... That's enough..." The arms released him, dropping his body to the ground with a thud.

The name sounded familiar, causing Jason to pause - before memory crashed down on him. Didn't that broken-nosed hooligan say that his Terra went missing?

There was silence, until someone said, "Keys..."

Jason, snapped out of his shock, quickly patted down the groundskeeper. It was difficult to see in the thin crack of light from the doorway. In his waist pack - a pack of cigarettes, a lighter, a stone carved in the shape of the corpulent mother... and a set of keys. Spying a large, old-looking iron key on the ring, Jason thrust it into the lock. It clicked open, clattering with the chain to the floor.

As the iron cell door screeched open on rusty hinges, the prisoners piled out of the cell, their faces a mix of relief and fear.

Jason held up the rifle, "Anyone good with this?" An older gentleman said, "Give 'er here, lad," his voice gruff and steady.

Jason took the bloody knife from Terra, hoping he would not have to use it, his hand shaking slightly.

Katie moved to the doorway, looking around. Then turned back, her voice low and urgent. "Quickly... but quietly."

They made their way out of the prison, pulses racing.

Jason, Katie, and the prisoners hurried out of the abattoir and down the tunnel, their footsteps echoing off the damp walls. The hairs on the back of Jason's neck stood on end as he heard noises behind them, a sickening realization settling in his gut that they were only moments ahead of their pursuers.

They raced down the ramp past the string of lights and into the dim cavern junction, their breath coming in ragged gasps. Lights flashed down the tunnel behind them, the beams cutting through the darkness like knives.

Jason ran deeper into the dark cave where the lights didn't reach, his eyes straining to see in the oppressive gloom. He came to a low fence, the sound of livestock beyond. "Come on!" he whispered loudly at the others, his voice tight with urgency as he leaped over the fence.

The pasture ground was wet and filth-covered, the stench of decaying waste assaulting their nostrils. As his eyes adjusted to the darkness, Jason noticed low, pale shapes clustered together, their forms indistinct and unsettling.

The last of the prisoners clambered over the fence as the first groundskeeper's lights burst from the tunnel, sweeping into the vast cave, the beams dancing across the rocky walls. From another tunnel, two more groundskeepers raced in with lights, their faces etched with confusion and alarm. "What is it?" one blurted, his voice echoing in the cavernous space. "We heard the shot..."

Jason and Katie moved deeper into the pen, the sound of the animals grunting and whining as they approached setting their teeth on edge. Barely able to see their surroundings in the darkness, they ducked down among the ruminating beasts, their fear hammering in their chests.

Trying to keep low and watch the pursuers, a beast bumped into Jason, its skin cool and clammy against his own. He jerked back, a wave of revulsion washing over him at the unnatural touch. The hairless, pale, flabby beast let out an annoyed mewling sound, unlike anything Jason had ever heard before.

A groundskeeper growled, his voice low and menacing, "Probably more Feral-Ones after the livestock again." A light shone into the pasture, the beam cutting through the darkness like a blade.

As the light hit the herd, they all suddenly stood upright, dozens of repulsively pale-fleshed things shrieking, hissing, and groaning as they recoiled from the brightness, their movements jerky and unnatural.

Jason gasped as he saw one of the things up close, his mind reeling with horror. It stared at him with huge, unintelligent glassy eyes, set disturbingly far apart in a cranium-indented skull. Rolls of greasy fat hung from its jowls, arms, breasts, and gut. Its chest was broad, and it had a malformed, hunched posture, its body a grotesque parody of the human form. Its long, black hair hung in wet, moss matted patches from its skull, the strands glistening in the dim light. It stood and swayed with its herd, shuffling away from the encroaching brightness, its movements slow and labored. One clear thought cut through Jason's shock - these things were human.

One of the Anchester captives, coming face to face with another of the creatures, inhaled sharply, preparing to scream. Instantly, another captive slapped a hand over her mouth, stifling the shriek before it could escape.

Another groundskeeper stomped down the ramp, his voice booming in the enclosed space. "The prisoners have escaped!" The four began pointing down tunnels and splitting into groups, their movements precise and coordinated.

Jason's mind spun with the implications of what he was seeing. These were the things from his dreams, being butchered by the Green Man's sickle. The bones they had found, they were from these pathetic, malformed humans. Not malformed... Devolved. Like some kind of sub-race left to live in the lightless underground. How long would it take for a species to become so adapted? Hundreds of years? Thousands? And why? Why keep them? The carcasses in the abattoir flashed through his mind, the horror of realization crashing over him like a wave. Food. To feed their cannibal religion. To feed those rats...

One of the devolved made a bleating cry and staggered away as an Anchester captive moved too close, its movements clumsy and uncoordinated.

Hearing the noise, two groundskeepers approached the pens, their boots squelching in the muck. As they drew closer, their sweeping lights agitated the shuffling, devolved humans, the beams sending them into a frenzy of fear and confusion.

Jason, seeing the panic in the beasts' eyes as the light touched them, was struck with an idea.

The groundskeepers opened the gate to the pen, straining to see in the darkness, their faces tense with focus.

Jason opened his phone and navigated to his alarm app, his fingers trembling. Turning the volume to maximum, he triggered the alarm. Suddenly, the screen began strobing white, and a deafening klaxon pierced the quiet. The devolved, terrified by the blinding and deafening cacophony, began to panic, loping away from Jason with surprising speed.

The herd began fleeing rapidly towards the open gate, their bare feet slapping on the muck strewn floor. As the stampede hit the surprised groundskeepers, they were knocked aside into the filth of the pen, their bodies disappearing beneath the tide of pale, flabby flesh. Jason and the others ran for it, their hearts in their throats.

Over the screams and bleats of the devolved, Katie grabbed Jason's arm. "This way!" she shouted, her voice barely audible over the din. Jason recognized the tunnel back to the cistern, the other prisoners close behind, their faces etched with terror.

The darkness swallowed them, the only light the faint glow of Katie and Jason's phone lights as they ran, their breath coming in ragged gasps.

Several huge oily rats scampered up from the impossibly deep cracks, their eyes glinting in the darkness. They hissed at Jason as he approached, their teeth bared in a snarl. He kicked at them, his foot connecting with one, sending it flying. It exploded into chunks of fur and black, gooey ichor, the sight making his stomach heave. Others squished the rats underfoot as they chased behind, the sound of their bodies bursting like overripe fruit.

Getting to the water pool, they leaped into the frigid stream, the icy water stealing the breath from their lungs. They squeezed through the narrow crack and into the cistern chute, their bodies scraping against the rough stone.

"Up! Climb! Quickly! Go!" Jason heard himself shout, his voice high and tight with panic, the words tearing from his throat.

Seeing if any more prisoners were in the tunnel, Jason saw a light and heard shouts, sending a jolt of fear through his body. He and Katie scrambled up the cistern ladder, their hands slipping on the rungs, slick with sweat and damp.

Climbing from the well and into the well-illuminated nighttime gardens, the freed prisoners ran in all directions, their frantic movements trying to save themselves.

The priory erupted in powerful searchlights as groundskeepers rushed into the gardens, their voices raised in shouts of alarm and anger.

Jason and Katie crouched with the two remaining Anchester captives, unsure of what to do. The group flinched as gunshot thunder rolled across the gardens. The panicked group raced deeper into the gardens, their feet pounding on the manicured grass.

Fleeing through the topiary, they heard the bay of hunting hounds, the sound chilling them to the bone. Red flares popped in the sky, bathing the gardens in a hellish red light, making flickering shadows in the eerie glow.

They reached the standing stone henge clearing with many exits, their breath coming in ragged gasps. A gunshot roared, and one of the Anchester captives fell, his body crumpling to the ground like a marionette with its strings cut. Terra shrieked, the sound piercing the night. Katie grabbed her as they ran back through the maze, their blood pounding in their ears.

Another bestial howl came from behind. As a flare popped overhead, a monstrosity appeared crouched on a stone wall, its form silhouetted against the red sky. It looked like the thing Jason had seen out the window, all pale flesh, long emaciated limbs, and claws. It leaped onto Terra, knocking her off her feet and pinning her to the ground with its claws, the sound of her screams filling the air. It shrieked at her, its head encased in a wire metal cage affixed to a metal collar on its neck.

Jason and Katie turned to help, but two more of the creatures had leapt onto the wall, growling and barking at them, their eyes glinting with a feral hunger.

Overcome with terror, the two fled through the narrow maze of bushes and stone walls, the sound of the creatures approaching over their own ragged breathing, the air thick with the stench of fear and desperation.

Turning a corner, they came to a dead end, an ancient statue of a Roman legionary staring down at them, its face impassive and uncaring.

The two creatures rounded the corner behind them, bathed in the red flare light, their forms twisted and grotesque. Naked humanoids with taut, pale-white skin stretched over twisted coils of muscle, they moved like quadrupeds on human hands and feet, their movements fluid and unnatural. Their chests were barrel-like, heaving with each breath, the sound of their breathing filling the air. Bones from their spines pronounced the ridge of their backs, the sight making Jason's skin crawl. Metal cages covered their heads with thick metal collars, the metal glinting dully in the light. One stood and bellowed a strange barking bray into the sky before again crouching menacingly, its muscles coiled and ready to spring.

Pressed up against the statue, Jason put himself in front of Katie, brandishing the long knife as the two things stalked towards them in a fluid predatory motion.

One darted at Jason, its movements lightning-fast. He swung the knife wildly, but it darted back, its reflexes inhuman. In a well-trained unison, the other threw itself at him, knocking Jason down, the knife skittering away into the foliage. The thing's claws scraped his shoulders as it fruitlessly tried to bite at him, its metal cage slamming into Jason's face as saliva splashed into his eyes.

Suddenly, it let out a cry as Katie stabbed its side with the knife, the blade sinking deep into its flesh.

Fighting with the thrashing thing, Jason wrestled it onto its back, its clawed feet slashing at his legs, tearing through his jeans and drawing blood. It kicked him back, the force of the blow sending him stumbling.

Katie moved to his side as the two things circled them, their eyes glinting with predatory focus, their muscles coiled and ready to attack.

A man came around the corner, spinning his hunting rifle towards them, the barrel glinting in the red light. He raised the barrel and commanded, "Heel!" his voice sharp and authoritative.

The two creatures immediately leaped away towards their master. As he moved forward, they nuzzled at his legs like loving cats, their eyes fixed on his face. One rose on its legs, and Caleb patted it on its caged head, the gesture almost affectionate.

Katie stammered, her voice trembling with fear and disbelief, "C-Caleb?" The two creatures crept behind their master on all fours, their eyes glinting in the darkness. Several groundskeepers moved in behind them, their faces impassive and their weapons at the ready.

Caleb sighed, his voice dripping with condescension. "It would have been so much easier if you had just stayed in the priory."

As the groundskeepers saw the two, one fired a flare gun into the sky twice, the bright red hell-light bathing the scene.

The two robed men approached Katie, and she swung her knife at one, the blade flashing dangerously in the light. Unconcerned, he grabbed her arm and backhanded her with a fierce blow, throwing her to the ground with a wet crack.

Jason screamed in rage, but was hit in the head with a rifle butt, the blow connecting with the same spot that the cricket bat had hit days before. Jason went out like a light, his body crumpling to the ground as the darkness claimed him.

CHAPTER
34

$\mathcal{A}$ mist-laden primeval forest. Twenty Roman Legionaries, clad in segmented armor, march through the overgrown wood. Soldiers hack at the tangle of ferns with their gladius, pushing ever forward into the unknown.

The banner held by the standard-bearer displays that they are a detachment from the Second Augustan Legion. They are weary from long marching, their left arms aching from the scutum shields they bear.

The commander senses his men's anxiety. They are deep in barbarous territory, having lost contact with the rest of their legion. This place is ancient and foreboding. And far too quiet. He feels as if the shadows themselves are alive.

From the unceasing forest before them comes a shrill whistle. The scout has returned. The men stop as the scout approaches the commander. Taking a knee, he reports that there is a shrine of standing stones ahead.

The men realize what this means. Barbarians. They will sack their primitive temple and take what supplies they might offer.

The commander gives the order to continue marching.

Soon the dense woods open into an overcast clearing. Tall granite cliffs rear behind a semicircle of standing stones. They approach the stones cautiously, searching for any primitive worshipers. There is just the cold breeze and the clank of their armor.

From inside the stone circle, a vast cave entrance yawns at the base of the bleak cliffs. The commander gives a silent order to press on.

As the men move towards the cave entrance, the commander spies something and calls a halt. The cave floor ends in a yawning pit, like a chasm into the mouth of Orcus.

His men notice them before he does. Gallic warriors dressed in black furs appear silently from the foliage around the clearing. They are surrounded.

The commander calls his men into a phalanx, closing their ranks with shields and outstretched spears. More black-clad warriors appear from the treeline. Thirty? Forty? They are outnumbered. He shouts for his men to hold their ground.

The barbarians do not approach. They stand like silent sentinels. They will teach these savages a lesson!

The order to advance catches in the commander's mouth as he sees them. The women in the cave. They seem like apparitions with long dark hair and gauzy dresses. One woman stands out among the others. She is tall and lithe, with a golden tiara on her impossibly beautiful head. She bears a stone pendant around her long neck.

The commander stands transfixed. The other legionaries soon notice the women and lose all thoughts of battle. The priestess smiles at the commander. The other women slowly creep from the cave towards the Romans, like nymphs to awaiting satyrs. Struck dumb, their weapons and shields drop to the ground, as the women begin to touch and embrace them.

The priestess glides directly towards the commander, legionaries and women parting as she walks barefoot. She stops before him and holds out a delicate hand. He takes it in his, his blood surging. She leads him towards the cave. Each of his men is partnered with a woman and follows behind in procession.

At the edge of the cavernous pit, the priestess beckons them down stone-carved stairs, winding down into the torch-lit underworld.

Arriving at a deep amphitheater, the Romans are bid to be seated at a row of feast tables. At the direction of the priestess, the women bring forth food and drink. Loaves of bread, casks of wine, and towering plates of meat. Having been marching on half-rations for a week, the soldiers devour the meal and drink heavily of the spirits.

Soon the feast turns into a celebration, as the Romans begin embracing their maidens. As the sounds of the carnal celebration echo in the chamber, the priestess stands and once again bids the commander to follow her.

Down they walk, past black fissures in the earth and into winding cave tunnels. They enter a tremendous chamber of tree-sized stalactites and oily black water. A towering statue of the corpulent mother looms over them.

The priestess points up at the statue. "Mater Kubileya," she says in reverence.

The commander recognizes this goddess from his schooling. This is a primitive form of the Great Mother. He points at the dominating statue and says, "Cybele. Magna Mater."

She smiles at him and puts her arms around his neck. He holds her close.

Later, at the entrance to the cave, the Roman Legionaries stand silently in black furs among the other warriors. Their commander walks forward to address them, his priestess at his side. The commander slowly takes off his Roman helmet and discards it into the dirt. He then takes from the priestess a large mask and affixes it. He puts on a long white robe and holds a shepherd's staff, turning back to his followers. His chant is muffled by the Green Man mask. "Magna Mater!" The warriors and women erupt in the cry, chanting it like screams to reach the depths of the pits below.

$\mathcal{P}$ain. It was the first sensation that greeted Jason as his eyes fluttered open, his vision blurry and unfocused. He found himself being dragged across a tiled floor, his feet scraping against the cold surface. The men on either side of him held him in a rough grip, their hands digging into his arms as they carried him down a dimly lit tunnel. Electric lights drifted past his foggy senses, their pulsating glow causing his head to throb. The taste of bloody iron filled his mouth, and he felt something tight cutting into his wrists, binding them together.

Jason drifted in and out of consciousness, the pain causing him to black out repeatedly. Each time he came to, he saw his feet being dragged over a different surface - from the smooth tiles to a rough, rocky floor illuminated by flickering firelight. Time seemed to lose all meaning as he was hauled through the winding passages.

Finally, he was dumped unceremoniously onto a hard floor. Struggling to see in the dim light, Jason realized he was in a dark chamber with a brazier burning in the corner. A shadowy figure stood just beyond his blurry focus, clad in white robes that seemed to glow in the dim firelight.

"Clean him up. Get him prepared," the figure commanded, their voice cold and authoritative, muffled as if behind a mask.

Rough hands seized Jason, stripping him of his shirt and trousers. He found himself crouching on the cold floor, nearly naked, as the lights continued to spin in his vision and skull. Suddenly, a shock of icy water hit him in the face, causing him to gasp and inhale some of the droplets. He coughed fiercely, the cold sensation clearing his head momentarily.

As clarity returned, Jason felt the two men approach once more. They yanked a long, coarse robe over his head before lifting him to his feet. Jason swayed, still disoriented. One of the groundskeepers gripped his chin, forcing him to stare into his face. The second held up a small dish, placing his thumb into it and smearing black paint over Jason's eyes and nose. A strange pointed cap was placed on his head, followed by a crown of linked golden disks that felt heavy and unfamiliar.

Yanked to his feet, Jason was prodded forward, stumbling and shuffling out an ancient wooden door. He emerged into a darkened cobblestone street, surrounded by dilapidated medieval buildings on all sides. Confusion gripped him. Where was he? Where was this place? A strange, moaning chant echoed through the night, sending chills down his spine.

What he first mistook for a tree revealed itself to be a stone pillar, fluting upwards into a blackened sky. Jason gasped as realization dawned on him - it wasn't a sky at all. They were underground. To his horror he realized he was beneath the priory. Stalactites and stalagmites created a forest of stone, descending into the throat of an enormous cavern. Sheer vertical chasms dropped into the stygian blackness below. A bright orange glow illuminated the cavern he was being forced towards, its light both mesmerizing and foreboding.

As they passed through the village, Jason noticed that the buildings grew older and more decrepit with each step. The medieval houses gave way to marbled, pillared Roman dwellings, which in turn led to primitive wood and stone huts. Eventually, even those structures were replaced by raised mounds of dirt and stone, a testament to the ancient nature of this subterranean world.

The source of the glow came into view - a towering amphitheater dome carved into the stone of the cave. The flattened stage floor was raised, with several stone stairs spanning up and across the impossibly deep chasms. An ominous stone altar stood at the center of the amphitheater..

Dozens of hooded figures stood in a hemisphere around that central altar, carrying torches or burning incense. They swayed to their own chanting cadence, their deep voices reverberating off the stone walls. Jason was taken past the standing worshipers and dropped heavily to his knees on the open stone before the altar. The stonework was smooth, appearing melted from sheer age.

Behind the altar, piercing the amphitheater's wall, was a vast opening into a void - the mouth of a pit made even more sinister by the fang-like stalactites dripping over its opening. It seemed to beckon, a gateway to an unfathomable darkness.

Over the chanting, Jason heard a mewling, bleating cacophony of grotesque sounds. Turning his head, he saw a cluster of flabby, white creatures being shepherded by groundskeepers. Their hunched and bloated bodies cowered in the torchlight, their wide-set eyes staring indifferently, like unintelligent farm animals.

"Jason!" a familiar voice cried out.

He looked up at the sound, his heart leaping. "Katie!" Two groundskeepers dropped her nearby, dressed in robes similar to his own. Red painted markings adorned her face, and she wore a tall, elaborate headdress. Her hands, like his, were bound.

They crawled towards one another, desperate for comfort. Jason longed to hold her, but his bindings prevented it. Instead, they leaned against each other as the chanting intensified. Tears streamed from Katie's reddened eyes. "What is all this? What is happening?" she murmured through bouts of terrified crying.

Kylie was brought out next, bound and gagged, struggling against her captors with muffled screams. She was dropped next to Jason and Katie, her eyes wide with fear. She tried to scramble away from the altar, but a groundskeeper held her in place, his grip unyielding.

From behind them, Alexia and Caleb strode towards the altar in full ceremonial attire. They were dressed in silk robes and adorned with golden finery, the polished corpulent mother pendants gleaming around their necks. With an air of pride, they took their places directly before the altar, their faces etched with a dark anticipation.

As the chanting thrummed like machinery, a white robed figure wearing a Green Man mask and holding a wooden shepherd's staff glided out from the crowd. He took his place behind the altar, his presence commanding and otherworldly. Jason, Katie, and Kylie were roughly lifted to their feet and pushed to stand near Caleb and Alexia before the high priest.

With a rap of his crooked staff on the stone floor, the chanting abruptly ceased. The Green Man intoned a sermon in a strange, melodic language filled with hard, guttural "ch" sounds. The cultists chanted in unison to punctuate his statements, their voices rising in a haunting chorus of "Mater Kubileya." The amphitheater resonated with their combined voice, the harmonics creating an eerie, palpable energy.

From the nightmare opening at the back of the amphitheater, a dark shape began to rise. More of a mass than a distinct form, its undulating black surface shone like oil in the bright firelight. It poured over the lip of the stage, a flood of churning, slime-covered rats that moved as one.

This was what Jason had witnessed in the abattoir - they did not move like any ordinary rats. The black swarm roiled over itself, moving like a singular, coordinated entity. It expanded and contracted, its movements reminiscent of cells in a protoplasmic pseudopod, a grotesque parody of life.

The Green Man made a gesture with his staff towards the groundskeepers controlling the cluster of devolved creatures. With prods of their shepherd's crooks, the docile, naked things shuffled forward, their movements sluggish and uncoordinated. As they neared the writhing mass, a wave of rats rose up and cascaded upon them in a frenzy of hunger.

Croaking cries emitted from once-human throats as the creatures struggled to comprehend the horror engulfing them. Heads and limbs would sometimes peek out of the horde, screaming and flailing, only to be swallowed again. In a matter of seconds, they were gone, devoured by the seething swarm of rats. Jason choked back nausea, his stomach turning at the gruesome sight.

Slowly, the mass of rats subsided like a tide, leaving no trace of the creatures it had consumed. "She is satiated," the Green Man's voice thundered through the amphitheater. "Let the choosing begin!" The screaming roar of the cultists' chants reverberated in Jason's brain, the sound almost physical in its intensity.

Staring into the squirming horde of rats, a horrible realization dawned on Jason. "She." The Green Man referred to these things as "She." These were not rats - they were a part of something else, something far more sinister and ancient.

The Green Man motioned to Kylie, and she was pushed forward, towards the flowing throngs of rats. She stood trembling, paralyzed by fear as the mass streamed across the floor, surrounding her feet. The rats churned about her, as if deciding whether or not to devour her. After a few tense seconds, the tendril of rats pulled back, retreating from her quivering form.

Alexia, without prompting, stepped forward, prostrating herself before the black heap of squirming vermin. Again, the rats extended towards her, forming a circle around her legs, sizing her up. Several of them stopped to sniff at her ankles, their movements deliberate and unsettling.

Suddenly, the rats broke away from Alexia, hopping and slithering over the floor towards Katie. Katie kicked at them in fear, her eyes wide with terror. Alexia lifted her head, her expression a mixture of shock and rage as she witnessed the scene unfolding before her.

As the stream of rats surrounded Katie, they began chittering and squeaking, standing on their hind legs and hopping in place. Their behavior was erratic, almost celebratory. Alexia shouted, her voice raw with anger, "No!"

The rats retreated, flowing back into the squirming mound behind the altar. The Green Man's voice rang out, "The Great Mother has chosen her Voice!"

The cultists cheered and cried out in a frenzy of devotion, "Magna Mater! Magna Mater!"

Alexia clenched her fists, her body shaking with fury. "It's me, goddamnit!" she screamed, her voice cracking with desperation. Enraged, she began to stomp towards Katie, her eyes blazing with a manic intensity. A forceful hiss emanated from the mass of rats, stopping Alexia in her tracks. Another feral hiss, and she backed down, her face contorted with barely contained rage.

Caleb stepped forward to the altar, glancing at Alexia with a smirk. "Tough luck, babe," he said, his voice dripping with condescension.

Once more, an oily group of rats spilled towards Caleb. The lead rats rose, sniffing at him, their movements curious and probing. He held out his arms in anticipation, his eyes gleaming with a dark hunger. But the rats recoiled, their interest fleeting. In an instant, they streamed towards Jason, their eyes fixated on him with an unnerving intensity. They began to squeak and dance, their shrieking echoed by the squirming mass behind them.

The Green Man shrieked, his voice rising above the cacophony, "The Atys has been chosen!"

The cultists shouted and gave praise, their voices rising in a frenzied chant of "Attes! Attes!"

Alexia glared at the stunned Caleb, her lips twisting into a bitter smile. "Sorry, babe," she said, her voice dripping with sarcastic satisfaction.

Over the chanting, the rats retreated, flowing back into the heaving mound. They slowly slipped back down the chasm from whence they came, their shiny dark forms disappearing into the depths.

Caleb threw off his cap, his face contorted with anger. He shouted at the Green Man, his voice raw with frustration, "What the fuck, Maz? You said I would be the Atys! I've been waiting for years for this bullshit!"

The Green Man raised a hand, his voice calm and commanding. "Now, now. You will still have a long life to share with her glory. Be happy, Caleb! This is a time for celebration! For the first time in centuries, She will have both Voice and Atys! All her gifts will be ours to use."

Lowering his staff at the assembled groundskeepers, the Green Man shouted ceremoniously, "Prepare them! We will begin the ceremony tonight!"

Jason, Katie, and Kylie were each pushed away from the altar, off the stone stage, and across the stair bridges. Kylie fought against her captors, thrashing and screaming, her voice muffled by the gag. Jason struggled to see Katie, his heart pounding in his chest.

She seemed overcome with fear, her eyes wide and staring, her limp body being dragged by the groundskeepers.

As they reached the village area, the group began to split up. Jason cried out for Katie, his voice hoarse with desperation. Katie snapped awake, shouting his name in return. He struggled against his captor, but a blow from behind sent stars dancing across his vision, the pain exploding in his head.

Jason was led into a cottage and through a door that opened into a bulb-lit stone tunnel. His wrist binding was cut and with a final, rough shove, he was thrown bodily into a cell.

The door slamming shut behind him with a resounding clang. It was the only sound, save for his breath, he would hear for hours.

After dark hours of clawing at the door and slamming his body against it, Jason collapsed in fear and exhaustion, breathing the stale air in heavy gasps. The sturdy cell door might as well been solid stone. Time passed, and without the strength to make an escape, his mind was left to try and comprehend his dire situation.

Regret washed over him. After the events in Anchester, he should have taken Katie and left. But where would they have gone? Home? He had nothing left to go back to. The thought of making a home somewhere with Katie. The thought caused him too much pain to continue. They should have just gone anywhere, as long as it was far away from this nightmarish place.

Jason's thoughts raced as he tried to make sense of everything he had witnessed in the last few hours. Albino pig people being eaten by rats, a cannibal cult that worshipped them - it all seemed too surreal to be true. He wondered how long Maz had been collecting people from his bloodline, luring them to this place. And for what purpose? To show them off to his bizarre cave rats?

A shudder ran through his body as he recalled the thing he had seen. His conscious mind wanted to keep believing it was just a swarm of rats, but his subconscious knew better. These were not some kind of intelligent rat swarm - they were not rats at all. They were a singular creature, a THING that defied explanation. Jason shook his head, trying to dispel the cognitive dissonance that threatened to overwhelm him. He knew that succumbing to that belief would lead to madness.

A sudden wave of drowsiness washed over him, urging him to sleep, to dream. It was more than just exhaustion; he felt a pull. Something was actively luring him towards slumber. Jason caught himself nodding off and shook himself awake fiercely. Whatever was urging him to sleep filled him with an inexplicable sense of dread.

Slowly rising to his feet, Jason knew he had to escape, find Katie, and get out of this place. He began to search his surroundings again for anything that might aid in his escape. The light from beyond the door suddenly flickered as something moved outside his cell. Through the narrow viewport, Maz's face appeared, looking down at him.

"I'm surprised," Maz began, his voice calm and measured. "I had groomed Caleb and Alexia so thoroughly. Yet, you were chosen." He shrugged, a nonchalant gesture. "But no matter, so long as Cybele has a Voice and Atys."

Jason rose to his feet, his voice tinged with anger and desperation. "How many, Maz?" he asked, swaying slightly. "How many more people have you lured to this place?"

Maz gave a nonchalant laugh. "Far too many to find what I needed."

"Why?" Jason demanded, his building rage beginning to focus him. "Why us?"

"Your blood, of course," Maz said with a smile. "This whole priory, and what stood here long before that...", he made a grand gesture, "this was the home of your ancestors. Her worshippers. She is... familiar with you."

Jason growled, his voice dripping with contempt. "You seem to be familiar with her! Why don't YOU go worship that pile of ooze and leave us the fuck alone!?"

Maz smiled and slowly shook his head, muttering, "Forgive him his blasphemies." He took a long breath before continuing. "I have worshipped her - been her servant, her high priest - for a very long time. I rose to the highest of her devoted, but I am not of your blood. My first temple was sacked by those who feared her gifts, feared our powers. They destroyed her as the temple burned." He made a reverent sign with his hands and bowed his head. "It took me a very long time to find her again, barely alive, in this magnificent place." He spread his hands, his voice becoming passionate. "And soon, with her Voice and Atys restored, her godly powers will return."

Jason stood there, stunned by Maz's words. What he was saying was completely insane, delusional. Yet, it was clear that, delusional or not, Maz was a true believer.

Sensing the apprehension in Jason's face, Maz chuckled. "You will come to see, my young De la Poer." He turned and walked away, his voice echoing behind him. "You will see..."

Gritting his teeth, Jason was determined to get out of this nightmare. He continued to search his ancient cell for any means of escape. The cell was a small, natural cave grotto, with only the dim electric lights from beyond the cell door providing any illumination.

In a small pool, he found the crumbling remains of a table and chair, now reduced to a heap of rotting wood. However, one of the chair legs looked solid enough to serve as a potential weapon.

The sound of footsteps echoed down the tunnel, growing louder as they approached his cell, accompanied by the clinking of keys.

Grabbing the wooden leg, Jason stood by the door, anticipation pounding in his chest. Through the bars, the groundskeeper eyed him with suspicion.

As the latch was thrown and the door swung open, Jason lunged at the man, bringing his makeshift club down onto his neck with all his might. The chair leg shattered on impact, but to Jason's horror, the blue-robed man barely flinched. A look of annoyance crossed his blank expression, and with a swift backhand, he knocked Jason to the damp stone floor.

Spitting blood from his mouth, Jason tried to catch his breath as the groundskeeper wrenched him off the floor and forcibly shoved him to his feet.

As they moved through the tunnels, Jason attempted to go limp, but the man's strength was inhuman, lifting him effortlessly by his mantle. "Where am I going?" Jason stammered, his voice trembling. "W-where are you taking me?" A sturdy shove was his only response.

Approaching an intersection, Jason caught sight of a shadow darting quickly away. As they passed the junction, a low hissing growl emanated from the darkness. The groundskeeper stopped abruptly, his blank expression flashing to one of fear.

With a shriek, a white shadow leapt from the nearby corridor. Jason was knocked to the ground as two emaciated, human-like creatures tackled the groundskeeper. One grabbed the large man's legs, sinking its teeth into his calf, while the other silenced his cry of fear with a crushing bite to the neck. Jason backed away, watching in horror as the gurgling man's body twitched in the grip of the abhorrent creatures.

As the man let out a final, sputtering gasp, the eyes of the two predators turned towards Jason. Their bloody maws opened, letting the heavy body drop limp to the floor. They began to step towards him on all fours with guttural growls.

"Heel!" The command came from the darkened corridor, causing the creatures to wince, yet they remained ready to pounce. Caleb emerged from the shadows, his voice stern. "I said, heel!"

The creatures turned and loped to his side, their movements swift and obedient. From his coat, Caleb produced a parcel wrapped in butcher's paper and tossed it to the floor. The creatures darted towards it, their claws tearing the paper aside to get to the red meat within.

Jason stared dumbly up at Caleb, who was now dressed in modern clothes. Caleb looked down at him with his irritating smirk. "Well, let's go then."

The creatures hissed and snarled as they fought over the scraps of meat. Jason, confused by the unexpected aid, hesitated. Caleb quipped, "Fancy a nap instead?" He extended a hand, his voice calm. "Let's go, cousin."

Hesitantly taking Caleb's hand, Jason rose from the floor. Caleb made a clicking sound with his tongue, and the creatures immediately stopped to look at him. He pointed at the corpse, then down the opposite corridor, and whispered, "Take." The creatures darted to the body, biting into its shoulders and leg, and began dragging their victim down the passage.

"This way," Caleb said, taking a passage leading down.

Jason followed Caleb down the age-worn stone tunnels, a string of intermittent overhead lights their only illumination. Caleb moved quickly, taking turn after turn. Jason struggled to keep up, his panicked mind focused on flight, not thought.

Finally, Jason gained enough composure to speak. "Why are you helping me?"

Caleb answered without looking at him or missing a stride. "Honestly, I just don't like competition. I'm more of a take-what-I-can-get sort."

Caleb must have sensed Jason's apprehension. He stopped and, with a wry smirk, added, "Listen, you don't want to be here, I don't want you to be here... it's kind of a win-win if you just fuck off."

"Besides, us De La Poers have to stick together, right?" he added with a wink before continuing quickly down the sloping corridor.

Jason nodded hesitantly before hurrying after him. "I have to get to Katie. Where..." Without warning, he slipped on something, barely grabbing the rough wall as he stumbled. A reeking odor bloomed around him. He covered his nose from the awful smell.

Caleb backtracked to him, crouching beside him. "Droppings," he muttered. "Ferals this close to the pens? Brazen little pricks." He stood and swept the tunnel with his rifle. "'Bout time for another sweeping..."

"A feral what?" Jason hissed, trying to wipe the spoor off his feet.

"Just food that learned to fight back." Caleb began moving forward again, more cautiously. "Sometimes the little piggies escape their pens and get lost in the tunnels. Sometimes they die. Sometimes they survive." He spat. "Sometimes, they breed."

Jason started, making the connection. "Those dog things of yours...?"

Caleb pointed his rifle down a dark corridor as they passed. "They took a while to train, but they're loyal - so long as you keep 'em fed and don't turn your back on them."

Memories of the devolved human-things flashed into Jason's mind - the implications staggering. "How long..." Jason started, "How long have they been here?"

Caleb shrugged. "I don't know. As long as these tunnels, I'd wager." He took a deep breath. "This place is old. Really fucking old. Maz thinks they are descendants from the very first captives of the Cybele cult, ancient druids and shit, held here since prehistoric times." He shrugged again. "Maybe he's right."

Jason's head, still swimming, remembered the prisoners they tried to free. "If you already have all these captives in the pens, why do you need to take people from Anchester?"

"For sport, of course!" Caleb turned to see the abject anger in Jason's eyes, and smiled. "Only a joke, cousin!"

Jason stopped, raising his voice. "WHY?"

Caleb turned and approached him. "Easy, mate. Let's not get loud right now." After eyeing him for a moment, he continued, "Sometimes the old families just won't get in line. Sometimes one of the ferals gets to the surface and starts causing rumors." He paused ominously. "Sometimes She wants some variety..."

Caleb turned away as Jason stood in shock. He continued conversationally, "All we've done to clean up that town has done wonders for our political situation. You'd be surprised the kinds of favors we're owed..."

Jason, overcome with anger, coiled to lunge at the madman before him. Suddenly, a distant noise froze Jason in place. It was a howl - long, mournful, and powerful - that rolled through the tunnels from up ahead. Even Caleb stopped in his tracks. Jason had heard that cry before at dinner, echoing through the priory like distant thunder. "Is that..." he stammered.

"Ehren," Caleb shook his head. "Stupid bastard."

Jason whispered, "Maz's son?"

Caleb spoke loudly, as if trying to shout back. "First-class fuck-up, if you ask me. All he wanted was his daddy's power, but wasn't willing to wait for it. Greedy bastard." Seeing Jason's confusion, he added, "He just kept eating, and eating. He didn't become powerful, he just became... like Her."

Another wailing howl rumbled through the hall. "His father was too soft to put him down," Caleb added before continuing.

They walked in silence for a long time. The walls of the corridor had become brickwork with arching vaults. Jason finally broke the quiet. "Those rats - that thing - what is it?"

"You mean, who is SHE!" Caleb chuckled. "Pronouns, lad." He withdrew a corpulent mother pendant from under his shirt. "She's something old. I mean, like before mankind old. She was worshipped by the Romans, the druids, who knows how far back. Even the Hittites, if you believe Maz's crazy bullshit. He thinks She's some kind of ancient god." He tucked the pendant back. "Me, I don't give a shit what She is. I only care about what she can do for me."

Jason scoffed. "You mean bestow powers?"

Caleb gave a knowing laugh. "I didn't believe it either at first. I thought this place was full of brain-washed nut-fuckers!" He glanced back at Jason, his voice heavy. "Then I saw it. The impossible made real."

Jason frowned, unimpressed.

"Haven't you seen it already?" Caleb continued forcefully. "Maz and those soldiers he calls groundskeepers? How did they get so fucking strong?" He grinned. "You know how old they really are? You wouldn't believe me."

Jason recalled the army photos in the groundskeeper's barracks.

"Strength!" Caleb continued like a chant. "Health! Even immortality!"

"Bullshit," was all Jason could say.

Caleb began to walk faster, as if closing on their destination. "You've already had a taste." Seeing Jason's puzzled look, he added, "Hanwell? That beating you took should have straight-up killed you, not given you a little headache."

Jason refused to believe, stammering, "But...how? I didn't..."

Like a cat taking pleasure in a mouse's torment, Caleb again turned to him. "That's the best part, cousin. We feed her, and she feeds us. What she doesn't eat, she leaves for her followers."

Caleb whispered in Jason's face, "You see, we INGEST her powers. We take in a tiny bit of her with each... little... nibble."

Jason's mind broke. Visions of the banquet's main course flashed in his head. That over-seasoned meat. He had eaten it. He had some of HER inside him.

Turning back with a smug look, Caleb merrily sang, "You are what you eat!"

Jason's head swooned. He fought back nausea. His nightmares - his visions. They had only begun once he had eaten the food Maz had offered him...

"Katie," Jason coughed. "I've got to get to Katie!"

"Almost there," Caleb said in a chipper voice.

The hall opened onto a stone bridge spanning a large vaulted room of crumbling masonry and pillars.

Spanning the bridge, Caleb began to slow. They must have been near the surface by now. Jason needed to get out of this place.

Jason moved next to Caleb. "Listen. Once Katie and I escape, we'll..."

"Escape?" Caleb asked quizzically. "Oh, this isn't an escape..." With that, he pushed Jason into the ancient stone railing. Jason flailed as it broke into a cloud of dust and falling debris. He landed with a crunch of dirt and stone on the vaulted chamber floor.

The pain in his body was almost too much for him, his vision turning to tight circles. The cloud of dust that surrounded him made it impossible to breathe. After several seconds of struggling, Jason finally coughed through the moldering air.

"You still alive, Cousin?" Caleb's voice seemed to come from far above. "I did say that I didn't like competition."

Jason spat the dust and blood from his mouth. He turned on his side, grunting with the pain. Caleb continued, playing with his prey. "I guess there's only one choice for Atys now. I mean, what good is living forever if you don't have all the power too, am I right?"

Jason tried to sit up, but crumpled back to the floor. He looked up and could just make out Caleb's form looking over the rails, taunting him. "Now I'll have some plausible deniability! Oh, I guess his guard got eaten by ferals. I guess poor Jason got lost in the tunnels and ran into..."

There was a scraping sound. Then a heavy thud. Something moved in the darkness of the chamber.

"Ah, here he is!" Caleb clapped his hands joyously.

The clank of sturdy metal chains echoed in the vault. Heavy, bellow-like breathing began. A cold terror washed over Jason as he realized the danger he was in.

Caleb waved a goodbye. "Play nice with your food, Ehren!"

CHAPTER

38

Chains clattered in the darkness, followed by another stomp.

Jason held his breath as a form lurched slowly towards him. Its silhouette resembled a man - an impossibly large man - whose limbs and torso bobbed and swayed like a ripped rag doll with bare stitching. It stopped at the edge of the light, affixing Jason with a hidden stare.

Jason was paralyzed with fear, the thunderous beating of his heart drowned out by the deep, ragged breathing of the thing across the room. He glanced around his surroundings for something that could help him. Refuse and broken masonry covered the dirt-laden stone floor. Piles of bones were arranged along the edges of the vault, like children's decorations.

The creature sniffed at the air, slowly, as if savoring the scent, swaying with its elongated torso. Jason pulled himself to his feet, fear overcoming his agony.

And then it stepped out from the shadows.

The abomination only bore a semblance of a man. Its entire form was swollen and distorted. The pale, bloated flesh was riddled with thin, pulsating black veins that writhed beneath the surface like parasitic worms. Its massive arms, legs, and torso were grotesquely disjointed, separated by masses of squirming, tar-black tendrils that seemed to have violently burst forth from within, shredding the thing's body into a mockery of human shape.

At first, Jason thought it had no head. Then he saw it.

Atop a long, undulating stalk extending from its neck, the creature's hideously normal human head lolled and twitched. Its lower jaw hung unhinged, swinging slackly as guttural groans emanated from its gaping maw. Its very human eyes, wide and bulging, darted around the chamber with a horrific, hungering intelligence.

It took another thunderous step forward, dragging an enormous steel chain from its manacled ankle.

Jason fought to keep his panic under control as Ehren plodded towards him. The pillared vault did not contain any exits, just vaulted alcoves. The stone bridge that spanned the room seemed to be the only way in or out.

Another crushing step forward. One side of its split torso was a tangled mass of flailing black appendages, resembling a twisted cage of jutting ribs, nightmarishly whipping and curling with a life of their own.

Jason was going to have to climb to the bridge to get out. Keeping his eyes on the creature, he took a cautious step towards the wall.

Ehren's head immediately shot up on its neck-tendril. From its drooling maw, it bellowed a howl that shook dust loose from the ceiling. It lunged at Jason, moving far faster than he could have imagined. In an instant, Ehren was across the room, reaching his surprisingly coordinated arms towards Jason.

Jason leapt with all his might, barely avoiding the creature's grasp. Ehren staggered to a stop and slowly turned to stare at Jason with those hungering, blinking eyes.

Jason darted for the wall, hoping to scramble up to the bridge. Ehren moved with superhuman speed, interposing himself between Jason and his climb. Again, the eyes on that lolling head stared at him, like this was a game he very much enjoyed.

Jason ran from it, trying to get to the back of the chamber, to see if there was anything that could help him. Ehren kicked out his shackled leg, causing the heavy chain to sweep across the floor. It hit Jason at his knees, and he fell hard to the floor.

Ehren let out a chuffing sound that resembled mirth and began striding towards Jason again.

Jason scrambled to his feet, moving with a limp. As he passed the enormous central pillar in the vault, he noticed that Ehren's chain was attached to a reinforced steel ring inset in the pillar's side.

As Jason raced to the back of the vault, he thought of a plan. Not a good plan. It probably had no chance. But he had to try something.

Ehren moved slowly around the pillar, corralling Jason into a corner of the chamber. Thick drool cascaded from its maw as it meticulously approached. Again, Jason saw its eyes observing him, but noticed something different. It had more than an expression of hunger - it was one of longing. He was more than just a meal to it. It wanted something from him...

Then it clicked in Jason's mind. He knew what he had to try.

"You sense Her, don't you?" Jason taunted. Ehren stopped, his head tilted in curiosity. Jason continued, "You can feel Her in me. Her gifts running through my blood." It emitted a low, gurgling growl.

"If you catch me, maybe you can gain a little more of her power." Jason lazily moved clockwise around the central pillar, keeping Ehren's attention on him. "But look what Her promises have done to you... what you have done to yourself."

Ehren lunged at him, but Jason continued his spiral around the pillar. The creature's mannerisms began to change, its body spasming in tremors of rage.

"Your ashamed father stuck you down here all alone." Ehren thrust out his arms to swat at Jason, but he kept the pillar between them. "When I leave here, I will be granted all Her gifts, while your father forgets you ever existed."

Ehren moved faster now. Only a few more steps. Jason made ready to run. He hissed at the creature with all the venom he could muster, "I will be her Atys, and your father, her high priest. Like the father and son you never were."

The scream of fury was blood-curdling. Ehren jumped at Jason, a tendril slapping at his back. Jason had turned and ran back towards the bridge. With a roar, Ehren gave chase, but then tripped to one knee. Glancing at the pillar, it took only seconds for it to realize his chain had wrapped around it. Ehren shrieked an unholy cry, dozens of mouths opening within his pulsating black seams.

Jason sprinted towards the wall beneath the bridge, the monster flailing behind him. It crashed forward, pulling at its chain, stones and dust falling with every titanic jolt.

Jason leapt onto the wall, but found no purchase, sliding back to the floor. With a final furious jerk, the room's central pillar shifted. Stones and dirt began to crash around Ehren as ancient supports broke under the monstrous strain. The ceiling began to collapse with a roar.

A cloud of dust exploded from the vault, engulfing and blinding Jason. Something heavy hit him in the shoulder, knocking him backward. He was pummeled by debris.

Slowly, as the dust began to settle, he saw that the chamber had collapsed, a massive pile of rubble piled in the center of the vault. The intermittent clatter of falling stones and trickle of dirt were all he could hear.

Jason rose and moved towards the wall again. The fallen dust had made it slightly easier to maintain his grip on the damp bricks.

Only a few feet off the ground, Jason heard a noise. The rubble shifted. Something was moving beneath it. As Jason frantically climbed, he glanced at the rubble. A broken and bloody hand had pushed through the rubble, supported by thick, ropy tendrils. More black lashes whipped out from between the stones, flailing through the cracks.

Jason reached a hand to the bridge and pulled himself up. He ran as fast as his broken body could take him out of that chamber.

A deafening cry of hate roared from the beast below.

Jason just ran.

He did not know how long he had run, or how far he had gone. He just kept moving forward, taking whichever passage sloped upwards.

Finding himself in a narrow brick tunnel, he spied a ladder leading up. Without thinking, he climbed, shoving the wooden trapdoor above him open with a shoulder. He was in a groundskeeper's hovel. He shuffled to the door and threw it wide. He was immediately blinded by the brilliant noonday sun. Still, he ran, through the gardens and towards the main gates of the priory.

He needed to find Katie. To save her from all this. But he knew he couldn't do it alone.

Determination and fear overcoming exhaustion, he raced from the priory grounds, heading towards Anchester town.

$\mathcal{H}$e ran.

His body screamed at him. His vision blurred. But all he could do was run. Katie needed him.

Down the old road, past copses of trees, from gravel onto paved road. His lungs gasped for air. The noonday sun punished him with its gaze.

In his delirium, he saw the forest darken around him as a sea of rats covered the area. A young girl was being led by the vermin towards him - towards the pits beneath the priory.

He put down his head, focusing on staying upright. One foot before the other.

Finally, with grimy sweat dripping into his eyes, he saw the buildings at the edge of Anchester come into view.

He staggered through the streets, pressing up against the building walls to support his bruised and exhausted body. He saw three people on the sidewalk ahead, and, mustering his will, hobbled towards them. He could see them pause with concern as he lurched closer to them. He could only pant under his breath, "Help..."

The three stared disapprovingly at what they clearly thought was an addict. One took a step back, the other put a protective hand over the third.

"I need... The police..." he croaked between gasps of air. They began backing away, finding a new direction to avoid the obviously deranged man. As Jason took a step towards them to follow, one thrust out a hand and pointed, "Down there." As Jason turned to look, they hurried off.

Limping in the direction given, Jason spied a small building with the stenciled words, "Anchester Police Department" on the window. He had made it.

Jason burst through the front doors, finding a nearly empty office with a startled woman behind a front desk.

"Help... I need help!" Jason pleaded with the desk officer.

"Easy, sir!" she said, standing abruptly. "Was there an accident?"

Jason coughed, shaking his head, still out of breath. "No. They have her." He saw the look of apprehension at his disheveled appearance. "You have to stop them!" he pleaded.

A uniformed officer entered from the back of the station, walking to the coffee maker. He paused at the scene, eyeing Jason curiously.

The desk officer said, "Okay, sir. Just calm down. Breathe with me. Are you okay?"

Jason gulped some air, trying to calm himself. He ran a forearm across his head and felt the grime of catacomb rubble streak on his sleeve. He realized what he must look like to her. He realized that they wouldn't listen to him if he sounded crazy. Well, MORE crazy. How could he make them understand?

The female officer sat slowly back at her desk. "Now, start from the beginning."

Jason took a deep breath, trying to choose his words carefully. "My friend... distant cousin... Katie and I came here a few days ago. We were invited to stay at the priory by Maz... ah... Mazhar Something."

She had a yellow notepad and began writing. "You are from the priory?"

"Yeah. Well, kind of. They invited us to stay there for... a vacation..." He tried to formulate a sentence that wouldn't make him sound insane.

A second officer entered the room, heading towards the coffee pot.

Jason continued slowly, "There's something beneath the priory. They need us to... feed it." The officer raised an eyebrow. "They need my family. My bloodline to..." He broke off, realizing that every word was making her less likely to help, and more likely to get a straitjacket.

One officer holding a mug of coffee approached her desk. He leaned down to speak closely. "You need any help with this one?" he asked, clearly insinuating that Jason might be a threat.

She nodded to the other officer in affirmation, waving him off but not taking her eyes off Jason. As the officer leaned back, a golden pendant slipped from his shirt collar. A thin chain carrying a shepherd's crook.

Jason's mind froze. He couldn't breathe.

"You need to feed something?" the woman officer continued to inquire. "Is this some kind of livestock dispute?" She eyed him as he felt sweat trickling down his cheek.

Jason began to panic. The officer slowly walked back to the coffee pot, glancing over his shoulder at Jason.

The desk officer continued. "Okay, so your family was asked to come to the priory for a vacation. Then what?"

"Then..." Jason was unable to answer. The two officers at the coffee pot began talking to each other in low voices. They both leaned casually, but continued to stare at Jason.

A part of Jason's mind wondered how far the cult reached. The rest of his mind was screaming at him to flee.

Jason willed himself to be calm. "Then..." he stammered, "...we had a lovely time."

The officer's stare flickered with annoyance. "Sir, why are you here? Why are you covered in dirt?"

Jason slid his chair back and slowly stood. "Dirt?" He patted himself. "Uh, yeah, we were exploring the... ah... catacombs beneath the place. They're filthy."

"Woah. Take it easy..." she said forcibly, beginning to stand again. "Take a seat."

Jason noticed that the two officers at the back of the room had stopped talking, simply staring at him with suspicious anticipation.

"You know, it's okay! I think the heat of the day just got to me. No, don't get up! I'll just fetch a ride back," Jason said with a smile. He backed away from the desk with a grin that probably made him look more crazy than sincere.

Her hand slipped down towards her handcuffs. "Sir? I can't help you if you..."

"No need! Thank you, officer! I'm all good." Still smiling and waving like an imbecile, Jason backed out the station door.

Once outside, he turned and ran.

Turning down alley after alley at random, he tried to put as much distance as possible between himself and that station. There were no sirens. No calls for alarm. But he knew that they were looking for him.

His legs finally gave out from sheer exhaustion. He sat heavily on a discarded wooden pallet in a dingy alley. He took deep gulps of air, trying to think of something he could do. Katie was in trouble, and she was running out of time.

Jason then realized his only option - the only person he could think of who hated the priory as much as he did.

Old Alice.

It took Jason a while to find "Antiques, Curios, and Whatnot". He shuffled to the front door. As he reached for the handle, he realized that the windows that before held leering hooligans were now empty.

As he pulled open the door with a tinkle of chimes, a pair of arms thrust out, grabbed him by the neck, and pulled him forcibly into the shop.

Jason was slammed roughly against a wall. He felt something cold, metal, and sharp against his cheek. A man with an eye patch glared at him angrily, holding the knife towards his eye. "Where is Butch?" he demanded. Jason put up his hands, but the thug slammed him against the wall again. "Butch, goddamnit! What have you done with him?"

Jason remembered the fight at the asylum. The deafening shotgun blast. It now seemed like so long ago.

"He's dead..." Jason began. Rage filled the face of his attacker, his knife flicking towards Jason's eyelid. "Caleb! He shot him at Hanwell Asylum. The others that came with him as well. They're all dead."

For a long time, the one-eyed man held the knife on Jason, trembling with fury. A wrinkled hand slowly rose up and took hold of the man's arm. "Brennan. You know he didn't do it."

"He was my mate, 'gam," Brennan said, a tear rolling down his face.

"I know, sweetie," old Alice said in a motherly voice. "Butch always went off half-cocked. He just picked a fight he couldn't win." She pulled at his arm. "Let him go."

Brennan gave one last shove before taking a step back. He wiped his face while flicking his knife closed. "All he was trying to do is get his Terra back."

Jason was struck with guilt. "I'm sorry," he began with sincere sympathy. "Terra is dead too."

Brennan spun back at him, raw hate flaring in his eye. He started for his knife again, spitting, "Devil-spawned witch-blood!" Old Alice shifted between Jason and the hooligan. Brennan stared at her before turning and storming off.

Jason gave a sigh. "Thank you..."

Old Alice spun on him, finger raised. "You've got one chance," she growled. "Tell me what happened, and you'd better make me believe."

Jason told her the whole story. How he found Katie. How they were invited to the priory. The rats. The cannibal cult. The devolved things they fed on. The terrifying ritual. About the Voice and the Atys. About his narrow escape.

A crowd had gathered behind Alice, listening incredulously to Jason's tale. Alice stood silently, hands on her hips, with a grim expression.

"They still have Katie," Jason finished. "After that ritual, Maz told everyone to prepare for tonight. Whatever is going to happen, it's happening tonight."

Alice silently eyed him up and down.

"Please," Jason whispered to her. "I've got to get her back..."

Alice raised a hand. Slowly, she exhaled. "I believe you, kid."

Jason sighed in relief.

"Brennan!" Alice shouted. "It's time!"

The one-eyed man began shouting orders. "You heard 'gam! It's going down! You lot, start bringing the crates to the loading dock! Kennith! Get that rusted lorry to the ramp! Stop faffing about and GO!"

The warehouse became a flurry of activity.

As Old Alice walked away from him, Jason asked, "What are we going to do?"

Alice cracked a grin as she lifted up the cover of a crate bearing the label "Explosives".

"We're going to blow that priory off the face of the bloody earth."

The sun once again began to dip below the granite cliffs rising like battlements over Exham Priory. Hazy shadows stretched over the stone walls in the orange glow of dusk.

The one-eyed man named Brennan looked through an antique spyglass, scanning the priory grounds from a distant copse of trees. The three trucks were parked there, the hooligans shifting restlessly, checking weapons, loading clips of ammo, and waiting for orders.

"It looks like they're having some kind of party," Brennan said. Jason and Alice looked at one another. "The courtyard is full of cars... but I don't see anybody..."

"What about guards?" Alice asked between puffs of her cigar.

Brennan was quiet. "...not a one." He collapsed the spyglass. "Wherever they are, they're not worried about the front gate."

Alice scratched her chin. "Good. We'll take advantage of their overconfidence." She made a short whistle between her teeth, "Alright boys, grab the stuff, we're going in."

As the men slung their rifles and bandoliers of bullets, Jason hesitated, "What's our plan?"

"We sneak in, set up the explosives, sneak out, then BOOM!" Alice made a theatrical explosion with her hands, "No more priory."

Jason shook his head. "That's not going to solve anything..."

Brennan angrily growled at Jason, "I think a smoking crater would be a step in the right direction!" Several of the hooligans chuckled.

Jason glared back at him, "It's not the priory - it's what's BENEATH the priory." The hooligans, not accustomed to people standing up to Brennan, waited for the inevitable fight to ensue. "The ceremony is happening in the caves below. That thing..." Jason's voice caught, "Katie is down there. She's running out of time..."

Alice closed her eyes, taking a long drag. "The boy's right. I can feel the evil down there."

Brennan's heated stare softened a bit. "How?" he finally asked. "How do we get beneath that?"

Jason thought for a second. "I know a way... but you're not going to like it."

Jason, Alice, and the men made their way across the overgrown field abutting the edge of the gardens. They moved low and cautiously, their leather satchels and burlap sacks overladen with explosives.

As they slipped into the gardens, each was on edge, expecting an alarm to be raised at any moment. But none came. When the garden lights came on with a loud thunk, they scrambled for cover among the hedges. They hid, not breathing before Jason ventured,

"I, uh, think the lights are automated..." They exhaled a sigh of relief and continued to follow Jason through the topiary.

They reached a row of medieval-looking hovels. After a quick scan, no guards were around. They crept across the open space and made cover next to the walls of the hovel. Jason opened the door. Moving into the spartan domicile, flanked by armed men, Jason walked to the standing partition. He bent and lifted up the trapdoor in the floor as the rest of the hooligans crowded into the small house. The ladder in the floor faded into inky blackness below.

"Torch," Alice said, holding out her hand. The men's confused looks said it all.

"We didn't think we'd need 'em..." came a pitiful voice from the back. The look on Alice's face was murderous.

Jason fished out his phone and activated the light. "Come on," he said as he began descending the ladder.

Slowly the group moved down the ladder, arduously lowering each sack of explosives down to waiting hands. After far too long, they found themselves in a narrow tunnel. Several of the men snapped on their own phone lights, the damp bricks glistening in their weak beams.

Jason led the way through the darkness. The tunnel opened into the vaulted and pillared halls of the catacombs. They moved quietly, sweeping the area with their meager lights. "I had no idea all of this was down here," one of the men voiced. "Must have been built centuries ago..." another said.

"Shut up, the both of ye," Alice hissed. Even her unflappable demeanor seemed to be on edge. They continued to move downwards. Always downwards.

A howling bellow echoed down the throat of the hall from somewhere in the depths. The group froze as the wail of anguish and rage subsided. One of the men whispered frightfully, "What WAS that!?"

"You don't want to know," was Jason's only comment. The man crossed himself before continuing to follow Jason into the depths.

Eventually, the stonework of the catacombs became rough natural cave walls, the passages winding and uneven. Everyone was tired, but too terrified to ask for a rest.

Long thin cracks would sometimes snake across the floor. "Watch for these," Jason said, flashing his light down one of the chasms for effect. "It's a long way down." The hooligan's eyes went wide as they saw no bottom to the fissure, only the black void of the abyss. They walked far away from the edges of those cracks, watching their steps with renewed caution.

One of the hooligans cried out from behind them, waving his light around frantically. He had dropped his sack of explosives and was waving his rifle towards his light. "I... I saw something," he sputtered, "Something watching us..."

The group searched with their lights, but found nothing. "What was it?" one inquired.

"I dunno. I just saw these shiny eyes looking at us..."

A feeling of foreboding washed over Jason. He thought he heard the scampering and rustling of tiny feet all around them, just beyond their lights. "We gotta go," Jason ordered. "Now."

A dull sound was rising through the tunnel, its rhythms pulsating and reverberating. The passages up ahead were lit by strings of electric lights. "Not a sound now, boys," Alice whispered. They switched off their lights, and readied their rifles.

Their tunnel opened into a vast cavern of stalagmite columns. Their path became winding stairs cut into the stone floor, leading towards ancient dilapidated buildings stuck haphazardly along the road like a small village. Several of the men gasped in sheer awe at the sight.

The cavern was lit by an intense yellow-orange glow at the back of the cavern. Jason knew it was coming from the amphitheater at the far end. The strange throbbing sound became even louder here, clarifying into low human vocalizations like a guttural chant.

"The ceremony must be happening!" Jason said to the group, "We've got to go!" Alice held her head in pain, but nodded her affirmation.

Alice winced, "This place is wrong..." The men began fawning over her, asking if she was alright. "I'm fine!" she barked, "I've just never been this close is all..."

They made their way down the main street, using the buildings for cover. They did not worry about making noise, as the chanting was almost deafening, yet each time they filed across the street, they expected a shout of alarm to go up. As they scanned the buildings for any sign of guards, they found none. "Must all be at the ceremony," one man offered. Another shrugged.

Jason moved recklessly, his thoughts only of Katie. He would turn back to see the hooligans giving him annoyed hand signs to slow down. He knew he had no time, yet waited fitfully for them to catch up.

Jason glimpsed movement in the shadows between buildings. Rats. Their cloudy eyes staring at them from a perch. Before Jason could act, they leapt down and scampered away. Jason's foreboding turned to dread. He had the sensation of a distant storm closing in on him.

He ignored the others and raced ahead.

As he reached prehistoric cairn-like mounds, the amphitheater came into his view.

Massive braziers of flames roared before the raised stage, casting everything in hot firelight. Before the stage, dozens of people in hooded white robes stood, danced, and sang chants, reveling in the fervor of the ceremony. A few groundskeepers in their blue-gray robes stood passively at the edge of the crowd, watching over the bacchanal.

Atop the stone altar at the center stage stood an elaborate stone throne. A woman in a white dress was being held by two groundskeepers at the front of the stage, facing towards the swaying cultists.

Jason caught his breath. "Katie!" She was slumped in the arms of her captors, her head rolling.

In front of the throne, the High-Priest in his leering Green Man mask shouted to the crowd, his cries of devotion whipping them into a frenzy. Maz's voice was deep and mesmerizing, and he punctuated his chants with the waving of his shepherd's crook. "Too long has Cybele been without a Voice! With no words, her secrets have been kept hidden from her beloved followers. But now, she has a new vessel! A vessel deemed worthy enough to speak through!" Cries of elation emanated from the jubilant cultists.

Alice and her hooligans finally caught up with Jason, taking cover behind the mound with him. Alice looked at the ceremony with revulsion. She whispered to herself, "There's so many more than I thought..."

Jason turned to her with pleading eyes, "Katie! She's still okay. I have to save her!"

Alice, seeing his desperation, gave a curt nod. She turned, "Brennan!" and gave him a gesture.

Brennan barked to the rest of the group, "Drop the explosives, lads!" He brought up his semi-automatic rifle. "We're gonna do these devil worshipers all personal-like." A mixture of fear and excitement was on the faces of the men as they dropped their explosive sacks in a heap and took up their rifles.

Maz continued with building passion, "Our great mother has chosen her Voice AND her Atys! Together they will bestow her godly powers unto her disciples!"

Another jolt of fear shot through Jason. He looked up at the Green Man on the stage.

"And now her Atys has come!" Maz shouted. He lowered his shepherd's crook right at Jason. "There!" he shrieked. The cultists began to cheer.

Jason was paralyzed in terror. Alice and the others were too occupied to pay attention to the high-priest's words.

Maz raised his staff, "Witness! Cybele bestows powers unto her followers..."

Jason cried out, "They know we're here!"

Maz's voice carried through the Green Man mask, "She gives us Strength! Longevity!" He gave a gesture with his hand, "AND VISION!"

A gunshot rang out, and one of the hooligans sprawled to the floor in a heap. "Now lads!" Alice shouted as their rifles erupted with return fire.

More gunfire exploded in the dirt around them. Men cried out in pain. "Behind us!" someone shouted. Jason saw a dozen groundskeepers bounding from their cover in the buildings, firing and covering one another with military precision.

The hooligans returned fire, but their shots were panicked and inaccurate. The groundskeepers assaulted their position, firing intermittently. Jason realized that they were not firing to kill - but to wound. They were to be taken alive...

Jason stumbled to his feet and raced towards the stage - towards Katie. He had never fired a rifle before, but he was out of his mind with fear and determination. Suddenly, a blazing agony shot through his head. Intense images flashed past his eyes and he stumbled. He checked to see if he was shot, but there was no blood. Again, the visions hit him, like a migraine stabbing into his brain.

He shouted for himself to get up and move, but could barely get to his knees. Behind him, he saw the groundskeepers reach the hooligans. One shot a groundskeeper at point blank, but it barely caused a reaction before he hit the shooter with the butt of his rifle with a sickening crack. Brennan was swinging his rifle like a club, only to have it broken in two with a single blow from a grey-robed cultist.

Jason's brain was slammed again by excruciating visions, driving him to the ground. He was barely aware of the groundskeepers grabbing him under his arms and dragging him towards the amphitheater.

They dragged him over the stone floor and past the cultist revelers who glared at him with mirth, intoxication, and awe. Jason's head swooned, but under the cultist's hoods, he thought he could make out their faces. The officer in the police station... the tattooed barista in the coffee shop... people he had seen in stores and on the streets of Anchester!

He felt his mind snap as unconsciousness fell over him.

Jason awoke with a start, warm liquid splashing on his face. He sputtered and coughed as the wine poured down his face. The Green Man stood before him, an empty glass of wine in his hands. Jason was being held from behind. He struggled, but the vice-like grip squeezed pain into his wrists until he stopped. Maz chuckled, "Oh, how you fight us now. You will soon know the honor bestowed onto you."

Through throbbing pain, Jason looked around for Katie. He saw her and his heart sank. She was seated on the stone throne at the center of the stage. She swayed groggily, barely aware of her surroundings, as if she had been drugged.

"Katie!" Jason shouted up at her.

Her limp head rolled towards him. He could not hear her over the chanting, but saw her mouth speak his name. Tears filled her eyes and flowed down her cheeks. Jason's heart broke. He pulled against the groundskeeper, but had his head roughly pushed down in a bow.

Cheers from the assembled cultists went up as three figures entered the stage. Caleb and Alexia were again dressed in ancient finery. Kylie was screaming and fighting against a groundskeeper who was dragging her behind them. They took up positions next to Maz before the throne.

Maz gave a gesture to the crowd and the wild chanting was muffled to silence. In the quiet, Jason could hear the crackling roar of the braziers. From deep below, there was a rumble. A shudder in the rocks that slowly became stronger.

From the pit behind the stage, an oozing black mass bubbled and twisted, rising into a towering mound. The black ooze slowly slithered towards the throne. Rats burst forth from greasy nodules on its surface, scampering out and forming a pool of oily vermin around its base. The shape reached the back of the throne and slowly began surrounding it. Katie tried to scream, but was all but paralyzed. Ropy and pulsating tendrils reached out from the mass, looking like malformed monstrosities. Each settled on either side of the throne and began to shake off excess ooze. What emerged from the embryonic sacks of goo were immense black lions. They shook open their foamy mouths and emitted a gurgling roar. The cultists cheered at the spectacle.

The flood of rats pooled around the throne, thousands of wet glassy eyes darting about. Cries of horror and wonder escaped from the assembled cultists.

The high-priest raised his staff, bellowing, "All praise the Great Mother!" The cultists began to sway and cry rhythmically, "Mater Kubileya! Mater Kubileya!"

The squirming swarm of rats began to envelop the throne, streaming and twisting like tentacles from behind. Jason watched in horror as the mass engulfed the throne, and the struggling Katie sitting on it. Jason screamed and thrashed against the man holding him, but to no avail.

The chanting grew louder. "Mater Kubileya! Mater Kubileya!"

The throne had been completely enveloped. Jason had begun to sob. He had failed her.

Slowly, the writhing mass began to part, exposing Katie's form. She sat upright and unmoving on the undulating ooze of her throne. Her eyes were rolled onto their whites, staring emotionlessly forward.

The High Priest shouted, "Praise the new Voice of Cybele!" The cultists cheered.

Jason looked at Katie for any sign of life. He chest expanded rhythmically. She was still breathing. She was alive.

"She is whole once more!" Maz shrieked over the din of celebrating cultists.

After a while, the Green Man gestured to the crowd to be calm. "And now," he said with a grand gesture, "we praise the descendants of the blood!" He pointed at the groundskeeper holding Kylie, and he dragged her before him, holding her down.

Maz produced a thin knife from inside his robes. With a quick flick, he drew the blade across Kylie's chest. She screamed and cried, kicking against the groundskeeper.

The pooling black rats began to squirm excitedly, like a quiver of anticipation.

Finally, with defiant rage in Kylie's eyes, she spat at Maz, the droplet dripping from the Green Man mask. Maz gestured, and the groundskeeper tossed Kylie towards the churning mass. "That's what you deserve!" shouted Alexia.

As the rats began to close around her, Kylie kicked and slapped at them, screaming fiercely. She cursed at them unafraid, crushing several with her hands. The chanting of the cultists became confused. The churning rats began to pull away from her, standing on their legs hissing and squeaking at her. She screamed at them, her long pent-up fear becoming belligerent fury, "You won't have me! Fuck you!"

Both Caleb and Alexia shook their heads at Kylie's defiance.

Finally, Maz ordered in an irritated voice, "Take her!" As the rats pulled away from Kylie, the groundskeeper hauled her to her feet. A defiant smile spread across her face. "If you would shun Her gifts," Maz shouted to the crowd, "then instead you will satiate her hunger." He pointed away and the groundskeeper dragged Kylie down the stairs, her maniacal laughter filling the chamber.

"Now then," Maz continued striding up to Caleb and Alexia. "For the two I have groomed for so many years. It is finally time." They bowed reverently to the writhing mass before turning to face Maz. Caleb stood with his chest out proudly, as Maz walked to him. He gently placed his hands on Caleb's shoulders. "I bestow Her gifts unto you." A groundskeeper moved beside him. Maz leaned forward and whispered, "All the things you will witness... I envy you."

The blade was in Maz's hand before Caleb knew it, slicing a deep cut across his chest. Caleb jumped back, but was caught by the groundskeeper.

"What the fuck!?" Caleb shouted incredulously, holding the gaping wound and staggering back.

As Maz stepped towards Alexia, her eyes went wide with shock. "No!" she screamed trying to move away, but another groundskeeper held her. Her screams turned to cries of pain as Maz dragged the knife across her from clavicle to clavicle. Blood began to flow down her white dress.

The black mass began to churn wildly, rats squirming out of its protoplasmic flesh.

Caleb, breathing heavily, panted, "You fucker! You - you fucking lied to us!"

Maz, still looking at him with admiration, said, "You were to be Her Atys. I said if you were not chosen, you would still get to live forever."

The black mass began fulminating and flopping towards the two.

Maz said, "And you will... inside of her."

The mass surged into a roiling wall of writhing black rats, crashing like a wave over Caleb and Alexia. Her scream was cut off as the swarm enveloped her head. Caleb's wild eyes and thrashing arms were the last Jason saw of him. The two forms could barely be identified as the twisting mass receded back behind the throne.

Katie suddenly began to rise from the throne, her arms outstretched like a motherly embrace. A thick tendril had anchored to the back of her head, raising her body off the throne and suspending her in the air above it, over the flailing tendrils of the towering black ooze below.

The cultists began a deafening cheer and cry, as their out-of-time chanting created a cacophony of noise echoing riotously within the cavernous amphitheater.

Jason was stunned at the sight. He wanted to run, but the impossibly strong man still held him in place. As Jason looked at Katie's body, suspended on the pillar of pulsating slime, he wept in hopelessness.

Maz raised his staff, commanding silence. "And now," he intoned, "We will finally unite her with her consort... her lover... her Atys!" The cultists began chanting "Atys! Atys! Atys!" with feverish devotion.

Jason looked up at Katie again. His sobs caught in his throat. She was looking at him. Her eyes blinked, rolling back to her irises as she stared at him. Although he couldn't hear her, he saw her mouth make the word "run".

Jason's sadness and terror broke with razor-sharp clarity. Katie was still in there. She could be saved. Jason was not about to give up on her.

He realized that he had not struggled against his captor for a while. He was aware that the groundskeeper's grip had loosened. He let his head sink and looked down at the floor. They were near the edge of the stage - surrounded by yawning chasms... He had to move now.

Jason suddenly threw his whole body against his captor, knocking him off balance. Jason continued to press into him, running with all his strength against him, pushing him backwards, building momentum, towards the ledge. Stepping back into air, the groundskeeper let out a shout as he pitched over backwards, flailing his arms to grab Jason. He barely avoided being dragged over the edge with the robed man. The screams of the falling groundskeeper were muffled by celebrating cultists.

Wasting no time, Jason bolted, running to the edge of the stage where a winding stone stair led down towards a dark tunnel.

As Jason ran, he heard Maz screaming behind him, "Stop him! Get him!"

A gunshot whizzed past Jason's arm, exploding the tunnel's wall into dust.

"Idiot!" Maz was screaming, "Do not kill him!"

Jason leapt into the tunnel, Maz's voice echoing behind him, "She needs her Atys alive!"

Jason ran through the darkness. Warm, wet air clung to his clothes. He tripped on the uneven floor, grinding his knees into the stones, but fear pushed him to rise and run again. He could hear the sounds of voices behind him, the barking of orders, the thud of boots.

Jason ducked down tunnel after tunnel trying to escape his pursuers. He wheezed and came to a stop, catching his breath, trying not to cough too loudly. His fiery lungs inhaled greedily, the humid air made him gasp for breath.

Behind him, a beam of light swept down the passage. Then another. They were coming.

In the reflected light, Jason could make out some of the features of the cave. A narrow break in the wall created a natural crevice. Hearing quiet voices approaching, he had no time for other options. He squeezed into the crack and hunkered down. Something dank and sticky littered the floor. He pressed his back against the wall, trying to control his breath as a putrid fragrance billowed around him.

The lights became brighter, sweeping the cave, looking for him. He heard the shuffle of boots as they spread out, searching. There was another sound, that of bare feet slapping against the cave floor.

The sound of sniffing and a guttural inhuman growl. Jason was struck with terror. They had one of those trained creatures with them - Caleb's hunting dogs. He realized that no amount of running and hiding was going to save him.

Suddenly, the creature sniffed and let out a meek hissing-bark. The men froze in place, becoming completely silent.

Then a deep growl reverberated through the cave. Then another. Jason could hear the clatter of the men readying their rifles. Jason risked a peek from his crevice. Six robed men formed a tight circle, their guns leveled and their torches sweeping the walls. A muzzled naked human form crouched fearfully between them. Its muzzled head darted from wall to wall, mewling frantically.

There was a blood-curdling shriek. Pale shapes darted from the cave walls, racing toward the men. Flashing gunshots strobed the horrible scene. A few Feral Ones exploded with blood, their bodies thrashing on the ground. Several of the devolved creatures reached the men, claws tearing through robes. For each the cultists battered aside, more creatures came at them.

One of the groundskeepers fell with a scream, two of the loping creatures dragging him off into the darkness. The cultist holding the hunting dog's chain fell, and the beast ran back out of the cave, two more Feral Ones chasing it.

There was an explosive pop, followed by a blinding red light. The Feral Ones shrieked in pain, scrambling away from the flare shot. Two of the robed men hauled a visibly injured third behind them, fleeing the cave.

Jason saw one of the things racing towards him. He tried to hide, pressing his body against the cave wall. The creature pulled itself through the narrow crevice and dropped to the ground next to Jason.

Jason was frozen in terror, expecting it to shriek and tear out his throat. Instead, it only crouched there, fidgeting. It was blinking its watery eyes, rubbing them with the backs of its long clawed fingers. It was blinded.

Jason held his breath. As the cultists disappeared through a tunnel, darkness returned to the cave. Only a lone dropped torch shined from the cave floor. The thing's skin was so pale, Jason could still make out its semi-glowing form next to him.

The thing began to sniff at the air. Jason tensed. It shuffled a bit closer to him, cocking its head towards him... Then with a whispering hiss, it vanished, silently moving out of the crevice.

Jason waited in silence for a long time. He slowly turned to look out of his hiding spot. A robed body lay on the floor, his dropped rifle nearby. Jason chanced it. He shuffled through the narrow crevice and back into the cave room.

He crept up to the body and quietly picked up the rifle and torch. Slinging the firearm, Jason rolled the body over. A bandoleer of bullets crossed his chest. A small leather case was on his waist. Quietly unzipping the case, Jason saw a bright orange flare gun with several loose flare shots inside.

Jason began trying to slip the bandoleer from the robed man, when he heard a scrape on the floor. He stopped moving. In the glow of his torch, he spotted a crouching white humanoid form at the back of the cave. It let out a low chuffing growl as it crept towards him. Jason realized that it was returning for the body he was standing over.

Trying to move slowly, Jason reached for his slung rifle. It glared at him like a stalking predator, flashing its jagged teeth in a snarl. Jason leveled the rifle at it and found the trigger. It crouched lower, splaying its clawed hands on the ground, ready to pounce. Jason pulled the trigger.

Click.

The rifle was empty. Jason realized sardonically that this was probably what killed the cultist...

Jason was hit full force from the creature's leap, knocking him off his feet. His dropped torch spun wildly. He could feel its dirty claws tearing at his sides. He held up the rifle defensively as the thing's jaws snapped at his face.

Mustering whatever adrenaline-fueled strength he had remaining, Jason smashed the butt of the rifle into the thing's head, tossing it off him. It flopped to the ground and squirmed in pain, still trying to claw at him. With anger and revulsion, Jason swung the rifle at the creature again and again. Even when it stopped moving, Jason continued to club it until only wet sticky sounds remained. Jason stood over the thing, panting victoriously.

Another growl emanated from the darkness. Jason could make out another Feral One crawling towards him. He reached for the rifle ammo, only to notice that his rifle was bent at a peculiar angle. Fear again washed over Jason. He scrambled to open the case and take the flare gun as the thing moved closer. He fumbled for the ammo, spilling the contents across the floor. He cracked the barrel open and slammed the flare into it, just as the creature reached the edge of his torchlight. He closed his eyes and fired.

Red light erupted in the cave with an explosion of smoke. Jason heard frenzied shrieking. He looked down the cave. His flare burned in a wall, illuminating several Feral Ones closing in on him. They dropped from the walls and fled, hissing and screaming their frustration.

Jason grabbed the torch and raced down an empty tunnel.

Jason continued down the warm tunnels, slick with moisture. He had no idea how far he was from the amphitheater above, but he did not hear any more search parties looking for him.

"Jason!" He spun around. It was Katie's voice.

"Katie?" he whispered, incredulously. The voice had come from another passage. Jason held up his light and proceeded down the tunnel.

Jason's light settled on a recess in the wall ahead. It was a door, made from thick wooden planks that had long since mildewed and rotted, but surprisingly intact. Iron hinges streaked trails of rust down its face, while an ancient-looking padlock was rusted to the frame.

With a slight push, the door groaned and splintered. The padlock broke with a clatter. Somehow the hinges kept the door from falling.

Inside, Jason's torch lit a square room carved from the rock of the cave. Old wooden barrels lined the walls, stacked to the ceiling. Some of the barrels were rotted through, spilling their contents to the floor. Baskets and chests were stacked haphazardly in the corners.

Inspecting one broken barrel, his light glinted off the metal trinkets scattered on the ground. He saw keys, coins, rings, jewelry, utensils, small trinkets. He bent over to pick up a tarnished coin, scraping away the grime with his thumb. It glittered like silver.

Jason waved his light around at the barrels brimming with melee weapons, random pieces of armor, moldering fabrics, and other miscellany. Jason chuckled. He had found a treasure room.

He looked through the barrels and chests, hoping to find something of use. A comb. A necklace locket. A signet ring. A slow realization dawned on him. This was not a treasure room - it was the personal belongings of the cult's victims across the centuries. With a trembling hand, he shone the light on the horde of containers. How many people had died in this place? Hundreds of thousands? How long had the cult been here, hiding away from civilization, ensnaring anyone who came too close...?

Jason tried to push the thoughts out of his mind. Maybe there was something here he could use. He searched through the mounds of weapons, but each had decayed into iron flakes long ago. He had just about given up the search when he spied a long wooden chest set apart from other containers. He pried at the rotted chest lid, which broke into pieces in his hand. Shining his torch inside, he gasped.

Lying on a moldy velvet cushion was a sword. Its polished blade scattered his light along the glittering edge. Entranced by the weapon, he took the hilt in his hand and lifted. It was heavy for one hand. He touched the edge of the double-edged blade. It was still sharp after all this time.

A memory drifted into Jason's mind of a Norse leader who once carried this sword, hundreds of years ago.

Here in this relatively safe space, Jason felt the pull of sleep. His body ached, and exhaustion sapped him of strength. But, there was something more. Something called to him, gently bidding him to rest.

Jason threw a pile of fabric in a corner and lay on it. Within seconds, his eyes had closed and rhythmic breathing carried him to sleep.

"Oh my love!" He heard Katie's soothing voice near him. "We have so much to talk about."

Jason was alone. He knew he was dreaming, but still felt Katie's presence alongside him. "Katie?" he asked.

"Yes," came the slow response, "And so much more."

Jason was confused, "Where are you?"

Katie's laughter swam around him. "I am with you, my love."

Jason's dream became more focused and lucid.

Bonfires blazed in the standing henge circle. A Green Man with a shepherd's crook sang among primitive revelers. A bound line of captives was being led into a fire-lit cavern in the side of the mountain. Katie assured him, "I have always been with you."

Visions of lands covered by dead and diseased crops, while the local fields are lush with harvest. "I have always fed you," Katie cooed.

Hostile warriors made plans of invasion around a campfire, while thousands of beady-eyed rats spied on them from the darkness. "I have always warned you of dangers," Katie whispered tenderly.

Grey robed men holding tall clay jugs knelt over a pool of black oil. A squirming lump slithered into each of the jugs with a wet plop. "We have traveled to the corners of the world together," Katie said excitedly.

The Emperor of Rome and his Empress bow to the scantily clad women dancing beneath the Cybelline statue. "Many in the world have seen us as gods," Katie said amused.

The scene became a debaucherous feast of intertwined bodies in a deep underground cavern. "I have always given you strength and longevity." Katie's voice was building, becoming more serious.

A Green Man priest stood over three stone altars, each with a naked victim strapped to it. "And all I ask for..."

A wave of rats wheeled up around the altars, descending upon the bodies, devouring all. "...is blood."

Jason snapped awake, those final words still tangible in the air. He had no idea how long he had slept, but was too full of dread and anxiety to continue. He sat up, musing on the visions he had received.

He had felt something building - like storm clouds about to erupt with lightning. He had felt violated, like something forcibly looking through his thoughts, trying to persuade him to succumb to its desires.

Whatever this ancient thing was, it was sending him dreams, trying to speak to him, to make him understand. Now that Katie was a part of it, it used her voice to speak to him. "Her Voice," he said out loud, finally understanding.

It wanted him - and would not stop until it had him.

He had to stop it. To kill it. To put an end to this nightmare. But how?

He thought of Katie, suspended in that unholy mass. Was she dead? Or could he still save her?

Jason realized that if that thing wanted him, it would have to bring him to it in person. He thought of the sacks of explosives that must be nearby...

Jason stood with resolve. He would find a way to save Katie. He would find a way to kill that thing.

Wrapping his sword in scraps of fabric, he ventured back into the caves, trying to find his way back to the amphitheater.

Jason heard the sounds of a crowd up ahead. His tunnel ended in a natural balcony overlooking the amphitheater. Jason lowered to the ground and crawled out to the edge, trying to remain hidden.

The Cybele-thing had apparently retreated from the stage, taking Katie with it. Only the Green Man and an empty throne remained.

The rabble of cultists were milling about in front of the platform. They looked to be a combination of bemused and bored, their revelry spent. Several cried out angrily towards the high-priest.

Maz stood at the edge of the stage, waving his staff theatrically. "Brothers and sisters! The ritual is almost complete! You will witness history!" However, the crowd seemed uneasy at his promises.

From a lower passage, two groundskeepers dragged a third behind them, their robes bloody and tattered from long claw marks. One split off to speak quietly to Maz.

Maz shouted shrilly at the man, "I don't care! Wipe them all out if you have to! Just bring the Atys to me alive!" Maz shoved the bowing man in obvious frustration.

Jason scanned the cave, but could not see where Alice and her hooligans were being kept. He hoped they were still alive.

Seeing the dead groundskeeper being dragged down another passage, Jason got an idea. He slowly crept away from the ledge and made his way down the winding tunnels.

Jason returned to the small cave where the groundskeepers had been ambushed. Thankfully, his torch revealed the robed body still sprawled on the floor. He began removing the bloody robe from the man and inspected it. Several jagged tears along the side turned the thick cloth into ribbons. Dark blood had pooled around the side and stomach. Jason donned the robes and began tucking and folding the bloody cloth so it was less visible. It wasn't perfect - or even passable - but it would have to work.

Jason searched the ground for the flares he had dropped. He only recovered two shells. Better than nothing.

He slid his sword under his robes, tucked the flare gun in his waist sash, and searched for the way back to the amphitheater.

Jason came out of the narrow passage along the side of the stage. He put the hood up over his head and stood tall as he walked purposefully into the crowd of cultists. Many had their hoods off, speaking to one another in conspiratorial voices. A few were coming off their drug-fueled high, while others smoked impatiently. As Jason moved past them, they wordlessly made way for him.

Maz was still on stage. He was turned towards the back of the stage, genuflecting in prayer. "Oh Great Mother, we have brought your Voice to you. And soon your Atys will follow!"

A rumble shook the stage, like a barely perceivable earthquake. Maz bowed deeply, "I beg for your patience and mercy! I will not fail you."

Jason lingered near the stage, searching the vast cavern for any sign of the Anchester captives. Maz turned back to the crowd and moved towards Jason. For a tense moment, he thought he was spotted. Then Maz shouted for his groundskeepers. Two approached as Jason tried to blend with the cultists.

Jason could hear Maz talking gruffly to his followers. "Yes she is unhappy! This has become a shit show!" He cracked one of the men with his staff. He put a hand onto the forehead of his Green Man mask and sighed. "Bring in the sacrifices. That might get this crowd alive again. Maybe it will even sate her anger for a while." He pointed for the two to go. They bowed and left quickly, pushing through the crowd. Jason followed.

Jason shadowed the two men, trying to look occupied whenever they looked back. They exited through a rough tunnel of dim lights. Jason peered into the passage behind them and slipped in. He could hear the men in the tunnel ahead, but was far enough behind not to see them.

Katie's voice sounded next to him, startling him. "Where are you going, my love?" Jason ignored the hallucination and continued ahead.

Jason followed the sounds of their boots, until they stopped. He hesitated, hoping they had not heard his own footsteps. A second later, he heard the clack of a metal latch and the squeal of rusty hinges. After hearing a heavy clang of a closing door, Jason hurried down the hall.

The metal reinforced door had a barred view hole in its center. Jason peered inside. In a small cell, Alice and her hooligans were crammed inside. One of the groundskeepers approached the cell door with a loop of keys while the other covered the prisoners with a rifle.

"Oy! You here to take our lunch orders, gov?" one of the hooligans joked.

"I think I fancy a ham sandwich, myself," another chimed in.

"Shut it," the groundskeeper growled, putting his key in the cell lock. Among the huddle of men, Jason spied Alice and Kylie packed in with them.

"Wot, no lunch, then?" said one hooligan pressed against the cell bars. "I'm sorry, but I'm going to have to launch a complaint with your manager."

"That just might drop a star off your overall rating, I'm afraid," another mocked.

The groundskeeper swung the door open, "Get out." Jason saw that the prisoners' hands were bound, a steel chain linking them through their manacles. When no one moved, the robed man reached into the cell, grabbed Kylie by the wrists and pulled her out the door. Kylie screamed in pain and anger. "I said get out!" he commanded.

Brennan lunged forward and body-checked the groundskeeper, but the big man barely moved. With a ham-like fist, he knocked

Brennan to the cell floor. The one-eyed Brennan spat blood onto the filthy floor, grinning with red-stained teeth. "Why don't you take these off me and we can have a proper scrap, yea?"

The groundskeeper dragged him to his feet and shoved him out of the cell.

As Jason peered through the door, he finally caught Alice's gaze. She raised an eyebrow at him and slowly nodded her head. "That's enough Brennan," Alice snapped. "Let's just do what these nice men want us to do."

Jason saw the rest of the hooligans glance at one other, as if understanding a secret code.

Jason hid behind the heavy door as the groundskeepers led the prisoners out. Jason drew the sword from beneath his robes, letting the makeshift fabric scabbard fall.

The groundskeeper covering the group with his rifle was at the rear, closing the prison door behind them. As the door swung shut, Jason did not hesitate. He thrust forward with the sword, burying the blade to the hilt in the chest of the surprised groundskeeper. The man stared at Jason with a look of bewilderment. Jason pulled back and the sword slid easily out of the wound, proceeded by a fountain of blood. The man dropped to his knees, blood pouring from his mouth, streaking down his robes. Jason kicked the rifle from his hand.

The corridor broke into a melee. The Anchester thugs piled onto the lone groundskeeper, hitting, kicking, biting, and lashing with their chains. Still, none could contend with his brute strength. He grabbed one hooligan and threw him so hard, three others were knocked down with him. He kicked one of the thugs into a wall hard enough to knock him unconscious.

Jason ran towards the cultist. Brennan was grappled onto the groundskeeper's back, legs around his chest, trying to strangle him with his length of chain. The robed man stood up with impossible force, grabbed Brennan and tossed him into a wall.

With all the might he could muster, Jason grabbed the sword in both hands and swung it at the groundskeeper. Jason had expected more resistance, as the sword cleaved clean through the man's neck, the blade's momentum spinning Jason around. With a sickening thump the groundskeeper's head fell to the floor, followed shortly by the thud of his body.

Jason stood there, panting. He glanced at the others, and they were all watching with wide-eyed surprise.

"That was some proper Excalibur type shit, mate!" one of the hooligans said in awe.

They helped the wounded to stand. Alice fished out the keys from the beheaded groundskeeper's robes, unlocking the chain that held the prisoners together.

"Where are the explosives?" Jason demanded.

One of the men turned down the passage, pointing to a door. "I think I saw them haul our guns in there."

Jason nodded and started moving to the door. "Woah! Where are you going?" Brennan held a hand to Jason's chest. "It's done mate! It's time for us to go!"

Jason stared into his eye. "I'm going to get Katie back," he said forcibly, "And I'm going to kill that thing." He pushed the hand aside. "You can help me, or you can run." Jason glared at him. Brennan simply stared.

Finally, Brennan grinned and said to the crowd, "Look at the pair of brass clangers on this one." He extended his hand courteously. "After you, mate."

Jason walked to the heavy wooden door. He pushed firmly, and to his surprise, the door swung open. Their belongings were lying haphazard on a table in the center of the storage room. Without hesitation, the hooligans took their rifles, checking and loading them. Their sacks and satchels of explosives were dropped beside the table. The cultists obviously didn't know what they contained. "Overconfidence", Alice said smugly. "We'll teach 'em not to count us out."

Jason hefted a sack and opened it. The inside was packed with what looked like red capped thermoses wrapped with caution tape. Jason looked up at Alice, quizzically. "Sapper Sticks," she had said with a grin. "For blowing up tree stumps. Each one's basically a stick of dynamite."

Jason took one of the charges in his hand, eyeing it uncertainly. "Look", Alice came to his side. "Just snap off the safety cap, twist this top, and you have about 30 seconds to get the hell away." Jason put the canister back and slung the sack over his shoulder, surprised at the weight.

"Oh", Alice ventured, "I got most of these at a discount... Something about a manufacturing defect or some such. All the ones we've used before worked just fine. Just...", Alice paused, "be careful not to drop them too hard, yea?"

Jason nodded and turned to leave, but Alice grabbed his shoulder. She eyed him with respect. "Go get your girl, lad. We'll hold 'em off on this end."

Kylie was near, shaking her head at their folly, "Her rats are her eyes and ears... She sees everything. She will know you are coming..."

Jason nodded. "I hope so." He turned and raced out of the storage room.

Behind him, Alice barked, "Move your arses! We came here to kill these devil-worshiping pricks, and there's still too many alive for my liking!"

CHAPTER
44

"Come to me, my love."

Katie's voice echoed in Jason's head. He felt her presence deeper within the ancient cave tunnels, beckoning to him.

Jason had made his way through the crowd of gathered cultists and back into the lower tunnels of the black pits. The sack of explosives weighed heavy on his shoulder. He stowed his sword beneath his robes and scanned the darkness with his torch.

More than once Jason had to hide to avoid a group of searching groundskeepers. They were clustered tightly together, moving rapidly, and on edge. It was the first time Jason saw an actual emotion on their faces - fear.

"You are getting closer, my love," Katie whispered into his head, "I am waiting for you."

Jason kept moving forward, taking whichever passage sloped downwards. He was being pulled closer to Katie. He could feel her anticipation to see him again. To be reunited.

Ahead of him was a junction of tunnels. Without warning, three hunched pale shapes scampered in from a side passage. They stopped mid-passage as one spied him. It let loose a low intimidating growl. Jason began fumbling through his robes for his flare gun.

Suddenly, the three Feral Ones cocked their heads in unison, as if listening. One stood upright pensively, then gave a high-pitched shriek. The three immediately ran off down another passage. No more than a second later, a horde of rats flooded down the tunnel they had stood in. The black wave of fur and teeth squirmed and chittered, chasing after the creatures.

The rat swarm disappeared as fast as it appeared, leaving the tunnel empty once again.

"Come my Love. I won't let anything harm you," Katie intoned in a soothing voice.

Jason continued walking downwards. The humidity of the claustrophobic caves was beginning to take its toll. Jason sat against a wall to catch his breath. The cave's stone walls were damp and cool to the touch.

"Rest, my love. We will be together soon," Katie comforted.

"Katie?" Jason said out loud, "Can you hear me?"

"I can feel you," she whispered back, "I can feel when you are excited. When you are anxious. When you are passionate."

Jason felt Katie's presence near him when he thought of her. Yet, he knew that whatever was speaking to him was not her. "Katie, is this you? Or is this... Cybele?"

Katie's voice laughed musically. "There is no Katie. There is no Cybele. There is only us, and our love for one another."

Maybe it was his exhaustion, but Jason still could not comprehend what was being said. Finally, he exclaimed, "Why me?! Why do you want us?!"

Feelings of warmth and tenderness washed over Jason. "Oh, my love. I have always loved you."

Jason once again felt the pull towards sleep. He shook his head to resist her.

The adoring voice continued, "You always seem to forget, my sweet De La Poer. But I still remember the man who taught me how to love..."

Jason struggled against the silver-tongued voice. "I feel your confusion," Katie purred in his brain. "Let me show you..."

Jason felt his consciousness slipping, his eyes involuntarily fluttering shut. Blackness overtook him.

A vision slowly faded into Jason's head. He saw a rocky desert steppe with thorny bushes scattered in the dry cracked dirt. A small pool of black liquid sprawled under the branches of green palm trees. It appeared to be a grassy oasis surrounding a tar pit. Jason could feel the age of this place, ancient and far away.

A black-furred rat sat on a rock near the edge of the pool. A shadow streaked over the dusty ground. The swooping eagle grabbed the rat with both talons, taking flight again. With the speed of a serpent, a black tendril lashed out, pulling the raptor into the liquid before it could let out a cry. The rat then crawled back into the pool.

"Before I met you, my life was an eternity of waiting and scavenging."

A young woman approached the pool, picking the reeds and flowers that were growing there. The liquid surged. Her scream was cut short. The banks of the pool were once again deserted.

"But then you came into my life."

A young man dressed in primitive furs approached the pool, his wooden spear held with trepidation. Had he heard the woman's cry?

The woman slowly emerged from the water before the man, her long disheveled hair covering much of her naked body. The man was shocked, but was transfixed at the sight. As he approached the edge of the pool, he was unaware of the thick black tendril lifting the woman from the back of her head.

"Then, I felt something for the first time. A longing to be with you."

The woman glided closer to the man. She pressed her ooze-filmed lips onto his mouth. He dropped his spear and embraced her. The two dropped into a passionate tangle in the grass.

Mercifully, the vision faded. When it continued, it was night under a crescent waning moon.

Three primitive men approached the pool with torches. One was the man who was in the earlier vision. He was leading the other two towards the oasis. Had he boasted to his friends of the lady in the pool? When they did not believe him, did he decide to show them?

The man pointed at the pond. The other two looked at each other before laughing out loud. The man angrily shouted at them, moving to the edge of the pool.

Slowly, the woman rose through the viscous liquid, her body glistening in the moonlight. The two men immediately grabbed their spears in fright. The other man jumped to his feet and gestured to hold back.

One of the two men pushed the man aside with his spear, as they thrust the weapons at the woman threateningly. One lunged forward, stabbing the woman in her stomach. She let out a scream of pain echoed by a thousand mouths.

Incensed, the man grabbed his spear and jammed it into the ribs of one of the other men. He fell in a bloody heap onto the grass. As the second man turned his spear on the defending man, the surface of the pond surged, hitting the spearman with a wall of churning black, engulfing him with thick froth. As the wave receded, only an oily smear remained on the bank.

"You protected me."

The man dropped his spear in shocked revelation of his actions. Was he afraid of his deeds being discovered by others?

She sensed his anxiety. Oily tendrils emerged from the waters, dragging the body he had murdered into the pool. She smiled at the man.

"All I wanted was to show you my love."

A fleshy lump breached the surface of the pond. A partially digested body part floated to the surface, being dragged to land by a tendril. It came to rest before the woman. She daintily bent down and took the limb into her hands. She bit firmly into the slime-covered chunk. Blood dripping from her mouth, she offered it to the man.

At first, he was repulsed, but eventually, he took the flesh from the woman. With her urging, he bit into it. The man jerked upright and gasped. He stared at his hands, seeing them begin to writhe, like serpents beneath his skin. His body trembled as the ooze flooded his system, pushing against his muscles and tendons.

Power filled his body, energy like he had never felt before. He smiled incredulously at the woman. He grabbed her, pulling her body close, kissing the oily grey mire coating her skin. She held him as well, tendrils wrapping their bodies, as they lay on the ooze covered grass.

Jason felt the vision releasing him. His brain reeled at the revelations shown to him. He felt queasy and repulsed... but also in awe.

He forced himself to his feet. Katie was just ahead. He had to reach her.

"We are immortal, you and I," the voice scintillated in his waking mind. "I have seen you in many forms, many times. I have seen the hundreds of faces you have worn over the eons of your bloodline, but they are all you... My first... My consort... My Atys... My love."

The tunnel became a winding stone stairway, each step worn smooth with the passage of time. A dark opening loomed at the bottom of that stairway. Jason took an uncertain breath and descended the stairs.

The darkness beyond the opening was almost absolute. His torch illuminated only a vast void. Jason could hear the drip and slosh of water. As his eyes adjusted, he realized the void was actually a vast cavernous basin. The path from the stone stairs continued down to the edge of a great underground lake. The black liquid seemed to move and swirl in the light of his torch.

With a great sloshing sound, the waters churned and parted, uncovering a stone bridge leading deeper into the pool. He suddenly realized that he had seen this terrible place in a vision. The Roman commander had stood on this very bridge.

Katie's voice sang joyously in his skull, "So close, my love! I can almost touch you!"

With no other way to proceed, Jason again hefted his sack and slowly moved onto the slime covered stone bridge. Clutching his torch, he looked down to watch his foot placement. His light caught a bulge in the thick liquid at the edge of the lake. It swelled, then burst open, spilling forth hundreds of squirming mucus-covered rats. They immediately scuttled away, disappearing into the crevices of the cavern.

Shining his torch about, Jason could see more of the massive chamber. The massive stalactites frozen in time as they flowed down the walls and ceiling. At the far side of the bridge stood a titanic statue of primitively carved stone. Its shriveled arms and legs stuck out from oversized breasts and impossible hips like an afterthought. It had no face, only rough bead-like spheres clustered around what should be a head. This was the Corpulent Mother. The Magna Mater. The visage of Cybele.

Jason stopped on the bridge as the statue loomed over him. The water around him began to bubble and froth. A bulge rose before the base of the statue. A form pressed and distended the bubble. The surface sloshed away, revealing Katie slowly rising through the muck. Her pale skin was coated in slime, and her eyes were rolled back to their whites - but still she smiled at him. Delicately, her body was lifted into the air, held aloft by a thick black tentacle grasping the back of her head, undulating back into the water like an unholy umbilical cord.

Katie spoke to him, but her mouth did not move. "We are reunited again, my love!"

Jason gasped as feelings of longing and adoration welled up inside him. He truly did love Katie. This was still Katie, wasn't it?

Katie drifted closer to him. "So long have we waited for the right Voice and Atys. So many of our blood have come before." Her smile turned to a frown. "Most presented to us could barely stand each other. They never had what we have - our love."

Even full of fear, Jason was still overcome with devotion to her. A reverence bordering on fanaticism.

She waved a hand towards the waters. "Still, they are a part of our blood..."

Jason shone his torch at the base of the statue. Floating in the murky liquid were solid forms. Jason's breath caught. They were bodies. Dozens of bodies roiling lifeless against one another like dead fish.

"...and they still remain with us.", Katie continued. "Our gift of immortality fulfilled."

Jason saw that one of the bodies was Alexia. As he turned the light on her, her eyes suddenly flicked open. She stared at him in panicked horror, acutely aware of what was happening to her. As fast as they appeared, the bodies were sucked back beneath the oily mass.

Jason reeled. How many of his family were down there? How long have they been kept alive? As sheer terror washed over him, whatever spell that gripped him was broken.

Jason took the sack from his back, holding it to his chest.

Katie landed gently on the stone bridge before Jason. "How long it has been since I felt your touch?" She reached out and caressed Jason's cheek. He tried hard not to recoil from her.

Jason dropped the sack of explosives onto the ground next to him.

Katie said seductively, "Let this be like our first time - a new beginning for our love." She moved forward to kiss him.

Jason put one hand under his robes.

"Let us be together for all time..." Katie embraced him, moving to consummate their reunion.

Jason opened his eyes and focused on the thick tendril attached to Katie's head. With one swift motion, Jason flung open his robe and swung the Norse sword, scything through the tentacle holding Katie. She dropped to the stone bridge like a marionette with cut wires.

The scream was deafening. Thousands of mouths shrieked in pain and rage. The severed tentacle flopped across the bridge like a headless snake. The entire cavern shook with a tremor.

Jason pulled Katie to her feet. Her eyes blinked open and she coughed deeply. "We have to run. Now!" Jason shouted at her over the din. She nodded groggily. They began a staggering run back towards the stairway out.

Jason knew that his thirty seconds was almost up.

Just as the lake began to surge towards them, the explosive he had set detonated, causing a chain reaction with the entire sack. The roar of the blasts were drowned out by thunderous screams of fury and agony.

Jason did not look back. He knew his paltry explosives could not kill it. He just prayed that they had bought them some time to flee.

Jason and Katie fled up the tunnels of the black pits, their feet pounding against the damp stone floor. The air was thick with the heat and falling debris.

"WHY! WHY HAVE YOU SCORNED ME!"

The words erupted in Jason's head with an intensity only unrequited love could elicit. The pain was searing, threatening to split his skull.

"HER?! YOU WOULD BE WITH HER?! INSTEAD OF ME?!" Flashes of Walter's mother stabbed into Jason's vision, her face contorted with rage and betrayal. "YOU ARE MINE! FOREVER!"

Katie stumbled, and Jason caught her arm, pulling her along. They could hear sounds of gunfire and explosions ahead, the echoes distorting in the winding passages.

As they burst into the amphitheater, they were met with chaos. The ancient cavern had become a war zone. Alice and her remaining hooligans were entrenched behind fallen debris, firing relentlessly at the groundskeepers. The air was thick with smoke and the acrid smell of gunpowder. Hooligans reached into their satchels and threw their charges. Explosions rocked the cavern, sending showers of stone and dust raining down.

Cultists ran in terror, their screams adding to the cacophony of destruction. Maz stood amidst the mayhem, barking orders to his men, his voice barely audible over the din of battle.

Jason and Katie reached Alice's position, diving behind cover as bullets whizzed overhead. "You must have pissed it off!" Alice shouted, a manic grin on her face.

Before Jason could respond, the entire cavern shuddered violently. A deafening roar filled the air as the opening behind the amphitheater exploded outward. From the gaping hole vomited a writhing mass of slapping tentacles, each one as thick as a tree trunk and glistening with viscous slime.

The beast's thrashings smashed against the walls, sending stone fragments exploding in all directions. Everyone, cultist, groundskeepers, and hooligan alike, ran in terror from the monstrosity. Its tendrils lashed out indiscriminately, dragging screaming victims back into its pulsating mass, leaving only bloody smears behind.

Jason was knocked to the ground by a sweeping tentacle, his flare gun and sword clattering across the rough floor. He watched helplessly as Kylie snatched up his sword and disappeared into the chaos.

The voice in his head returned, dripping with venom. "After all I have done for you! You could have been a god, but instead you are just meat! Meat like the rest of them!"

"We gotta get outta here!" Brennan shouted, his voice cracking with fear.

"No!" Alice bellowed back, her eyes blazing with determination. "I've waited for this fight my whole life!" She stepped forward beyond the cover, standing with arms outstretched before the abomination.

"I know you", Alice hissed. "I have felt your presence for years. I will be your end. You..." In a heartbeat, a massive tentacle crashed down upon her. The sickening crunch of bones was lost in the creature's roar. The hooligans froze in disbelief.

Amidst the carnage, Maz strode forward, holding his staff high before the writhing monstrosity. He seemed oblivious to the sporadic gunfire from the hooligans, the bullets tore into his robes but barely fazed him. "Be calm, oh Great Mother!" he intoned, his voice carrying an eerie resonance. "We still have your chosen Voice! And your Atys! All you desire is within reach. This time, I will ensure they cannot fight against your will. Let me bring them to you. We will rebuild the..."

His words were cut short as a sword burst through his chest. He turned slowly, disbelief etched on his face, to see Kylie gripping the hilt of Jason's sword. "You..." he burbled, blood frothing from his lips.

"Just die already!" Kylie shrieked, raising the sword high and bringing it down with all her might. The blade cleaved through Maz from neck to sternum, a fountain of gore erupting from the wound. His body fell to its knees, but still gurgled breath.

Cybele's rage thundered through the cavern, the very stone seeming to heave with her fury. Kylie sprinted back to the hooligan's cover, her face spattered with Maz's blood. The group opened fire on the writhing mass, their bullets tearing chunks of flesh from its form, but seeming to cause it only pain and annoyance.

Brennan shouted over the din, "That was proper epic, love, but we might be greased if we don't get out of here right quick!"

Jason's mind raced. "Throw your explosives at it!", he yelled, scrambling for his fallen flare gun. "Now!" Without hesitation, the hooligans lobbed their remaining charges at the creature, the satchels being enveloped and trapped within its sticky body.

As Jason took aim with the flare gun, a massive pseudopod crashed into their position, crushing one of the hooligans with a sickening crunch. "Run!" Jason cried, his voice raw with desperation.

Jason sighted the explosives and fired a shot, the bright red flare embedding itself in the creature's undulating flesh, glowing beneath the slimy membrane. Nothing.

Jason steadied himself, aiming carefully. One shot left. He squeezed the trigger just as a lashing tentacle crashed into him, knocking the wind from his lungs and sending the flare careening into the ceiling.

Tendrils wrapped around Jason's legs, pulling him to the ground. He heard Katie and Kylie scream as they too were ensnared by thick whips of ooze. They were dragged across the ragged floor towards the pulsating mass.

Jason's fingers scrabbled for purchase, finding a small cleft. He grabbed for Katie's hand, straining to hold both her and Kylie against the creature's relentless pull. His muscles screamed in protest, tendons threatening to snap under the pressure.

Suddenly, Alice's voice rang out behind them, challenging the beast. "I wasn't finished..." She stood like a battered warrior, bloodied and with one arm hanging uselessly at her side. Yet her face bore a manic grin, the fire of defiance burning in her eyes. "You are going to feel pain before I put you down."

The creature's tentacles lashed out, wrapping around Alice. She cackled in laughter as she was drawn into its shifting mass. As she was engulfed, Jason caught a glimpse of something clutched in her good hand - a red-tipped canister.

For a moment, all was still. Then, a bright light flared within the creature, like a depth charge detonating in its core. A geyser of fluids erupted from its hide, raining down on the survivors. In rapid succession, the other buried explosives began to detonate like a chain of firecrackers, each blast tearing new holes in the abomination's form.

The tentacle holding Jason went slack, thrashing uselessly on the floor. He scrambled to his feet, pulling Kylie up with him. Together, they lifted Katie, her body limp but still breathing. With blasts still erupting from the creature, they ran for their lives.

The cavern shook violently, great cracks spider-webbing across the ceiling. Cultists and hooligans alike fled in blind panic, their allegiances forgotten in the face of certain death. Behind them, explosions continued to rock the chamber as the creature thrashed.

Jason held Katie close, his legs burning with exhaustion, but he refused to stop.

Quakes rocked the passages as they climbed higher, the beast's anguished roars growing fainter. Dust and debris rained down as collapsing tunnels rumbled behind them, threatening to seal them in this nightmare realm forever.

They ran.

EPILOGUE

They stood on a nearby hill, overseeing the priory. Jason recalled it was the same spot Walter De La Poer had stood as he watched the estate burn hundreds of years ago. The weight of history pressed down upon them, a tangible reminder of the horrors they had endured.

Katie leaned against his side, holding him tightly, but saying nothing. A mixture of relief and lingering fear etched her face.

Kylie stood with Brennan and the few remaining hooligans, their faces haggard and drawn, but alive.

The priory grounds looked mostly the same, except for a few huge sinkholes that had opened across the once-pristine gardens. The manicured hedges and flowerbeds now bordered gaping maws in the soil, as if the very ground had tried to swallow the evil that dwelled beneath.

They all watched the grounds intently, as if waiting for the creature to rear up from beneath the earth. But nothing moved. The silence was oppressive, broken only by the occasional gust of wind.

"What now?" one of the men said, his voice barely above a whisper.

Brennan spat, his voice gruff. "We're gonna burn the whole place to the ground and salt the goddamn earth. We'll make sure no one ever tries to rebuild this place ever again."

Kylie nodded to him, her eyes hard with resolve. "I'll make sure no more of my family are lured to this place. Or any others like it."

They stood reflecting, the weight of their experiences making them thankful to be alive.

Brennan wiped a tear from his eye, his usual gruff demeanor cracking. "Gam always said that there are strange and unbelievably evil things on this earth - but sometimes the good guys win."

Kylie touched his shoulder. He cleared his throat, composing himself. "Come on, let's get to the trucks."

As Jason turned to leave, he heard a faint whisper clawing at his mind. "Ask yourself - have you killed me? I have survived worse." Jason tried to shake the voice from his head, but it persisted. "What if I did die? Do you think this was my only body? How many of my servants carried me across the world over the thousands of years? How long have I been allowed to grow and spread? How many other cults still live to serve me?"

Jason growled under his breath, his jaw clenching. "Maybe... But you won't have us."

As he followed the hooligans, her voice spoke its last. "I will see you again, my De La Poer - you are mine - FOREVER."

"So what do you remember?" Jason asked, his voice soft in the quiet of the airplane cabin.

"Not much," Katie shrugged in her chair, her brow furrowed. "I remember being captured and held captive. Then, I think they gave me some good drugs, because the rest is kind of a blur."

Clouds drifted past their window, a serene backdrop to the turmoil of their recent experiences. A stewardess offered them drinks and snacks. The whole ordeal had left them exhausted and somewhat famished.

"You missed... a lot," Jason said, his voice heavy with the weight of unspoken horrors. "Most of it not pleasant."

"Well," Katie stretched, a hint of her old playfulness returning to her eyes. "You have eight hours to fill me in."

"Maybe we should get some sleep instead," Jason offered with a smile, the dark circles under his eyes betraying his exhaustion.

She clutched his arm, her grip tight as if afraid he might disappear. "Too excited to sleep. I could probably talk to you the whole way home."

Within minutes, she was asleep, her head gently snoring on his shoulder. Jason reached for a blanket and placed it gently over her, carefully tucking her in. As he watched her sleeping form, a mixture of love and protectiveness washed over him.

She smiled in her sleep, muttering quietly, "Thank you... my love."

THE RATS IN THE WALLS

by H. P. Lovecraft

Written Aug-Sep 1923

Published in March 1924 in Weird Tales, Vol. 3, No. 3, p. 25-31.

On 16 July 1923, I moved into Exham Priory after the last

workman had finished his labours. The restoration had been a stupendous task, for little had remained of the deserted pile but a shell-like ruin; yet because it had been the seat of my ancestors, I let no expense deter me. The place had not been inhabited since the reign of James the First, when a tragedy of intensely hideous, though largely unexplained, nature had struck down the master, five of his children, and several servants; and driven forth under a cloud of suspicion and terror the third son, my lineal progenitor and the only survivor of the abhorred line.

With this sole heir denounced as a murderer, the estate had reverted to the crown, nor had the accused man made any attempt to exculpate himself or regain his property. Shaken by some horror greater than that of conscience or the law, and expressing only a frantic wish to exclude the ancient edifice from his sight and memory, Walter de la Poer, eleventh Baron Exham, fled to Virginia and there founded the family which by the next century had become known as Delapore.

Exham Priory had remained untenanted, though later allotted to the estates of the Norrys family and much studied because of its peculiarly composite architecture; an architecture involving Gothic towers resting on a Saxon or Romanesque substructure, whose foundation in turn was of a still earlier order or blend of orders -- Roman, and even Druidic or native Cymric, if legends speak truly. This foundation was a very singular thing, being merged on one side with the solid limestone of the precipice from whose brink the priory overlooked a desolate valley three miles west of the village of Anchester.

Architects and antiquarians loved to examine this strange relic of forgotten centuries, but the country folk hated it. They had hated it hundreds of years before, when my ancestors lived there, and they hated it now, with the moss and mould of abandonment on it. I had not been a day in Anchester before I knew I came of an accursed house. And this week workmen have blown up Exham Priory, and are busy obliterating the traces of its foundations. The bare statistics of my ancestry I had always known, together with the fact that my first American forebear had come to the colonies under a strange cloud. Of details, however, I had been kept wholly ignorant through the policy of reticence always maintained by the Delapores. Unlike our planter neighbours, we seldom boasted of crusading ancestors or other mediaeval and Renaissance heroes; nor was any kind of tradition handed down except what may have been recorded in the sealed envelope left before the Civil War by every squire to his eldest son for posthumous opening. The glories we cherished were those achieved since the migration; the glories of a proud and honourable, if somewhat reserved and unsocial Virginia line.

During the war our fortunes were extinguished and our whole existence changed by the burning of Carfax, our home on the banks of the James. My grandfather, advanced in years, had perished in that incendiary outrage, and with him the envelope that had bound us all to the past. I can recall that fire today as I saw it then at the age of seven, with the federal soldiers shouting, the women screaming, and the negroes howling and praying. My father was in the army, defending Richmond, and after many formalities my mother and I were passed through the lines to join him.

When the war ended we all moved north, whence my mother had come; and I grew to manhood, middle age, and ultimate wealth as a stolid Yankee. Neither my father nor I ever knew what our hereditary envelope had contained, and as I merged into the greyness of Massachusetts business life I lost all interest in the mysteries which evidently lurked far back in my family tree. Had I suspected their nature, how gladly I would have left Exham Priory to its moss, bats and cobwebs!

My father died in 1904, but without any message to leave to me, or to my only child, Alfred, a motherless boy of ten. It was this boy who reversed the order of family information, for although I could give him only jesting conjectures about the past, he wrote me of some very interesting ancestral legends when the late war took him to England in 1917 as an aviation officer. Apparently the Delapores had a colourful and perhaps sinister history, for a friend of my son's, Capt. Edward Norrys of the Royal Flying Corps, dwelt near the family seat at Anchester and related some peasant superstitions which few novelists could equal for wildness and incredibility. Norrys himself, of course, did not take them so seriously; but they amused my son and made good material for his letters to me. It was this legendry which definitely turned my attention to my transatlantic heritage, and made me resolve to purchase and restore the family seat which Norrys showed to Alfred in its picturesque desertion, and offered to get for him at a surprisingly reasonable figure, since his own uncle was the present owner.

I bought Exham Priory in 1918, but was almost immediately distracted from my plans of restoration by the return of my son as a maimed invalid. During the two years that he lived I thought of nothing but his care, having even placed my business under the direction of partners.

In 1921, as I found myself bereaved and aimless, a retired manufacturer no longer young, I resolved to divert my remaining years with my new possession. Visiting Anchester in December, I was entertained by Capt. Norrys, a plump, amiable young man who had thought much of my son, and secured his assistance in gathering plans and anecdotes to guide in the coming restoration. Exham Priory itself I saw without emotion, a jumble of tottering mediaeval ruins covered with lichens and honeycombed with rooks' nests, perched perilously upon a precipice, and denuded of floors or other interior features save the stone walls of the separate towers.

As I gradually recovered the image of the edifice as it had been when my ancestors left it over three centuries before, I began to hire workmen for the reconstruction. In every case I was forced to go outside the immediate locality, for the Anchester villagers had an almost unbelievable fear and hatred of the place. The sentiment was so great that it was sometimes communicated to the outside labourers, causing numerous desertions; whilst its scope appeared to include both the priory and its ancient family.

My son had told me that he was somewhat avoided during his visits because he was a de la Poer, and I now found myself subtly ostracized for a like reason until I convinced the peasants how little I knew of my heritage. Even then they sullenly disliked me, so that I had to collect most of the village traditions through the mediation of Norrys. What the people could not forgive, perhaps, was that I had come to restore a symbol so abhorrent to them; for, rationally or not, they viewed Exham Priory as nothing less than a haunt of fiends and werewolves.

Piecing together the tales which Norrys collected for me, and supplementing them with the accounts of several savants who had studied the ruins, I deduced that Exham Priory stood on the site of a prehistoric temple; a Druidical or ante-Druidical thing which must have been contemporary with Stonehenge. That indescribable rites had been celebrated there, few doubted, and there were unpleasant tales of the transference of these rites into the Cybele worship which the Romans had introduced.

Inscriptions still visible in the sub-cellar bore such unmistakable letters as 'DIV... OPS ... MAGNA. MAT...', sign of the Magna Mater whose dark worship was once vainly forbidden to Roman citizens. Anchester had been the camp of the third Augustan legion, as many remains attest, and it was said that the temple of Cybele was splendid and thronged with worshippers who performed nameless ceremonies at the bidding of a Phrygian priest. Tales added that the fall of the old religion did not end the orgies at the temple, but that the priests lived on in the new faith without real change. Likewise was it said that the rites did not vanish with the Roman power, and that certain among the Saxons added to what remained of the temple, and gave it the essential outline it subsequently preserved, making it the centre of a cult feared through half the heptarchy.

About 1000 A.D. the place is mentioned in a chronicle as being a substantial stone priory housing a strange and powerful monastic order and surrounded by extensive gardens which needed no walls to exclude a frightened populace. It was never destroyed by the Danes, though after the Norman Conquest it must have declined tremendously, since there was no impediment when Henry the Third granted the site to my ancestor, Gilbert de la Poer, First Baron Exham, in 1261.

Of my family before this date there is no evil report, but something strange must have happened then. In one chronicle there is a reference to a de la Poer as "cursed of God in 1307", whilst village legendry had nothing but evil and frantic fear to tell of the castle that went up on the foundations of the old temple and priory. The fireside tales were of the most grisly description, all the ghastlier because of their frightened reticence and cloudy evasiveness. They represented my ancestors as a race of hereditary daemons beside whom Gilles de Retz and the Marquis de Sade would seem the veriest tyros, and hinted whisperingly at their responsibility for the occasional disappearances of villagers through several generations.

The worst characters, apparently, were the barons and their direct heirs; at least, most was whispered about these. If of healthier inclinations, it was said, an heir would early and mysteriously die to make way for another more typical scion. There seemed to be an inner cult in the family, presided over by the head of the house, and sometimes closed except to a few members. Temperament rather than ancestry was evidently the basis of this cult, for it was entered by several who married into the family. Lady Margaret Trevor from Cornwall, wife of Godfrey, the second son of the fifth baron, became a favourite bane of children all over the countryside, and the daemon heroine of a particularly horrible old ballad not yet extinct near the Welsh border. Preserved in balladry, too, though not illustrating the same point, is the hideous tale of Lady Mary de la Poer, who shortly after her marriage to the Earl of Shrewsfield was killed by him and his mother, both of the slayers being absolved and blessed by the priest to whom they confessed what they dared not repeat to the world.

These myths and ballads, typical as they were of crude superstition, repelled me greatly. Their persistence, and their application to so long a line of my ancestors, were especially annoying; whilst the imputations of monstrous habits proved unpleasantly reminiscent of the one known scandal of my immediate forebears -- the case of my cousin, young Randolph Delapore of Carfax who went among the negroes and became a voodoo priest after he returned from the Mexican War.

I was much less disturbed by the vaguer tales of wails and howlings in the barren, windswept valley beneath the limestone cliff; of the graveyard stenches after the spring rains; of the floundering, squealing white thing on which Sir John Clave's horse had trod one night in a lonely field; and of the servant who had gone mad at what he saw in the priory in the full light of day. These things were hackneyed spectral lore, and I was at that time a pronounced sceptic. The accounts of vanished peasants were less to be dismissed, though not especially significant in view of mediaeval custom. Prying curiosity meant death, and more than one severed head had been publicly shown on the bastions -- now effaced -- around Exham Priory.

A few of the tales were exceedingly picturesque, and made me wish I had learnt more of the comparative mythology in my youth. There was, for instance, the belief that a legion of bat-winged devils kept witches' sabbath each night at the priory -- a legion whose sustenance might explain the disproportionate abundance of coarse vegetables harvested in the vast gardens. And, most vivid of all, there was the dramatic epic of the rats -- the scampering army of obscene vermin which had burst forth from the castle three months after the tragedy that doomed it to desertion -- the lean, filthy, ravenous army which had swept all before it and devoured fowl, cats, dogs, hogs, sheep, and even two hapless human beings before its fury was spent. Around that unforgettable rodent army a whole separate cycle of myths revolves, for it scattered among the village homes and brought curses and horrors in its train.

Such was the lore that assailed me as I pushed to completion, with an elderly obstinacy, the work of restoring my ancestral home. It must not be imagined for a moment tat these tales formed my principal psychological environinent. On the other hand, I was constantly praised and encouraged by Capt. Norrys and the antiquarians who surrounded and aided me. When the task was done, over two years after its commencement, I viewed the great rooms, wainscoted walls, vaulted ceilings, mullioned windows, and broad staircases with a pride which fully compensated for the prodigious expense of the restoration.

Every attribute of the Middle Ages was cunningly reproduced and the new parts blended perfectly with the original walls and foundations. The seat of my fathers was complete, and I looked forward to redeeming at last the local fame of the line which ended in me. I could reside here permanently, and prove that a de la Poer (for I had adopted again the original spelling of the name) need not be a fiend. My comfort was perhaps augmented by the fact that, although Exham Priory was mediaevally fitted, its interior was in truth wholly new and free from old vermin and old ghosts alike.

As I have said, I moved in on 16 July 1923. My household consisted of seven servants and nine cats, of which latter species I am particularly fond. My eldest cat, "NiggerMan", was seven years old and had come with me from my home in Bolton, Massachusetts; the others I had accumulated whilst living with Capt. Norrys' family during the restoration of the priory.

For five days our routine proceeded with the utmost placidity, my time being spent mostly in the codification of old family data. I had now obtained some very circumstantial accounts of the final tragedy and flight of Walter de la Poer, which I conceived to be the probable contents of the hereditary paper lost in the fire at Carfax. It appeared that my ancestor was accused with much reason of having killed all the other members of his household, except four servant confederates, in their sleep, about two weeks after a shocking discovery which changed his whole demeanour, but which, except by implication, he disclosed to no one save perhaps the servants who assisted him and afterwards fled beyond reach.

This deliberate slaughter, which included a father, three brothers, and two sisters, was largely condoned by the villagers, and so slackly treated by the law that its perpetrator escaped honoured, unharmed, and undisguised to Virginia; the general whispered sentiment being that he had purged the land of an immemorial curse. What discovery had prompted an act so terrible, I could scarcely even conjecture. Walter de la Poer must have known for years the sinister tales about his family, so that this material could have given him no fresh impulse. Had he, then, witnessed some appalling ancient rite, or stumbled upon some frightful and revealing symbol in the priory or its vicinity? He was reputed to have been a shy, gentle youth in England. In Virginia he seemed not so much hard or bitter as harassed and apprehensive. He was spoken of in the diary of another gentleman adventurer, Francis Harley of Bellview, as a man of unexampled justice, honour, and delicacy.

On 22 July occurred the first incident which, though lightly dismissed at the time, takes on a preternatural significance in relation to later events. It was so simple as to be almost negligible, and could not possibly have been noticed under the circumstances; for it must be recalled that since I was in a building practically fresh and new except for the walls, and surrounded by a well-balanced staff of servitors, apprehension would have been absurd despite the locality.

What I afterward remembered is merely this -- that my old black cat, whose moods I know so well, was undoubtedly alert and anxious to an extent wholly out of keeping with his natural character. He roved from room to room, restless and disturbed, and sniffed constantly about the walls which formed part of the Gothic structure. I realize how trite this sounds -- like the inevitable dog in the ghost story, which always growls before his master sees the sheeted figure -- yet I cannot consistently suppress it.

The following day a servant complained of restlessness among all the cats in the house. He came to me in my study, a lofty west room on the second storey, with groined arches, black oak panelling, and a triple Gothic window overlooking the limestone cliff and desolate valley; and even as he spoke I saw the jetty form of Nigger-Man creeping along the west wall and scratching at the new panels which overlaid the ancient stone.

I told the man that there must be a singular odour or emanation from the old stonework, imperceptible to human senses, but affecting the delicate organs of cats even through the new woodwork. This I truly believed, and when the fellow suggested the presence of mice or rats, I mentioned that there had been no rats there for three hundred years, and that even the field mice of the surrounding country could hardly be found in these high walls, where they had never been known to stray. That afternoon I called on Capt. Norrys, and he assured me that it would be quite incredible for field mice to infest the priory in such a sudden and unprecedented fashion.

That night, dispensing as usual with a valet, I retired in the west tower chamber which I had chosen as my own, reached from the study by a stone staircase and short gallery -- the former partly ancient, the latter entirely restored. This room was circular, very high, and without wainscoting, being hung with arras which I had myself chosen in London.

Seeing that Nigger-Man was with me, I shut the heavy Gothic door and retired by the light of the electric bulbs which so cleverly counterfeited candles, finally switching off the light and sinking on the carved and canopied four-poster, with the venerable cat in his accustomed place across my feet. I did not draw the curtains, but gazed out at the narrow window which I faced. There was a suspicion of aurora in the sky, and the delicate traceries of the window were pleasantly silhouetted.

At some time I must have fallen quietly asleep, for I recall a distinct sense of leaving strange dreams, when the cat started violently from his placid position. I saw him in the faint auroral glow, head strained forward, fore feet on my ankles, and hind feet stretched behind. He was looking intensely at a point on the wall somewhat west of the window, a point which to my eye had nothing to mark it, but toward which all my attention was now directed.

And as I watched, I knew that Nigger-Man was not vainly excited. Whether the arras actually moved I cannot say. I think it did, very slightly. But what I can swear to is that behind it I heard a low, distinct scurrying as of rats or mice. In a moment the cat had jumped bodily on the screening tapestry, bringing the affected section to the floor with his weight, and exposing a damp, ancient wall of stone; patched here and there by the restorers, and devoid of any trace of rodent prowlers.

Nigger-Man raced up and down the floor by this part of the wall, clawing the fallen arras and seemingly trying at times to insert a paw between the wall and the oaken floor. He found nothing, and after a time returned wearily to his place across my feet. I had not moved, but I did not sleep again that night.

In the morning I questioned all the servants, and found that none of them had noticed anything unusual, save that the cook remembered the actions of a cat which had rested on her windowsill. This cat had howled at some unknown hour of the night, awaking the cook in time for her to see him dart purposefully out of the open door down the stairs. I drowsed away the noontime, and in the afternoon called again on Capt. Norrys, who became exceedingly interested in what I told him. The odd incidents -- so slight yet so curious -- appealed to his sense of the picturesque and elicited from him a number of reminiscenses of local ghostly lore. We were genuinely perplexed at the presence of rats, and Norrys lent me some traps and Paris green, which I had the servants place in strategic localities when I returned.

I retired early, being very sleepy, but was harassed by dreams of the most horrible sort. I seemed to be looking down from an immense height upon a twilit grotto, knee-deep with filth, where a white-bearded daemon swineherd drove about with his staff a flock of fungous, flabby beasts whose appearance filled me with unutterable loathing. Then, as the swineherd paused and nodded over his task, a mighty swarm of rats rained down on the stinking abyss and fell to devouring beasts and man alike.

From this terrific vision I was abruptly awakened by the motions of Nigger-Man, who had been sleeping as usual across my feet. This time I did not have to question the source of his snarls and hisses, and of the fear which made him sink his claws into my ankle, unconscious of their effect; for on every side of the chamber the walls were alive with nauseous sound -- the veminous slithering of ravenous, gigantic rats. There was now no aurora to show the state of the arras -- the fallen section of which had been replaced - but I was not too frightened to switch on the light.

As the bulbs leapt into radiance I saw a hideous shaking all over the tapestry, causing the somewhat peculiar designs to execute a singular dance of death. This motion disappeared almost at once, and the sound with it. Springing out of bed, I poked at the arras with the long handle of a warming-pan that rested near, and lifted one section to see what lay beneath. There was nothing but the patched stone wall, and even the cat had lost his tense realization of abnormal presences. When I examined the circular trap that had been placed in the room, I found all of the openings sprung, though no trace remained of what had been caught and had escaped.

Further sleep was out of the question, so lighting a candle, I opened the door and went out in the gallery towards the stairs to my study, Nigger-Man following at my heels. Before we had reached the stone steps, however, the cat darted ahead of me and vanished down the ancient flight. As I descended the stairs myself, I became suddenly aware of sounds in the great room below; sounds of a nature which could not be mistaken.

The oak-panelled walls were alive with rats, scampering and milling whilst Nigger-Man was racing about with the fury of a baffled hunter. Reaching the bottom, I switched on the light, which did not this time cause the noise to subside. The rats continued their riot, stampeding with such force and distinctness that I could finally assign to their motions a definite direction. These creatures, in numbers apparently inexhaustible, were engaged in one stupendous migration from inconceivable heights to some depth conceivably or inconceivably below.

I now heard steps in the corridor, and in another moment two servants pushed open the massive door. They were searching the house for some unknown source of disturbance which had thrown all the cats into a snarling panic and caused them to plunge precipitately down several flights of stairs and squat, yowling, before the closed door to the sub-cellar. I asked them if they had heard the rats, but they replied in the negative. And when I turned to call their attention to the sounds in the panels, I realized that the noise had ceased.

With the two men, I went down to the door of the sub-cellar, but found the cats already dispersed. Later I resolved to explore the crypt below, but for the present I merely made a round of the traps. All were sprung, yet all were tenantless. Satisfying myself that no one had heard the rats save the felines and me, I sat in my study till morning, thinking profoundly and recalling every scrap of legend I had unearthed concerning the building I inhabited. I slept some in the forenoon, leaning back in the one comfortable library chair which my mediaeval plan of furnishing could not banish. Later I telephoned to Capt. Norrys, who came over and helped me explore the sub-cellar.

Absolutely nothing untoward was found, although we could not repress a thrill at the knowledge that this vault was built by Roman hands. Every low arch and massive pillar was Roman -- not the debased Romanesque of the bungling Saxons, but the severe and harmonious classicism of the age of the Caesars; indeed, the walls abounded with inscriptions familiar to the antiquarians who had repeatedly explored the place -- things like "P. GETAE. PROP... TEMP... DONA..." and "L. PRAEG... VS... PONTIFI...ATYS..."

The reference to Atys made me shiver, for I had read Catullus and knew something of the hideous rites of the Eastern god, whose worship was so mixed with that of Cybele.

Norrys and I, by the light of lanterns, tried to interpret the odd and nearly effaced designs on certain irregularly rectangular blocks of stone generally held to be altars, but could make nothing of them. We remembered that one pattern, a sort of rayed sun, was held by students to imply a non-Roman origin suggesting that these altars had merely been adopted by the Roman priests from some older and perhaps aboriginal temple on the same site. On one of these blocks were some brown stains which made me wonder. The largest, in the centre of the room, had certain features on the upper surface which indicated its connection with fire -- probably burnt offerings.

Such were the sights in that crypt before whose door the cats howled, and where Norrys and I now determined to pass the night. Couches were brought down by the servants, who were told not to mind any nocturnal actions of the cats, and Nigger-Man was admitted as much for help as for companionship. We decided to keep the great oak door -- a modern replica with slits for ventilation -- tightly closed; and, with this attended to, we retired with lanterns still burning to await whatever might occur.

The vault was very deep in the foundations of the priory, and undoubtedly far down on the face of the beetling limestone cliff overlooking the waste valley. That it had been the goal of the scuffling and unexplainable rats I could not doubt, though why, I could not tell. As we lay there expectantly, I found my vigil occasionally mixed with half-formed dreams from which the uneasy motions of the cat across my feet would rouse me.

These dreams were not wholesome, but horribly like the one I had had the night before. I saw again the twilit grotto, and the swineherd with his unmentionable fungous beasts wallowing in filth, and as I looked at these things they seemed nearer and more distinct -- so distinct that I could almost observe their features. Then I did observe the flabby features of one of them -- and awakened with such a scream that Nigger-Man started up, whilst Capt. Norrys, who had not slept, laughed considerably. Norrys might have laughed more -- or perhaps less -- had he known what it was that made me scream. But I did not remember myself till later. Ultimate horror often paralyses memory in a merciful way.

Norrys waked me when the phenomena began. Out of the same frightful dream I was called by his gentle shaking and his urging to listen to the cats. Indeed, there was much to listen to, for beyond the closed door at the head of the stone steps was a veritable nightmare of feline yelling and clawing, whilst Nigger-Man, unmindful of his kindred outside, was running excitedly round the bare stone walls, in which I heard the same babel of scurrying rats that had troubled me the night before.

An acute terror now rose within me, for here were anomalies which nothing normal could well explain. These rats, if not the creatures of a madness which I shared with the cats alone, must be burrowing and sliding in Roman walls I had thought to be solid limestone blocks ... unless perhaps the action of water through more than seventeen centuries had eaten winding tunnels which rodent bodies had worn clear and ample ... But even so, the spectral horror was no less; for if these were living vermin why did not Norrys hear their disgusting commotion? Why did he urge me to watch Nigger-Man and listen to the cats outside, and why did he guess wildly and vaguely at what could have aroused them?

By the time I had managed to tell him, as rationally as I could, what I thought I was hearing, my ears gave me the last fading impression of scurrying; which had retreated still downward, far underneath this deepest of sub-cellars till it seemed as if the whole cliff below were riddled with questing rats. Norrys was not as sceptical as I had anticipated, but instead seemed profoundly moved. He motioned to me to notice that the cats at the door had ceased their clamour, as if giving up the rats for lost; whilst NiggerMan had a burst of renewed restlessness, and was clawing frantically around the bottom of the large stone altar in the centre of the room, which was nearer Norrys' couch than mine.

My fear of the unknown was at this point very great. Something astounding had occurred, and I saw that Capt. Norrys, a younger, stouter, and presumably more naturally materialistic man, was affected fully as much as myself -- perhaps because of his lifelong and intimate familiarity with local legend. We could for the moment do nothing but watch the old black cat as he pawed with decreasing fervour at the base of the altar, occasionally looking up and mewing to me in that persuasive manner which he used when he wished me to perform some favour for him.

Norrys now took a lantern close to the altar and examined the place where Nigger-Man was pawing; silently kneeling and scraping away the lichens of the centuries which joined the massive pre-Roman block to the tessellated floor. He did not find anything, and was about to abandon his efforts when I noticed a trivial circumstance which made me shudder, even though it implied nothing more than I had already imagined.

I told him of it, and we both looked at its almost imperceptible manifestation with the fixedness of fascinated discovery and acknowledgment. It was only this -- that the flame of the lantern set down near the altar was slightly but certainly flickering from a draught of air which it had not before received, and which came indubitably from the crevice between floor and altar where Norrys was scraping away the lichens.

We spent the rest of the night in the brilliantly-lighted study, nervously discussing what we should do next. The discovery that some vault deeper than the deepest known masonry of the Romans underlay this accursed pile, some vault unsuspected by the curious antiquarians of three centuries, would have been sufficient to excite us without any background of the sinister. As it was, the fascination became two-fold; and we paused in doubt whether to abandon our search and quit the priory forever in superstitious caution, or to gratify our sense of adventure and brave whatever horrors might await us in the unknown depths.

By morning we had compromised, and decided to go to London to gather a group of archaeologists and scientific men fit to cope with the mystery. It should be mentioned that before leaving the sub-cellar we had vainly tried to move the central altar which we now recognized as the gate to a new pit of nameless fear. What secret would open the gate, wiser men than we would have to find.

During many days in London Capt. Norrys and I presented our facts, conjectures, and legendary anecdotes to five eminent authorities, all men who could be trusted to respect any family disclosures which future explorations might develop. We found most of them little disposed to scoff but, instead, intensely interested and sincerely sympathetic. It is hardly necessary to name them all, but I may say that they included Sir William Brinton, whose excavations in the Troad excited most of the world in their day. As we all took the train for Anchester I felt myself poised on the brink of frightful revelations, a sensation symbolized by the air of mourning among the many Americans at the unexpected death of the President on the other side of the world.

On the evening of 7 August we reached Exham Priory, where the servants assured me that nothing unusual had occurred. The cats, even old Nigger-Man, had been perfectly placid, and not a trap in the house had been sprung. We were to begin exploring on the following dlay, awaiting which I assigned well-appointed rooms to all my guests. I myself retired in my own tower chamber, with Nigger-Man across my feet. Sleep came quickly, but hideous dreams assailed me. There was a vision of a Roman feast like that of Trimalchio, with a horror in a covered platter. Then came that damnable, recurrent thing about the swineherd and his filthy drove in the twilit grotto. Yet when I awoke it was full daylight, with normal sounds in the house below. The rats, living or spectral, had not troubled me; and Nigger-Man was still quietly asleep. On going down, I found that the same tranquillity had prevailed elsewhere; a condition which one of the assembled servants -- a fellow named Thornton, devoted to the psychic -- rather absurdly laid to the fact that I had now been shown the thing which certain forces had wished to show me.

All was now ready, and at 11 A.M. our entire group of seven men, bearing powerful electric searchlights and implements of excavation, went down to the sub-cellar and bolted the door behind us. Nigger-Man was with us, for the investigators found no occasion to depise his excitability, and were indeed anxious that he be present in case of obscure rodent manifestations. We noted the Roman inscriptions and unknown altar designs only briefly, for three of the savants had already seen them, and all knew their characteristics. Prime attention was paid to the momentous central altar, and within an hour Sir William Brinton had caused it to tilt backward, balanced by some unknown species of counterweight.

There now lay revealed such a horror as would have overwhelmed us had we not been prepared. Through a nearly square opening in the tiled floor, sprawling on a flight of stone steps so prodigiously worn that it was little more than an inclined plane at the centre, was a ghastly array of human or semi-human bones. Those which retained their collocation as skeletons showed attitudes of panic fear, and over all were the marks of rodent gnawing. The skulls denoted nothing short of utter idiocy, cretinism, or primitive semi-apedom.

Above the hellishly littered steps arched a descending passage seemingly chiselled from the solid rock, and conducting a current of air. This current was not a sudden and noxious rush as from a closed vault, but a cool breeze with something of freshness in it. We did not pause long, but shiveringly began to clear a passage down the steps. It was then that Sir William, examining the hewn walls, made the odd observation that the passage, according to the direction of the strokes, must have been chiselled from beneath.

I must be very deliberate now, and choose my words. After ploughing down a few steps amidst the gnawled bones we saw that there was light ahead; not any mystic phosphorescence, but a filtered daylight which could not come except from unknown fissures in the cliff that over-looked the waste valley. That such fissures had escaped notice from outside was hardly remarkable, for not only is the valley wholly uninhabited, but the cliff is so high and beetling that only an aeronaut could study its face in detail. A few steps more, and our breaths were literally snatched from us by what we saw; so literally that Thornton, the psychic investigator, actually fainted in the arms of the dazed mem who stood behind him. Norrys, his plump face utterly white and flabby, simply cried out inarticulately; whilst I think that what I did was to gasp or hiss, and cover my eyes.

The man behind me -- the only one of the party older than I -- croaked the hackneyed "My God!" in the most cracked voice I ever heard. Of seven cultivated men, only Sir William Brinton retained his composure, a thing the more to his credit because he led the party and must have seen the sight first.

It was a twilit grotto of enormous height, stretching away farther than any eye could see; a subterraneous world of limitless mystery and horrible suggestion. There were buildings and other architectural remains -- in one terrified glance I saw a weird pattern of tumuli, a savage circle of monoliths, a low-domed Roman ruin, a sprawling Saxon pile, and an early English edifice of wood -- but all these were dwarfed by the ghoulish spectacle presented by the general surface of the ground. For yards about the steps extended an insane tangle of human bones, or bones at least as human as those on the steps. Like a foamy sea they stretched, some fallen apart, but others wholly or partly articulated as skeletons; these latter invariably in postures of daemoniac frenzy, either fighting off some menace or clutching other forms with cannibal intent.

When Dr Trask, the anthropologist, stopped to classify the skulls, he found a degraded mixture which utterly baffled him. They were mostly lower than the Piltdown man in the scale of evolution, but in every case definitely human. Many were of higher grade, and a very few were the skulls of supremely and sensitively developed types. All the bones were gnawed, mostly by rats, but somewhat by others of the half-human drove. Mixed with them were many tiny hones of rats -- fallen members of the lethal army which closed the ancient epic.

I wonder that any man among us lived and kept his sanity through that hideous day of discovery. Not Hoffman nor Huysmans could conceive a scene more wildly incredible, more frenetically repellent, or more Gothically grotesque than the twilit grotto through which we seven staggered; each stumbling on revelation after revelation, and trying to keep for the nonce from thinking of the events which must have taken place there three hundred, or a thousand, or two thousand or ten thousand years ago. It was the antechamber of hell, and poor Thornton fainted again when Trask told him that some of the skeleton things must have descended as quadrupeds through the last twenty or more generations.

Horror piled on horror as we began to interpret the architectural remains. The quadruped things -- with their occasional recruits from the biped class -- had been kept in stone pens, out of which they must have broken in their last delirium of hunger or rat-fear. There had been great herds of them, evidently fattened on the coarse vegetables whose remains could be found as a sort of poisonous ensilage at the bottom of the huge stone bins older than Rome. I knew now why my ancestors had had such excessive gardens -- would to heaven I could forget! The purpose of the herds I did not have to ask.

Sir William, standing with his searchlight in the Roman ruin, translated aloud the most shocking ritual I have ever known; and told of the diet of the antediluvian cult which the priests of Cybele found and mingled with their own. Norrys, used as he was to the trenches, could not walk straight when he came out of the English building. It was a butcher shop and kitchen -- he had expected that -- but it was too much to see familiar English implements in such a place, and to read familiar English graffiti there, some as recent as 1610. I could not go in that building -- that building whose daemon activities were stopped only by the dagger of my ancestor Walter de la Poer.

What I did venture to enter was the low Saxon building whose oaken door had fallen, and there I found a terrible row of ten stone cells with rusty bars. Three had tenants, all skeletons of high grade, and on the bony forefinger of one I found a seal ring with my own coat-of-arms. Sir William found a vault with far older cells below the Roman chapel, but these cells were empty. Below them was a low crypt with cases of formally arranged bones, some of them bearing terrible parallel inscriptions carved in Latin, Greek, and the tongue of Phyrgia.

Meanwhile, Dr Trask had opened one of the prehistoric tumuli, and brought to light skulls which were slightly more human than a gorilla's, and which bore indescribably ideographic carvings. Through all this horror my cat stalked unperturbed. Once I saw him monstrously perched atop a mountain of bones, and wondered at the secrets that might lie behind his yellow eyes.

Having grasped to some slight degree the frightful revelations of this twilit area -- an area so hideously foreshadowed by my recurrent dream -- we turned to that apparently boundless depth of midnight cavern where no ray of light from the cliff could penetrate. We shall never know what sightless Stygian worlds yawn beyond the little distance we went, for it was decided that such secrets are not good for mankind. But there was plenty to engross us close at hand, for we had not gone far before the searchlights showed that accursed infinity of pits in which the rats had feasted, and whose sudden lack of replenishment had driven the ravenous rodent army first to turn on the living herds of starving things, and then to burst forth from the priory in that historic orgy of devastation which the peasants will never forget.

God! those carrion black pits of sawed, picked bones and opened skulls! Those nightmare chasms choked with the pithecanthropoid, Celtic, Roman, and English bones of countless unhallowed centuries! Some of them were full, and none can say how deep they had once been. Others were still bottomless to our searchlights, and peopled by unnamable fancies. What, I thought, of the hapless rats that stumbled into such traps amidst the blackness of their quests in this grisly Tartarus?

Once my foot slipped near a horribly yawning brink, and I had a moment of ecstatic fear. I must have been musing a long time, for I could not see any of the party but plump Capt. Norrys. Then there came a sound from that inky, boundless, farther distance that I thought I knew; and I saw my old black cat dart past me like a winged Egyptian god, straight into the illimitable gulf of the unknown. But I was not far behind, for there was no doubt after another second. It was the eldritch scurrying of those fiend-born rats, always questing for new horrors, and determined to lead me on even unto those grinning caverns of earth's centre where Nyarlathotep, the mad faceless god, howls blindly in the darkness to the piping of two amorphous idiot flute-players.

My searchlight expired, but still I ran. I heard voices, and yowls, and echoes, but above all there gently rose that impious, insidious scurrying; gently rising, rising, as a stiff bloated corpse gently rises above an oily river that flows under the endless onyx bridges to a black, putrid sea.

Something bumped into me -- something soft and plump. It must have been the rats; the viscous, gelatinous, ravenous army that feast on the dead and the living ... Why shouldn't rats eat a de la Poer as a de la Poer eats forbidden things? ... The war ate my boy, damn them all ... and the Yanks ate Carfax with flames and burnt Grandsire Delapore and the secret ... No, no, I tell you, I am not that daemon swineherd in the twilit grotto! It was not Edward Norrys' fat face on that flabby fungous thing! Who says I am a de la Poer? He lived, but my boy died! ... Shall a Norrys hold the land of a de la Poer? ... It's voodoo, I tell you ... that spotted snake ... Curse you, Thornton, I'll teach you to faint at what my family do! ... 'Sblood, thou stinkard, I'll learn ye how to gust ... wolde ye swynke me thilke wys?... Magna Mater! Magna Mater!... Atys... Dia ad aghaidh's ad aodaun... agus bas dunarch ort! Dhonas 's dholas ort, agus leat-sa!... Ungl unl... rrlh ... chchch...

This is what they say I said when they found me in the blackness after three hours; found me crouching in the blackness over the plump, half-eaten body of Capt. Norrys, with my own cat leaping and tearing at my throat. Now they have blown up Exham Priory, taken my Nigger-Man away from me, and shut me into this barred room at Hanwell with fearful whispers about my heredity and experience. Thornton is in the next room, but they prevent me from talking to him. They are trying, too, to suppress most of the facts concerning the priory. When I speak of poor Norrys they accuse me of this hideous thing, but they must know that I did not do it. They must know it was the rats; the slithering scurrying rats whose scampering will never let me sleep; the daemon rats that race behind the padding in this room and beckon me down to greater horrors than I have ever known; the rats they can never hear; the rats, the rats in the walls.

ABOUT THE AUTHOR

Robert S. Campbell, or Scott to his friends, lives in sunny southern California and has worked as a professional game designer since 1992.

In all those years of creating game worlds and stories, he has built up quite a library of personal works. In fact, he has far more ideas than could ever be made into games! So, this book is the first of (hopefully) many stories that enable him to get his ideas out into the wild and in the hands of readers.

Thanks for giving this a read! I sincerely hope you like it!

www.RobertScottCampbell.com

Feel free to email me: AuthorRobertSCampbell@gmail.com